Penguin Books

Home and Away

Rosemary Creswell is a Sydney literary agent and consultant, and has also written a number of short stories.

Home and Away

Edited by Rosemary Creswell

Penguin Books
Published with the assistance of the
Literature Board of the Australia Council

Penguin Books Australia Ltd,
487 Maroondah Highway, P.O. Box 257
Ringwood, Victoria 3134, Australia
Penguin Books Ltd,
Harmondsworth, Middlesex, England
Penguin Books,
40 West 23rd Street, New York, N.Y. 10010, U.S.A.
Penguin Books (Canada) Limited,
2801 John Street, Markham, Ontario, Canada L3R 1B4
Penguin Books (N.Z.) Ltd,
182-190 Wairau Road, Auckland 10, New Zealand

First published by Penguin Books Australia, 1987
This collection copyright © Rosemary Creswell, 1987
Copyright in individual stories is retained by the author

Publication assisted by the Literature Board of the Australia Council,
the Federal Government's arts funding and advisory body.

Typeset in Garamond Book 393 by Leader Composition Pty Ltd
Made and printed in Australia by
Dominion Press – Hedges & Bell

CIP

Home and away.
ISBN 0 14 008075 9 (pbk.).
1. Short stories, Australian. I. Creswell, Rosemary, 1941 –
A823'.0108

Contents

Introduction

It is rumoured that Sir Henry Bolte, returning from an overseas trip, once remarked that he would have rather spent the time driving around the Dandenongs. This sentiment has been and still is expressed by many Australians returning from abroad. Fortunately though, not all Australians feel this way about the world beyond our shores, and many of them write about it.

The advent of packaged tourism has, though, created an argument about its effect on travel writing. The eminent American writer and critic, Paul Fussell, claims that it has brought about the demise of the whole genre. He makes a distinction between the traveller and the tourist, the former as one 'who seeks the mind working in history', the latter as he 'who seeks that which has been discovered by entrepreneurship and prepared for him by the arts of mass publicity'. As Australian writer Kate Jennings has said in an article on travel writing, that distinction is not the point; 'Surely it is all a state of mind, the spirit with which a journey is undertaken.' And, she maintains, 'travel can be edifying, arduous, a celebration of life or a running away from it. The reason for a journey can be spiritual, intellectual, or of-this-world.'

Certainly much of the great literature of travel has been written out of a spirit of pioneering and adventure – and perhaps the opportunities for this kind of travel writing have diminished as the world grows smaller through jet flight.

But despite entrepreneurship and mass publicity travel still provides adventures: spiritual, emotional, sexual, political. The diminution of the world through cheap fares and fast travel has been countered by the accessibility of myriad cultures to many more writers.

Busy, air-conditioned airports and 'international' hotels can provide just as fruitful a source of the travel experience as vistas of snow, wastelands of desert and the threatening landscape of uncharted territories. Moorhouse's Francois Blase, in his own way, can be just as terrified of the Bell Captain in a New York hotel as can Peter Matthiesson by a putative yeti in Tibet. The child in Nadia Wheatley's story can feel just as alienated in a modern hotel in Europe as does Elspeth Huxley's child in a British-run boarding school in Africa. And a love affair in Vanuatu in Carmel Kelly's story can provide potent material for reflection on the political state of the world, as do Swift's strange lands in *Gulliver's Travels.*

I have chosen stories that have been written or published in the 1980s, though I am aware of many fine Australian travel stories from earlier periods of our literary history. It is intended to be a collection of contemporary travel stories.

The broad basis of this collection is that of Australians travelling overseas in stories by Australian writers, and one of the essential ingredients is Australians defining themselves in some way against other cultures.

This sounds, perhaps, proscriptive; it rings perhaps of a high-minded seriousness. But these stories cover a wide range of styles and countries and, to the contrary, many – far from being serious – are comic tales in the best spirit and history of Australian short fiction. Nor has my definition of 'travel' limited me exclusively to stories about finite overseas journeys; a few of the pieces here are about the experience of Australians living in some kind of permanence in other countries. Transience is not the only perspective from which to view oneself or another country.

The stories are also set in a wide variety of places, though I did not select them on that basis. Given the number of journeys made by young Australians in Asia and the Pacific, it may surprise some readers that there are not more stories set in those countries. But for some reason there seems to have been less creative shaping of experience in such places than might have been expected. The pieces in this collection are set in Greece, Amsterdam, Frankfurt, California, Italy, Kampuchea, Belgium, Germany, New York, Rome, in-flight over Asia, London, Ireland, France and also in some 'foreign parts' of the mind.

I did not limit my selection to what might be termed fiction proper, although the majority of the stories here are certainly wrought in a way that has to be seen as fictional. But travel writing is surely a genre that invites transgression of narrative modes and some of the work here sits easily between fiction and fact, between the story and the travelogue, between dramatisation and diary entry.

Similarly, it is not easy to classify the themes of such writing, although some emerge with a certain clarity – perhaps the most obvious of which is sexual adventure. Exotic places seem to provide the setting, and perhaps the opportunity through cultural freedom or dislocation, for exotic sexual and emotional experience. Foreign places also set the scenery for unusual sexual attachments (Suzanne Falkiner); the background for permanent or temporary emotional breakups (Jean Bedford, Kate Grenville, Sylvia Lawson, Helen Garner); the ambience for emotional or sexual expectations which are disappointed (Pauline Marrington, Beverley Farmer, Andrew Taylor and Susan Pointon).

Other stories are used to define the political attitudes of the narrator or to confront him or her with the politics of other cultures (Sylvia Lawson and Allan Baillie).

Some of the pieces do not fall into any of these themes, especially the story 'Islands', by Angelo Loukakis which in some senses is an anti-travel story, reminiscent perhaps of the mode of Calvino's character Marco Polo in his account of his travels to Kubla Khan in *Invisible Cities,* where in fact every city is a version of the one city, Venice. Calvino contracts the actual world while expanding it in the imagination, whereas Loukakis writes of islands that repeat themselves infinitely so that they can never be known and the journey never finished.

But wherever these stories are set, and despite a rich abundance of physical descriptions in these pieces, they are not essentially travelogues. The writers, humorous or serious, adventurous or paranoid, urbane or naive, are cartographers of the hearts and the mind and the spirit. The stories are as rich in these elements as the travel writing that was generated from a world that was larger and less accessible and the landscape less conquerable.

Rosemary Creswell
Sydney

Blood and Wine

GEOFFREY BEWLEY

The X.E.N. cafeteria had the cheapest good food in Athens. At the counter Francoise took chicken and vegetables. He took soup, potatoes and milk because that was cheapest of all. They carried their trays over to one of the shiny tables.

'You have enough to pay for this?' Francoise said.

'I've got about three hundred drachs,' he said. 'I've got to spin that out.'

'That's not a lot.'

'That's why I'm going to the blood place.'

'I thought maybe you were joking about that.'

He shook his head. 'The word is you get five hundred drachs for a pint.'

'I think I would not do it in this city.'

'It's just one of those things you do when you're travelling. Once you've been on the trail a while you get used to it. You've got to do something every now and then to sort of tide you over. To make do.'

'You don't think it's a little bit dangerous?'

'Not really. I mean, everybody does it, so I know what I'm doing. I know what I'm letting myself in for. I'll get over it all right.'

'You think that much will be enough?'

'It'll do for a few days, and then I'll get the real money and I can head down to Crete. Because Athens is starting to drive me a bit crazy after all this.'

'Crete will be good,' she said.

'You'll be going there too. Have you figured out when you'll go?'

'I don't know. I think maybe in two, three days.'

'Maybe if my money was ready in time we could get the same boat.'

'That would be something.'

'I think if I sell the blood, then the money'll come straight away, just to show I didn't need to. That's the way it always goes.'

Francoise smiled. 'That's destiny, I think,' she said.

They'd finished the meal. They went out into Amerikis Street in the cold wind and walked around by Syntagma Square and down Mitropoleos to the hostel. He held Francoise's arm lightly the last part of the way and she leaned against him a little. They turned in at the narrow doorway by the furrier's.

He remembered there'd be a crowd upstairs. 'Just a minute,' he said. Francoise stood still and he kissed her lightly on the mouth. She didn't move and he didn't try too hard, but she was smiling when he stepped back.

Upstairs, their dormitories were at opposite ends of the floor. They shook hands goodnight. 'See you in the morning,' he said.

There were six bunks in his room. The others all had packs on them but the guys were still out. He took off his boots and jacket and lay on his top bunk. He took *The Lord of the Rings* out of his pack. He read a few pages for about the sixth time, and then put it aside. He really just wanted to think about Francoise.

He wished he could speak a bit of French to her. They were getting on all right in English, though. He thought she was very attractive. French girls could be attractive when they weren't pretty, but she was actually quite pretty. She had pale skin and big dark eyes, and thick dark curly hair. He liked the way it curled just above her white neck. She looked foreign but he liked that. He liked the way she always looked to be about to smile.

He kept thinking how lucky it was. He'd come overland through Istanbul and she'd come south from Paris. They were both travelling alone. She wanted to see Crete. He wanted to catch the last warm weather there before going up to London.

Except for the trouble with his money it was all working out.

He thought over how he'd kissed her just then. He re-enacted it in his mind. Maybe when they got to Crete things would get going. That was supposing he got the money in time. But he'd have to get the money.

Some of the others came back into the dormitory. He finished undressing and shook out his sleeping-bag. The other guys were talking about the crater at Santorini. In his bunk he turned his face to the wall and thought more of Francoise. He was trying to imagine her body. He pictured it pale and soft and well-shaped. He thought of her smiling. Only once he thought of the blood place. Otherwise he thought of Francoise until he fell asleep.

In the morning he woke late in the stuffy room. It was chilly and there was rain on the window. The German guy in the bunk below was coughing. Another guy had packed and left already.

When he was washed and dressed he looked for Francoise. Her pack was in her room but she was out. He went out too for bread, cheese, tomatoes and milk. He ate breakfast in the hostel kitchen, reading an old copy of *Newsweek* in a corner where he could watch the stairs.

He was finishing it when she came in. '*Bonjour,* Francoise,' he called. She slid onto the bench opposite him. She was smiling. She knew that was about all the French he could say.

'Good morning, Anthony. Are you going to give the blood?'

'Yep.'

'Today?'

'I reckon I'll go this morning. What'll you be doing?'

'I think I will see the Acropolis.'

'That ought to be interesting. When'll you be back?'

'Maybe at midday, I think.'

'Maybe we could go somewhere this afternoon, then. We could go and have dinner somewhere tonight. I'll shout you.'

'Shout?'

'I'll buy you yours.'

'You have not the money.'

'No, I'd like to. We could go somewhere in the Plaka.'

'All right, if you wish.'

'No, that's it. That's what we'll do.'

He finished his milk and pushed back his chair. He couldn't stop himself smiling. It was all working out so well.

'You go now for the blood?' Francoise said.

'Sooner I do it, the sooner I start getting over it.'

He stopped at the front desk to pay the bearded Dutch guy for another night. They went downstairs together. He gave Francoise a quick, clumsy hug at the street door.

'Good luck, Anthony,' she said.

She turned right up Nikis Street. He watched her out of sight. The Red Cross place was marked on his map near the Victoria subway station, the other way. He thought of getting the subway there but it would save drachs to walk. He looked in at American Express on the way, but the clerk said the money order hadn't come. He had to go through with it.

He walked on up the windy avenue. Grey rain clouds were low over the peak of Lycavettus and all the people were wearing coats. The wind chilled him. It was a long walk and by the time he found the place it was starting to rain again. He saw the Red Cross sign up Loulianou and found the waiting room inside.

He gave a grey-haired nurse some particulars and sat with his hands in his coat pockets. Now he had nothing to do but think about the needles and the blood. He hated the idea of it. He hated that kind of thing.

A tall bearded guy went into the doctor. He checked his watch. That one took eight minutes. A blond guy in a duffle coat and torn jeans and pebble glasses went next and he took nine minutes.

Now it was his turn. The grey-haired nurse showed him through. A short dark man in a white coat looked around. He wore thick glasses too. The nurse spoke in Greek. 'You speak English?' the doctor said.

'Yes.'

'Take this off please.'

He hung his coat over a chair.

'Bare your arm, please. Good. Lie down.'

He lay on the white padded table. 'I haven't done this before,' he said.

'This is nothing.'

He shut his eyes. He felt an icy swab and then the needle

went in. It hurt a little and he kept waiting for it to hurt more.

'Still,' the doctor said.

He tried not to notice it. He tried to think of the five hundred drachs and dinner with Francoise. Then Crete with Francoise when the money came. He tried to keep that fixed in his head. He tried not to think about blood pumping out of his body.

He made himself lie absolutely still. He counted the seconds, one thousand, two thousand, three thousand, four thousand. He noticed his right hand was clenched and he made its fingers bend open slowly. He practised lying still with them open. Once his eyes blinked open and he saw the doctor on the other side of the room. He shut them again fast.

Then somebody touched his arm. The doctor was there. The needle was already gone. The doctor was putting on a patch and plaster.

'You can get up now,' the doctor said.

The nurse led him over to one side. He rolled down his sleeves and put on his coat.

'Drink,' the nurse said. She handed him a bottle of orange soft drink.

'This is for the loss of sugar,' the doctor said.

He drank it quickly. He wanted to get out now. The doctor scribbled in a ledger and spoke to the nurse. She took money from a drawer and counted off some notes.

There were five fifty-drachma notes. 'I thought it was five hundred,' he said.

The doctor straightened his glasses. 'The payment is five hundred from a well-built person and two hundred and fifty from a lean person,' he said.

'I didn't know that.'

'It is a medical matter,' the doctor said. 'It is not for me to say, I'm sorry.'

After a year-and-a-half on the road he was lean all right. It was no use to argue. He crushed the notes down in his pocket and walked out with his hand over his hurting arm.

The arm throbbed as he walked the cold streets. He thought, it was a rip-off. It had gone for nothing, for half nothing, for as good as nothing. He had half what he'd reckoned on to last out.

He took two plastic bottles of milk up to the hostel. He drank one down and lay on his bunk. His arm still throbbed a little. He couldn't stop thinking about it. He realised if he'd known it was only two hundred and fifty he'd still have gone ahead with it. That wasn't the point, but it made him feel a bit better.

He remembered Francoise. Dinner didn't look like a good idea now. But he'd told her he'd take her, so now she'd expect it. She was French and if he let her down that'd be the end of it.

He slept a while. When he woke it was growing dark outside. He drank the second bottle of milk. He was still hungry but he could wait till the meal now. It was cold in there and he pulled his sleeping-bag over his legs. He lay back with the book in his hands and waited while night came on outside the window.

Then he heard Francoise. She was outside, talking to the Dutch guy at the desk. He couldn't tell what they were saying. He tossed the sleeping-bag aside and went out. They were talking at the desk. A thin guy in a green combat jacket and a beret was with them.

'Ah, Anthony,' Francoise said. 'You gave the blood.'

'I gave it but I didn't get the money,' he said. 'I only got two hundred and fifty.'

'That was not right, surely?'

'It was some rule they had.'

'I think I've heard of that one,' the thin guy said. He sounded like another Australian.

'Ah, Roger,' Francoise said. 'Anthony, this is Roger.'

They both glanced at Francoise as they shook hands. She smiled back.

'I've still got enough to go out tonight,' he said.

'You are sure you want to, so soon after?'

'I might as well do what I said.'

'You would like to come to Plaka?' Francoise asked Roger. 'Anthony, you don't mind if Roger comes?'

'The more the merrier,' he said. There was no other good answer.

Roger nodded. His dark drooping moustache hid his mouth. His eyes watched from behind wire-rimmed glasses.

'Ah well, we all go, then.'

Outside it was dark already. They walked down past the old church to Monastiriki, then up the hill under the Acropolis. The floodlights were glowing among the Acropolis pillars. In the Plaka the shops were closing and the cafes were open. Greeks and tourists were filling up the tables. In a big lighted place a band was playing bouzouki music.

They looked in a couple of places. One was crowded with Germans and the other was too dark. They both looked expensive.

'There is this one,' Francoise said. 'But it looks expensive also.'

'Take a chance,' said Roger.

They found a table in a corner away from the music. He let Francoise order first. When he saw the menu he thought, shit, two hundred and fifty drachs. But he had to keep on with it.

'Retsina,' he told the waiter. 'Two bottles.'

He ordered moussaka. The waiters brought lamb for Francoise and Roger. 'You are not eating much,' Francoise said.

'No, I had something earlier on.'

'But you must make up your strength.'

'No, I'll be right.'

He pulled the cork on the first bottle of yellow wine. They all clinked glasses. Roger said a toast in French.

'Your accent is improving,' said Francoise. Roger said something else in French and she laughed. They both started laughing.

He couldn't understand them. He only knew the usual few easy French words 'How many languages do you know?' he asked Roger.

'Just a little bit of French,' Roger said. 'But Francoise knows a lot.'

'Just a little English and some German,' she said.

'And French.'

'Ah yes, and French of course.'

'Let's practise some more,' Roger said. He started in French again, stumbling for words. Francoise was laughing still.

'Ah, you think so?' she said. 'Well, if you say so.'

He couldn't follow any more of it. He drank more wine. He watched Francoise across the table, her good skin and crisp hair and her figure under her pullover now she had her coat off. He finished eating while they were talking, and he poured more wine.

Roger was saying something about Crete. 'Yes, soon, perhaps, I think,' Francoise said. 'Yes, I think.'

They were into the second bottle now. He was doing most of the drinking. That was all right, because it was his wine. He was paying for it. He found he didn't like to see them getting it. He'd paid for it with his blood that day. It was his blood they were drinking. The bouzouki music was too loud. It was going through his head. Roger was smiling under his moustache and Francoise was laughing all the time.

'Oh, no,' she said. 'You must not think I am such a one.'

The second bottle of retsina was gone now. 'Do we want another one?' said Roger. 'No?'

'No,' he said. 'Waiter?' He handed the Greek four fifties for the bill.

'Wait a minute,' said Roger. 'What was mine?'

'No, don't worry about it.'

'No, come on.'

'No, it's all on me.'

'If you wish it,' said Francoise.

'Well, I wish it.'

The waiter brought his change. He left the silver on the cloth by his plate.

'You need the money,' Francoise said.

'I wouldn't worry about that either, if I were you.'

He saw they were both staring at him. He smiled at Francoise but it wasn't any good. It didn't matter anyway. He'd already known it was no good. He'd missed out and it was all over. It was all gone.

There was a stab of pain in his arm as he pulled his coat on. He led the way outside. In the dark street it seemed much quieter suddenly. The cold was doing something to his head. It felt hot and cushioned inside. He had to shake it to start to think.

'You look tired,' Francoise said. 'You should go back to your place.'

'Aren't you coming back?' he asked.

'No, my bags are not there any more.'

'Where are they now?'

'In a place close to here. I moved them this afternoon.'

He thought of her coming and going while he was nursing his arm. It was all too much.

'Well,' he said. 'Well, can I just say goodbye?'

He held her arm. She shook her head. 'I think maybe not,' she said.

He felt sick and sad because this was the end of it. He drew Francoise toward him. Her eyes widened and she pulled away.

'I think we'd all better just take it easy, eh?' Roger said.

Roger was holding his arm. He tried to shake free but Roger only gripped harder. Now he felt a great relief. Suddenly it was all easy. He let go Francoise and swung his fist at Roger, and hit him below the ribs. Roger tried to cover up and hold on, but he landed two more belly blows. Roger doubled over, leaning against the whitewashed wall. He punched Roger's head and hurt his knuckles on bone, and Roger went down.

Francoise was backing away. He took a step toward her. She looked ready to run down the dark street. It was no good. He lowered his hands. People were calling out somewhere up the hill. Roger was on his hands and knees.

'Go on, take him,' he said. 'He's all yours.'

'You're crazy,' Francoise said in a high voice. 'You must be crazy, you know?'

Roger was trying to get up. He knew he'd have to get out now. He didn't want to have to hit Roger again.

'Take him to Crete with you,' he said.

People were gathering around. A Greek at his elbow was shouting at him. He turned and lifted his fists, and the Greek's mouth shut under his black moustache and he backed off. There was a clear way down the hill.

He backed away from them with his fists up. Nobody was coming after him. Roger was leaning against the wall and Francoise was helping hold him up.

'Crazy,' he heard her saying.

He turned up a laneway, out of sight. His arm, where the blood had been taken, was hurting again. He was scared it was bleeding inside his sleeve. He held it tight and stumbled down the rough pavement. He didn't know where he was heading. He just thought Syntagma Square was probably somewhere ahead. He'd get back in the end.

He remembered the coins he'd left on the table. It made him feel sick. He couldn't work out how much he had left. More than a hundred drachs anyway. Maybe two hundred. Probably a bit less. But he'd have the money from home if it came. His arm still hurt. He could sell more blood too. He kept thinking, Francoise.

Two Tales of a Trip

JANE GRAHAM

Date   *20th November (After 1 o'clock)*
Place   *Plane. In the sky. (Boeing 707)*
Weather   *fine, cloudy*

Departed at 1 o'clock.
Had lunch at 2.30. Tomato Soup, a roll, meat, apricot
tart.
Darwin. Very hot. Brought back pamphlets.
The sunset took up the whole sky.
Saw lights of Singapore as I landed.
At Karachi met Shalah the ground hostess who told me
various things about Pakistan.
I slept through Calcutta and Bangkok.

I was eleven, and as it was summer in Australia I was sent to
Europe in a cream cotton dress with a border of pink and blue
ballerinas, a hat (white) made of plastic raffia, long white
socks, black lace-up school shoes (newly soled and capped),
and white gloves. In my white plastic handbag I had my new
passport, fifteen pounds worth of travellers' cheques, a letter
from my father saying that perhaps he would be unable to
meet me at Rome airport as planned; 'in that eventuality' I was
to take a taxi to the *Pensione So-and-So* on the *Via Wherever*,
and wait: he and the lady he had engaged to be my companion
would join me as soon as they could. . .

And also of course I had the little book with a plane and a

11

train and a palm tree and the words MY TRIP embossed on the cover.

I look at it now: the neat writing on the endpaper: wishing you a very happy trip, Your Loving Friend Judy. And my own neat writing, meticulously and boringly and in near-perfect spelling telling lies – or at least not the truth – for day after day through those weeks of November and December and later, through the countries of Italy and France and Monaco and Spain and Gibraltar and Andorra and France again and the rest.

As I wrote it, I saw it as a kind of code. I knew the 'lady' read it. Or could read it. So I put in asterisks to mark particular misery, sorts of scribbles for the fights, other marks for days of especial hatred, and something else for the loneliness of the fact that in that whole time I did not speak to another child, I did not play a game.

Reading it now, I can't always tell the difference between a sign and a genuine scribble over a mistake. The main thing is, it covered up what was happening.

Date   *Mon 21st November 1960 2.30 pm*
Place   *Rome*
Weather   *Sunny, a bit chilly*

Arrived on scedule at airport after smooth trip except
between Bahrain-Cairo.
Drove through countryside to Lake Albano, great
batheing place of Romans, where we had lunch. Drove
past vineyards and agricultural country to Rome
where we saw St Peters Square, the Colisseum
(visited), the old stone walls and many single, double
and triple towers and domes.

I arrived on schedule at the airport in a state of terror. I hadn't seen my father since my mother's death three years earlier; and I'd always feared him anyway. He was a sadist, in a peculiarly subtle, trivial and complicated manner. For example: once when I was perhaps three he brought home a new cup of pure white china. He showed it to me, saying: 'Look at the rose, down at the bottom.' I said I couldn't see one. He grew most insistent: 'Look at it, look, *look at it!*' He yelled:

'*Don't you see the rose!*' But I couldn't see it and I couldn't see it, and in the end fled to my room in a fit of coughing and crying, his voice behind me exclaiming at my mother that he didn't know what was wrong with her daughter.

Yes, I was a sook. And on the 21st of November 1960 I was frightened too of the lady. I was enough of an eavesdropper to have heard my mother's relations mention her.

But though I feared meeting my father and her, I was even more afraid that they wouldn't be there. I kept on taking out Daddy's letter and reading: take a taxi to the *Pensione* on the *Via*. . .

He told me too that I would have to cash a travellers' cheque to pay the taxi. . .

The man was a lunatic, I now think. Looking too at the account of the sightseeing which he dragged me off on that first day. . . Of all that, I remember the lunch, which was stale rolls and greasy white butter that my father had saved from wherever he'd had breakfast that morning, and ham that was too fatty and too raw. I was feeling sick. I was also cold. But at least I was no longer lost. For after wandering for an hour in the Rome terminal, approaching air hostesses who brushed past me, I was finally spotted by the lady, who had red hair and a red kilt.

'This is Glenda Ferguson,' said my father, 'who has kindly come to look after you. You can call her Auntie Glenda.'

On the 22nd of November (I read) *we visited the Wall, saw statues of Garibaldi, soldiers and fountains. Went to Vatican saw Sistine Chapel. Also saw lovely museum containing tapestries, books. On Tour saw Basilica St Mary Major; 'Mother of Churches' St John in Lateran; the Holy Steps; Catacombs where early Christians met; along Appian Way saw walls castles towers columns again; lovely Trevi Fountain (Three Coins in a Fountain).*

On the 23rd November 1960 it was a bit rainy and cold in Rome. We went to St Peter's and saw the Popes' Treasury. I liked the red cowboy hats. Later we saw the Pope give a speech in Italian, French and English. On a Tour we went to the Piazza Venezia, Square of the Capital, Roman Forum, the Collosseum where Christians were sent to fight beasts, St

Peter's arm-chains in St Peter in Chains, Michaelangelo's Moses, Basilica of St Paul outside the Walls where St Paul is buried, faniculum for a view of the city.

The Pope (I now know) was John. My eyes were on the level of everybody else's elbows. The room went dark and the floor tiles flew up to the ceiling. A football team cheered and cheered. My father wouldn't let me go out because we had paid. Behind a column, I saw a nun smoking.

In the pensione, Auntie Glenda had her suitcases in the same room as me, and slept there after about two in the morning. Before that, she was down the corridor in Daddy's room. I always stayed awake till she came back, because I was frightened. I always knew the time. My watch had once been my mother's.

On the Thursday we'd finished Rome, and drove to Florence via Siena in my father's grey Wolseley. Auntie Glenda knitted and smoked and handed me over sweets from the front seat. Daddy found it hard because they drive on the wrong side of the road, and it was raining heavily in patches . . . *white oxen pulling carts, ploughs, and being ridden. Olive and cypress trees form shade over vineyards and fields. Saw pig-girl in peasant clothes with pigs.* Yes, that pig-girl. The sun came out as we passed her, and she waved.

There was confusion as we booked into the pensione.

'*Un chambre à deux et un chambre à un,*' my father said. He spoke French and German, but not Italian.

Of course, they presumed that the Monsieur and the Madame would have the double, and the Madame's such a pretty daughter would. . .

'*Non non non non non. . .*!' my father blurted through the carrying of the suitcases. He tried to explain. '*La madame est l'amie de ma fille. . .*'

To his credit, I think that perhaps he blushed. Though he had always, right up to his death, roses in his cheeks.

Anyway, they dumped us into two rooms joined by a bathroom, and let us work it out for ourselves.

It is perhaps best to summarise things here, and to say that if I had to give one and only one memory of my trip, it would be the feeling of a full bladder. Not only was I caught again and again during the day: on a tour, in a museum, driving along a European road that was not flanked by the shelter of scrub as the roads at home were. But at night I lay with my legs pressed together, with the pillow pressed between my legs, with my hand on my crutch, with my mind desperately willing itself to think of something other than a toilet: for if Daddy's room were down the corridor, then we didn't have an en suite bathroom, and the toilet was down the corridor too. And of course I was too afraid to walk down a corridor in a foreign country in those hours of the night when Auntie Glenda was in Daddy's room. Yet if we had adjoining rooms and our own bathroom, I was still too afraid to go, for Daddy and Auntie Glenda would hear me, and know I was still awake.

When I heard Auntie Glenda start to come back, I used to pretend to be asleep, then pretend to wake up as she got into her nightie. . .

'You needn't try that,' she sometimes told me. 'I didn't come down in the last shower. I know you stay up listening to us. . .'

I'd deny it, grunt a sleepy grunt, stumble off to the toilet. . .

They got so fed up with me that they started not letting me have anything to drink with dinner. I loved mineral water: Vichy was my favourite. And because of the garlic and the oil, I'd get so thirsty. . .

From Florence I remember the bridges, and a leather factory. That's all. Yet I afterwards saw Florence as my favourite of all the places we visited (except Gibraltar). Perhaps it was because Florence was the first, and the nights of not sleeping and the days of looking and looking at the things Daddy was paying for me to see were only beginning.

Date   *Sat 26th November 1960*
Place   *In the car*
Weather   *Cloudy, Fine.*
Went to Pisa. Climbed tower. 252 steps. It really does
slope as much as it seems to. . .

Date   *27th November 1960*

Place Car
Weather Foggy. In afternoon sunny.
Travelled 148 miles from Bracca Pass to Montemiglia
for night. Drove along Italian Riviera. It is terrible.
The sand (the ten feet or so there is of it) is like pebbly
dirt. The waves are about a foot high, breaking about
20 feet from the so-called 'beach'. It was cold and
nothing half as good as Australia's worst beach.

Ah, my little Aussie chauvinist. It is at least a pleasant change
to hear your real voice.

Through the rain of the 28th we entered France. Drove to
Monte Carlo, which pleased my royalist tendencies. I bought a
postcard of the Family, and loved the flowers in pots in the gardens. Cyclamens, I now imagine: pink and rare. The next day,
back in France, we did a perfume factory at Grasse and Daddy
bought some for Auntie Glenda.
    'This can be my Christmas box,' she smiled as she accepted.
She'd said the same thing back in Rome when he'd bought her
a cameo pendant, and the same thing in Florence when he got
her a leather tooled box to put the pendant in.
    Something nice happened on the 29th: we washed the car
near a waterfall. The sun was out, and it was good to splash
around.

    Wednesday 30th: Monaco again: Oceanographic Museum.
I wrote: *Saw fish.* But next there was. . .

Date 1st December 1960
Place France-Spain.

It was in Spain that the real badness started. We travelled down
the Costa Brava (is that what it's called?) down through La
Scala to Tarragona, then 343 miles to Murcia through Valencia
where oranges are in abundance. On to Torremolinos and
finally on the warm and white-cloudy day of Monday 5
December settled at the Hotel Nicholas in Marbella, where we
were to stay until the 12th.

Daddy's room was on a different floor. At night, before she came back, the wind howled through the air-conditioning (I now suppose). The shutters were green and rattled. There was a wash basin in the room, and one night I tried to pee into my water glass, so I could then tip the pee down the basin. But it jetted out, splashing onto my bare feet, onto the floor. Luckily it was lino, so I wiped it up with my towel. Then was afraid: what if Auntie Glenda smelled my towel? What if the maid did? If I'd have been a boy, there'd have been no problems.

Footsteps travelled up and down the corridor. They were always going to stop at my door, to get in (yes, it was locked, but. . .); they'd have a knife, a strangling-thing, a mask, two eyes through the slit; the sound of them breathing. . .

The food came on a trolley at lunchtime, and you had to pick. It was pretty: green and red and black. But I always picked too much, and the wrong stuff, and had to eat it.

We made two day-jaunts to Gibraltar. The best bit of the whole trip: for I found a bookshop, and got my father to show me how to cash a travellers' cheque, and each time bought a book and a British schoolgirl magazine. (I'd wanted to blow a lot more money there, but wasn't allowed.)

On the Rock, Daddy was British enough to be easier. I have a photo of me in my overcoat with the too-short sleeves, Daddy in his long tweed and his Tyrolean travelling hat, both of us plump, stiff, self-conscious, standing on either side of a sign saying IT IS FORBIDDEN TO FEED THE APES. I hate resembling him.

Yet as soon as we left, the old dreadfulness was back. This is the sort of thing that is impossible to explain. Compared with the violence done to many children, it is nothing.

SCENE: INT/EXT AN ENGLISH CAR ON THE COSTA DEL SOL. WINTRY AFTERNOON.

A plump blonde child sits absorbed in a *Girls' Own Weekly*. A redhead smokes and chatters. A plump man in his early sixties steers fast and efficiently around the bends. The sea sparkles, little fishing boats putter, rocks jab out along the coast.

MAN

Do you think I've paid
for you to come to Europe

so you can sit and read a book?
Look at the sea!
The child closes the book, stares through tears at the Mediterranean (or whatever it is).

What was it? How, why did he have the power to destroy me with the slightest thing? Over something like that, I would sob and sob for hours. Calling for my mother inside me. And of this day in my book I have written:

> We set off and went to Gib (50 miles from Marbella) where we found we had left our raincoats in the Hotel. We stayed three hours in Gib then went back to Marbella then on to Seville by the inland route.

That night, we didn't arrive till late, for a drizzle was setting in, the roads were broken with winter potholes. We found a hotel, but walked around and around, looking for somewhere to eat. I'd hardly spoken since the afternoon, and was rebuked now for sulking. Auntie Glenda was in a bad mood because Daddy had blamed her for the raincoats.

MAN
. . . Well if you'd packed properly
we wouldn't *be* walking around a
strange town at midnight . . .
REDHEAD
What you don't seem to realise
is I'm a free agent. I can
go any time I want to.
MAN
Well go on then.
REDHEAD (storming off)
I bloody well will.

I panicked. I was terrified of having to travel alone with Daddy. Up till now, Auntie Glenda had always been kind to me, in ways such as giving me lollies and knitting me a cardigan and at least trying to crack jokes and talk in the car. Of course, I copped it sometimes from her at night when she came in: but then I somehow thought she was right. I should have been asleep. Please don't leave please don't leave please don't leave. The rain dripped off awnings, and my shoes were soaked. At last my father found a place. I ordered a chicken bouillon. It came with a raw egg sitting in a spoon. I was meant to stir it into the soup. I couldn't. My father forced me to. In foreign places you have to do foreign things. Everything is experience. This is what he'd paid for. (Years later I was to find, in an old album, a photo he had taken of an execution he'd gone to see while a tourist in Indonesia in the 1920s. The prisoner was standing, but there was air and a sword between his head and his neck.)

Of course, when we got back to the hotel I found she hadn't left. She was smoking cigarettes, hungry, waiting.

In that place, we had adjoining rooms, and this night they didn't care if I heard the row. I wasn't used to noisy hatred: the variety practised by my father and my mother had involved days, weeks even, of not saying a word.

Yet though this night was the first time I put the pillow over my head instead of between my legs, I was later to see December 12 as only a try-out, a minor skirmish.

Date   Tues 13th December 1960
Place   Seville (Sevilla – Spanish)
Weather   Fine, warm, cold-late.
Went on two tours of the city and saw a lot of old
places . . . In the afternoon we went to many
cathedrals and saw floats weighing 4 tons which are
carried by 48 men at Easter . . .

Date   14th December 1960
Place   Sevilla to Granada
Weather   Cold (snowy)
We travelled all day through scenery to Granada, the
old (maybe 2,500 years) Moorish capital, founded by
the Arabs years uncountable ago. We stayed at
Parador de San Francisco. It had an Alhambra Garden
but it wasn't a very big one.
On the way to Granada it snowed a terrible lot.

On the way to Granada it snowed a terrible lot . . . As I type the words, it begins to come back to me: that was a code for 'they rowed a terrible lot'. Over the next couple of weeks, until Christmas, as the rows got worse, I was to use the weather as a code sign for what was really happening behind the hectic looking at things. My personal discovery of the objective correlative. The trouble, however, with this system is that I can remember too that the weather was *really* getting worse as well. Sitting now, on a drizzly day, so many years later, I try to puzzle out the atmospheric from the emotional storms.

With Granada, however, there is no risk of confusion: it was the first time she turned against me too.

December 15th. We went to the Alhambra Palace, and something happened to set her off. She had what people see as a redhead's temperament: could suddenly fly, for no apparent reason, and you'd never know what you'd said or done. You'd question her: What have I done?

'You know very well. Don't play that game on me, miss.'

She waltzed outside and smoked a cigarette in short strong puffs, too cold to take her black leather gloves off.

My father told her she was being childish. Told me to see what I'd done now.

I couldn't speak for the tears that stuck in my throat. This was interpreted as my sulkiness by my father, as my high-and-mightiness by her.

Of the Palace, of the Gardens, I have no memory. Years later, however, watching the opera *Otello,* the cardboard Moorish sets, the shrieking of the dying Desdemona, I remembered that day.

Date   16th December 1960
Place   Granada to Alicante
Weather   Snowy, chilly, rain

Date   17th December 1960
Place   Alicante-Benicarlo
Weather   Cold. Rain.

Date   18th December 1960
Place   Benicarlo-Seo
Weather   Cold, sleeting

. . . A minute ago, outside in the real cold of now, chopping wood, I wondered if I were being fair. I tried to get into the mind of her, to see what she felt about this presence who was interrupting her European trip. One thing: she was a very affectionate, a very physical woman, and yet could not kiss and hug her lover because of his daughter. Another thing: her lover made her feel ignorant and common. And that namby little private school brat of his, with her reading and her writing in that bloody book, sly little bitch, butter wouldn't melt in her mouth, oh no, bloody up themselves the pair of them, and talk about cold, that kid hardly laughed, never cried, never fought you back, just acted real superior, yes please, no thank you, and him just whistling through his teeth as he drives, writing down the miles in his little book . . .

There were a couple of days respite when we entered Andorra. For 19th December (Seo to Andorra) I wrote: *Snowy, cold but lovely.* I was excited to be somewhere so little (Monaco had had the same effect), and the brochure said that smuggling was the second industry. We booked into the Hotel Internacional, got chains for the tyres, and the next day headed up the road to the Pas de la Casa.

> *The chain had a bit flying and it kept hitting the undercarriage and making a terrible noise (like tin cans, only worse). Anyway, we got about 3000 feet when we saw a barrier across the road and went to have a look. We saw a snow plough clearing the road, but it got stuck, so another one went to yank it out but it also got stuck, so we thought we'd better not go any further.*

This was most exciting, despite the dullness of my account. The next day, we got there; I wrote: *Snowy (and lovely). I am positive they take the photographs of fir trees, chalets and snow there for the Christmas cards.*

In fact, I was nearly busting with Christmas. To have a real white Christmas! I pushed myself into a state of such a high that there would of course be nowhere ultimately to go but down. On each of these next three days we drove up into the peaks. I would run off to make snowballs, and look down at them as they sat on the balcony of the restaurant, drinking coffees and brandies. Their words came out in little white puffs, like the balloons that comic people speak in. Sometimes I'd catch her watching me to see if I were watching her; if she thought I wasn't, she'd give him a kiss; he'd brush it off like a snowflake.

I got her to help me sneak off to a bank to cash a travellers' cheque, and to help me go into a shop and buy him a pair of socks. They had green diamonds up the sides. And I gathered all my courage and went into a sort of chemist shop and said *s'il vous plaît* and bought a cake of soap for her.

I desperately hoped that my gifts had been smuggled.

On Christmas Eve there was a dinner dance. I went to the dinner bit, and they stayed on for the dance bit. I could hear the music from my bedroom: Strauss, and lots of piano accordion, the odd gypsy violin. For the first time, I heard no murderers in the passageway. I must have dozed off. Later I woke to hear their muffled voices — for at the Internacional we had a two-room suite.

I checked the tone: it wasn't a row. Looked at my watch: at 2 am it was technically Christmas Day. I looked out the window at the moonlight shining on the snow banked up on the roofs. Then I took their presents in to them.

Her step-ins and stockings were on the floor, her green silk dress a heap beside them. Her bra, her slip, her warm undies.

We all looked at each other.

I walked out.

The reason this is difficult to write about is because it didn't mean anything. I had truly always believed that they'd played cards at night, as they'd told me. My mother and father had not in my knowledge shared a bed, so it meant nothing to see her lying with him. And I was absolutely ignorant as to why they would be together.

I had a pee. I was disappointed that I couldn't give them my presents. I had a pretty good idea what she was going to give me: a Spanish dancer doll, that I had obviously longed for. But what would he?

When morning came, we all pretended that nothing had happened. For me really, nothing had: it was all still to come.

She was edgy, kissing me too much, jollying him along. He was gruffer, pretending even more that he didn't know her.

We would have breakfast in our room, she decided. Then presents.

I would order, he decided.

At my private school, French was taught in sixth class primary, which I'd just done. My report said I'd come second. But I was not up to saying down a telephone: *'Trois cafés au lait, s'il vous plait, et cinq croissants et de beurre et confiture pour chambre vingt-et-un . . .'*

He asked me to order, told me to order, ordered me to order. I picked up the phone again and again, and my voice disappeared each time the phone talked to me.

She stuck up for me, and they had a row.

Then he stormed out, and she turned on me for making them row at Christmas: 'Before you came, we never used to!'

I watched the snowflakes fall outside.

He came back in and started to speak to me in French. I understood. She didn't. She turned on both of us for thinking we're smart.

She went to the bathroom for a long time, and we listened to her noisy sobbing.

My father said: 'See what you've done.'

He whistled through his teeth in that tuneless way he had, and went out for a walk.

I watched him from the window: his dark green hat with the feather, his tweed coat, his habit of rubbing his hands together, the little bounce in his walk. Three gypsy children carol singers grabbed at his sleeve: he shook them off, as my dog shakes the rain from his coat.

She came back in with new makeup on. She embraced me. 'Never mind, love,' she said.

For her, there was no history, no past. She began her life afresh from hour to hour.

She picked up the phone. 'Three cafés au lait, five rolls, all the works, for room twenty-one, grazias, yeah adios amigo!'

She grinned and lit a fag. If I'd have been the me of now, meeting her then, I might have liked her. (I suddenly think: I'm getting on for the age that she was then.)

And even then . . . well, I found her an improvement on

him.

She gave me the Spanish doll: red dress, and black mantilla.
'This is really from Daddy too,' she said. I knew it wasn't.
I gave her the soap and she acted well.
We knitted. She'd got me some cheap wool at Gib.
He bobbed in close on lunchtime.
All smiles.

'Give me your handy-pandies,' he said, taking my right hand
with his left hand, and then her left hand with his right, and
we processed out and along and down the three flights of
stairs and into the dining room. He could be charming.

And he was, that lunchtime. Only the best German dry
champagne. But of course we ordered the British Christmas
Special. The room was full, and there were French, Spanish,
German and British varieties of Christmas to be had. 'Or any
additional nationality you require,' the menu promised.

Halfway through the turkey I gave him his socks. I'd carried
them all day down the front of my jumper.

They made him pompous.

'Well, you know what your present is, don't you?'

'No . . .'

'Guess.'

'I can't.'

'I said: guess.'

I shook my head. He finally told me:

'Your trip.'

'Oh.'

'Well aren't you going to say thank you?'

'Thank you.'

'You mean: Thank you, Daddy.'

'Thank you Daddy.'

And she chimed in: 'And thank you too Daddy for my
Christmas boxes.' She was wearing the cameo and perfume.

My father smirked at her.

She smirked at me.

That was the first time I got pissed. The room shone, with
walls of light that seemed to come in from the snow outside.
Men wandered around with violins. A chef came out with a big
white hat on, carrying a huge plum pud in flames. All the
British Special eaters sang 'For He's A Jolly Good Fellow',

except Daddy and sort of me.

I didn't know whether to sing like Auntie Glenda, or be silent like him.

They took away my turkey plate and gave me a bowl of pudding. You don't get sixpences in it in hotels.

Daddy ordered, in German, another bottle of Sekt.

The name made me giggle, and I couldn't stop.

A couple from the next table asked if they could join us. They knew *her* from the dinner dance, they said.

My father looked cross.

They said they were from Adelaide.

In the introductions, the men said their full names and the ladies said their Christian names. Then they all called each other Mister and Mrs.

They called her Mrs Daddy's name.

That was my mother's name.

I'd heard no one called that for three years.

I got drunker.

She got drunker.

My father danced with Mrs Adelaide.

She danced with Mr.

I ran away for ever into the street. Hearing that name again made everything look drunk.

My mother had long black hair in a coil on the back of her head. She walked through the snow in a red hibiscus sunfrock, singing one of her army songs.

Eventually I went back to room 21. They were rowing in their room next door.

The woman said, she couldn't help it if people jumped to conclusions.

The man said, she bloody encouraged it.

Why shouldn't I, screamed the woman, I pick up after you and your brat. Why shouldn't I have a right?

Aren't I good enough, yelled the woman.

Well aren't I?

Well answer me!

Well aren't I?

That day of course I didn't write in my little book. Over the bit where I'd written in expectation *Christmas Day 1960* I find now a heavy scribble, and the date of the 26th.

> *Today Daddy suddenly thought we should go so we went from Andorra to Spain again and from Spain to France again. The road was very slippery going through the various passes.*

After that entry the book ends, for the bullshit was over. After Christmas there was nowhere to go but further on.

The Killing of a Hedgehog

SUZANNE FALKINER

I

In the park, ash-blond Dutch with pale milky skin walk their dogs. The leaves are still autumn colours, but the wind is icy. The walkers wear sheepskin coats, long woollen scarves, their pale hair is frizzed out by the cold. Dead leaves litter the paths, half-turned to decay by the frost.

When the strollers feed stale bread to the ducks in the cold lake, sea gulls hanging in the air above the clustering birds make sudden swoops, chaotic flickings of grey-white wings, and perform aerodynamically impossible manoeuvres to catch the crusts of bread in midair. The ducks, deprived, come out of the water and stand waiting sulkily at the bread-throwers' feet, shifting from one web to another, unable to compete . . .

Inside, they lie in bed. It is 3 o'clock in the afternoon.

'What did you do before?' she asks. Meaning: before this house overlooking the canal and the park.

'I was travelling,' he says.

But then he is on a different track, avoiding the subject, as usual.

'In summer you just walk down to 'Dam square and there's all these chicks who are only here for a few days, and they've all heard about Amsterdam and perhaps they're a little bit disappointed nothing's happening . . .'

A pause.

'There was one, an Italian chick who didn't speak any

27

English. . .'

He grins, his face transparently conveying his thoughts.

'So how did you get her back to your room?' she asks.

'Hashish is the same in all languages.'

He giggles. He finds himself amusing. She finds it unpleasant.

'In summer you just walk down to the square. In winter you've got no chance at all . . . American chicks are dumb, stupid. You start talking to them and they get into bed with you five minutes later. They think it's cool to know someone who lives here all the time . . .'

A pause.

'You, though. I thought I had no chance with you.'

In one corner of the room there is a pile of television sets. Viewed from the main body of the room their pale green faces stare blankly, but from behind they spill out an extravagant tangle of wires and multicoloured resisters, circuits and terminals soldered into a labyrinth of irregular, angular spiders' webs. At night, one of them, the one that works, lights the darkened room with a hum of tiny lights: a scale model of a city with illuminated highways connecting the major metropolises.

Above them, between the huge stereo speakers that hang from the ceiling (at such an angle that the exact intersection or focus of sound is the double mattress in the far corner) hang several pot plants, their leaves trained along the wires that lead respectively to the televisions, to an amplifier, to a turntable, an electric clock, a small electric coffee-grinder, a toaster, a percolator surrounded by crumpled filter papers, an architect's lamp, an infra-red globe in an inverted, suspended seven-inch terra-cotta flower pot and, less predictably, to a plastic model of a shrunken head with an unlit joint in its mouth.

The room is rectangular, much longer than it is wide, sufficiently so as to suggest a passage rather than a room. From behind the door a single shelf of books stretches along the wall for perhaps ten feet. Most of the names on the garish spines are unfamiliar: Poul Anderson, Fritz Leiber, Roger Zelazny, C. J. Cutcliffe Hyne, William Hope, Hodgson, Fred Hoyle . . . to the girl, they have the ring of pseudonyms. On their covers, dome-headed creatures stare moon-faced from the centres of vivid symmetrical lilies; green and violet women stand straddle-legged and threatening in front of space vehicles surrounded by miniature craters. Then there are several volumes of rock and roll encyclopaedias.

There is the mandatory mattress on the floor. The sheets are crumpled into hundreds of tiny creases, covered with coffee and semen stains. Faded orange. Sometimes she smoothes them out and tries to tuck them in, when he is not there.

He pulls out a fat plastic bag full of soft-green crumpled leaf, hardly any stalk, and rolls a fat, loose cigarette with three papers. He watches to see how she reacts. The end flares and he lights it, and a thick cloud of white smoke balloons up.

'We grow it on the roof,' he says. 'There are three more bags like this in the other room.'

II

He is getting up to go out.

Narrow shoulders, slight potbelly. Thin. Chin, not quite compensating for the jutting nose, covered by a sparse black beard. Big feet. His hair is soft and lank, also thin, and so he combs it into carefully arrayed disorder over his forehead.

He wears high leather boots outside his patched jeans. The boots are of the type of pale pink-yellow leather that turns to tan with age. He puts on a black shirt. Pale hands. His little fingers are bent inwards at the last joint. He was born like that, he says.

His right arm above the elbow seems misshapen and wasted away. A long scar seamed with stitch marks runs down it, where, he tells her, they cut some of the muscle away. That is how he lives, he says. He fell through a roof and now they have to pay him each month, as long as he stays where he is. Again the giggle.

He bends his knees and holds his front shirt-tails over his balls as he pulls his jeans up, neatly, and tucks the whole lot in. Zip. He never wears underwear. Then the olive-green waterproof army coat, shrugged on. He's going out to buy sliced white Dutch bread for toast. He lives on bread and coffee. Five spoonsfull of sugar in the coffee, because of his dope-smoker's craving for sugar. She likes the thick, crusty Dutch bread that he brings, but she can see he is drawn to the idea of something else, not available in these bakeries: the waxy paper, the thin dry slices all symmetrical and identical . . .

He is ready. He looks at her curled up on one corner of the mattress, under the loose blanket. 'Maybe I'll hurry back,' he says. Then he goes out.

She considers leaving while he is gone.

She hasn't been out of the bed for any considerable length of time in the past forty-eight hours. He, on the other hand, makes short forays into the cold to buy food. While he is gone she reads his trashy novels, has showers, peels tiny mandarins from a paper bag.

Sometimes in the afternoons he wanders over to the televisions, picks up an instrument which looks to her like a thick pen with a pointed tip, and starts methodically poking it into the exposed entrails. Little metallic sounds occur. He, also, hasn't asked her when she is going to leave.

When she has a shower the stone floor is cold under her bare feet, but the water is hot on her cold skin, and she shivers violently. Then the cake of white soap streaked with brown cracks glides over her wet skin and she washes every part of her body carefully. Her skin feels tender, as if she has been sick for a long time, like a child.

She feels weak in all the joints of her body, and lethargic from inactivity. She wonders when she is going to break the spell of him and leave. It is an effort to remember how long she has been there, trapped inside the radius of his demands. To her, the hours pass in a seeming stupor, a kind of slow-moving dance, and even then, sometimes, when she is half-asleep and dreaming, he is leaning over her body and his hand is gliding down over her belly and she can tell by the way his hand moves that she is moist, and the waves of feeling are starting to flow through her body yet again, against her will. His persistence amazes her.

But she doesn't like him.

It is occupied by squatters, the house. She has only seen one or two of them. In the next room a tall, blond Dutch boy with a gold earring plays a drum set, always starting about 4 o'clock in the afternoon and continuing for about an hour. He gets up about midday, so that allows time for breakfast, she supposes. A girl in a long velvet skirt taps away interminably on a typewriter. She doesn't look up as their naked figures walk past to the bathroom. Half-open doorways lead to other rooms. Sometimes there are other figures, only vaguely differentiated, lolling in armchairs. To the girl, the faces are always expressionless and impassive. They move slowly. In contrast, excited Schnauzers scramble on the staircase when a new arrival comes, claws clicking on the old linoleum. Presumably they belong to someone, they cannot be just a function of the house itself, but she doesn't know to whom.

It is three flights of stairs up to the room. Beside the front door is a door leading to the big old kitchen, where crumpled newspapers lie on the floor, saucepans with unidentifiable encrustations litter the table. The kitchen is not often used. It has the empty, listless look of an abandoned house. Cupboards yawn open, everything is still.

Tacked on the walls there are sheets of butcher's paper covered with what look like practice runs for lino-print posters. Everywhere else there is a junky accumulation of random objects from the street, stacked against walls and spreading out from corners like funghi. Beside the staircase stands a contraption resembling partly a bicycle, partly a wheelchair; it reveals itself as a three-wheeled carriage for invalids, powered by hand levers. Out of a window she has seen one of the occupants of the house proceeding jerkily down the street on it, after taking a short run and jump to get the thing going. Like an old movie. On the brick street. The carriage, like the boxes, broken radios, slightly damaged rugs and spare doors, has been brought in from the lane on the nights before the garbage run. But everything, amazingly, works. In the large, bare, white-tiled and grimy bathroom, hot water flows out of the taps, which always seems surprising to her. It is not long, he tells her, since the place was cracked, or broken into. (Walking down the street with her he looks at a pristine old house with a For Sale sign in front of it. The windows are clean, and through them one catches glimpses of bare white walls, tantalisingly empty rooms. 'It's a nice place,' he says, surveying it appraisingly, 'all it needs is someone to crack it.') Cupboards and chairs not wanted in the rooms stand in the hallways, their backs to the observer, long-forgotten chalk marks and stencilled numbers again exposed. The house is no longer one unit, doors close onto the separate camps of the occupants, keeping out the cold of the hallways.

'How old are you?' she asks him.

'It doesn't matter.' Defensively. To her, his probable existence before the house is just as much a mystery as that which will take place after it. A blank, with an island of the here and now.

III

'One time,' he says, 'we was in a different house, me and a mate. That was in England. Well, one day we haven't eaten anything for a couple of days because we don't have any money and it's too cold to go out of the house. So I go down to the vegetable market after it closes and get this big bag of vegetables for free. It was in the south of England, the house.

'Anyway, I go to the market and coming back on the road there's this little hedgehog running about. So I picks him up and puts him in the basket with the vegetables and when I get home me mate says, 'What've you got?'

'So I say, well, there's potatoes and carrots for a stew and tomatoes, and rhubarb for afterwards, and for meat I've got a hedgehog. Well, he thought I was flippin' mad.'

It is a long speech for him. She considers it.

'A hedgehog?'

'Yes.'

'And you ate it?'

'Well, we didn't feel like killing it right away so we ate the other stuff and went to bed. But the little bugger keeps running round the walls making little scratching noises and going squeak-squeak when it gets to the corners. Drive you mad, in the end.'

'Four o'clock in the morning, Bill yells out "shut that bloody thing up!", so I get up and have a go at it with a hammer, but every time I go to hit it, it curls itself up into a ball.'

'So after a while I turn the gas on in the oven and leave it in there for a while; but every time I open it up it's still running round in there and squeaking . . . Jesus, there's gas everywhere and the little bastard still isn't dead.'

'So what did you do then?' She isn't quite sure if she believes all this.

'I fill the basin up with water and try to drown it. But no matter how long I hold him under the bastard doesn't drown. And I got tired of holding him under after a while.'

'How did you hold it under?'

'Oh, I don't know . . . Couple of forks.

'Anyway, eventually I took this bloody great carving knife and tried to cut its bleedin' throat, holding it uncurled with a spoon and sawing away, but they've got skin like bloody leather . . . you just can't kill the bloody things.'

It is 12 o'clock at night. How long before morning? Ouside she knows that in the blackness the heavy grey clouds are pushing down on the city. She is fascinated by his weirdness. And asks: 'What happened in the end?'

'Eventually I got really wild and picked up this bloody great meat cleaver and . . . WHAM!'

'So you killed it.'

'I killed it.'

'And ate it?'

'And ate it.'

A pause.

'Hedgehogs are a great delicacy in England,' he says. And then he is turning to her again. Pinning her down on the mattress, touching her with his pale hands.

It's going to be a long winter.

Telephones

THOMAS SHAPCOTT

The Manhattan telephone directory (area code 212) of New York comes in three volumes. The White Pages begin on page 57 of the blue covered book, after the general information pages, Manhattan Zip Code Map and Customer Guide and an Open Letter to N.Y. Telephone Customers by William C. Ferguson, President and Chief Executive Officer, explaining new federal regulations.

I am looking for the name KOLLSMAYER.

On each page there are 5 columns of names, 125 names to a column. There are 1653 pages of names. Add that up.

So I find the K section. Little joy:

    Koller
    Kollinger
    Kollins
    Kollisch
    Kollifus
    Kollman

wait a bit

    Kollman
    Kollmer
    Kollmorgen
    Kollock
    Kollor
    Kolmad

There has to be a KOLLSMAYER. I try again. It is, after all, very small print and I am jet-lagged. I have just flown in from

Sydney, Australia, in a non-stop flight that got here shortly after dawn.

Esther Kollsmayer, 1110 Fifth Avenue, right opposite the Metropolitan Museum. She has to be there.

I cannot believe she would need a silent number. My own recollection of Esther, back in 1972, was of someone who lived because of the telephone. For three months she phoned me virtually every night, often for hours at a time, and usually well after midnight.

We never met.

After three months our conversations were extensive; we had become intimate. Her ex-husband in Los Angeles, her psychiatrist in Zurich, or myself, the young writer in the Hotel Tudor (eighteen dollars a night): Esther juggled each of us in turn after Royce left her apartment, heading for the Pickwick Arms and his unfinished playscripts.

Royce had been a Promising Young. Feted in Sydney, he'd been the darling of literary Bohemia. His poems and stories gave way to fragile and aching verse-plays. Critics spoke of a new wave. Ronald Duncan and Christopher Fry were avant-garde then, Eliot's *The Cocktail Party* was in the repertory. 'Kitchen sink' in theatre had not yet reached Australia. Royce wrote about delicate relationships among schoolteacher-poets and hypersensitive graziers' daughters in the harsh, lovely countryside beyond Tamworth or Coonabarabran. His creatures were dream-like, he required non-realistic sets: gauze and cheesecloth. His fame was based on practical considerations: he had achieved the first great post-war story sequence, drawing upon the life of his girlfriend, stories about her Macedonian family with its poetry and pathos, struggling in the parched Mallee hinterland. When I first read those stories I wept. Royce by that time had been taken up by *The Nation* and *The Observer*. Shortly after I met him he was elbowed to London with his new theatre piece, a 'significant development' nudging poet and moonlight into Kings Cross tenements, mid-city.

When his ship sailed, in 1961, he left the girl scrubbing floors in Sydney. An older man followed him over.

How Royce first met Esther I do not know.

When I arrived in 1972, naive on a Churchill Fellowship

and a cash loan from my dying father, Royce and Esther had cemented their routine. Each evening for cocktails he visited her apartment, which was then on the 57th floor of the Waldorf Astoria. She had patent rights to some of her ex-husband's inventions, including something in atomic missiles. Her apartment, Royce told me, was *above* that of the Windsors.

Royce was the first person in five years to entice her out of her unit. He saved her. He had persuaded her, one dreadful night, not to hurl the Pekingese out of her window, something all her friends agreed was a surrogate suicide bid. The Carnegie Hall concert, though, had been Esther's great turning point and it earned Royce a round of cocktail hour acquaintances across Manhattan. He was a marvel.

When I re-met him in 1972 he was dapper; the years in England had not been lost. His life had been crowded.

I only heard snippets, through friends.

Our first meetings, back in the fifties, were friendly and tentative. I sat at his feet. In my apprenticeship Royce was the only new voice, though I was drunk on the short stories, not the plays. When he left our country he was the sort of person for whom everything seemed possible.

Yet by 1961 his *Life of the Coven* was soon dead at the Royal Court Theatre. Nothing more was heard in the papers. He sent only muted Christmas cards. Artist friends sometimes relayed sad stories of staying in Royce's London flat: when they opened the bedroom wardrobe parcels of rejected scripts would fall out; or he would urge them to look for his name in small print in the list of television credits after some late night show.

When my son was born I wrote Royce a long, confused and passionate letter: he was far away. I needed to explain my anguish and apprehension, the sudden burden of responsibility.

Coraggio, coraggio, Royce wrote in reply.

I memorised that letter; he was still the poet-ancestor: 'We are like kangaroos thumping in great leaps on a red-dirt plain, we are impossible yet inevitable once the dream puts us there,' he wrote. '*Coraggio,* dear friend: to engender a son is to play games with numbers and telephones – some day a stranger will ring, saying *ancestor!'*

He was spending the summer, he wrote me, in Italy with a Princess who had a palace in Umbria. His world outdistanced me, I was delighted and envious.

Although he was mobile, I though of his life as not exotic but inevitable. I could dismiss the sad stories. I imagined rich masterpieces.

Yet when Royce returned from Italy to his shared London flat, he found the friend's suicide note with its bequest of the apartment. Then he found, still in the bath, his friend's body.

That year he did publish his first (and only) novel. A young student teacher, west of Tamworth, in New South Wales, distant Australia, encounters sad hints of incest; there is a grazier's daughter.

Royce, always the poet, was sent on a British Council tour to the States. He jumped ship. In 1972 he still had no legal status, though he seemed debonair about that when I finally tracked him down.

In New York, his accent sounded trim and English. He seemed in control of his life. He hinted that a major work was engrossing him.

I cannot recall how, at that time, I became entangled in the phone calls with Esther.

I recall everything. 1972: it is all still vivid – her voice, jewelled and imperious; myself listening, interrupting, explaining, my very accent rubbing some Australian distance into the polished cadence of Royce's voice, revealing for Esther strange hints of his shadowy past.

What did we talk about all those evenings?

I remember what we talked abut.

'You sound like someone who understands. I would do anything for Royce. He is like a son to me. I will look after him, he knows that. He is so thoughtful, so considerate, like a son like the son I could never have, ach, but the suffering, no one could understand that, I expect nobody to understand that. Royce understands a little, he is so *simpatico,* but not even Royce, not even my husband, not even in Zurich my doctor – but let us talk about you. Royce tells me you, too, are a writer. You are being successful, Royce says, only last week in the *New York Times* your poem, Royce showed me your poem and he said there have been others. I must apologise for not remembering your name, I must apologise, it is difficult to remember these things, you do understand, so many things to keep together. Royce tells me you are having successes. I am worried for Royce, he works did you know that, he works day after day, he is working and writing but what can he show for it? I tell him: you must publish, even if only in the *New Yorker*. Keep your name before people's eyes. I tell him, look at your young friend there, your young Australian colleague in the Hotel Tudor, how successful he is and nearly ten years your junior. I tell Royce this, I am honest. I am worried for Royce. And why does your young friend stay at the Tudor?, I say to him. It is not an atmospheric part of town, journalists, United Nations people, it has no colour. We have to invent our own city; I had to invent New York, I tell you. I had to invent Europe again and it was not easy, though I will never return to the old cities, I will never endure the grime and the bomb scars, I have suffered, but that is not suffering. I have to cling tight so as not to let go, and I do not let go, they will not make me let go. Royce is so thoughtful: flowers, he brings me flowers or he sends flowers. We have so much to talk about, Royce and I, I will take care of him, I will see that he does not suffer. And you. Tell me all about you, I am eager to hear of your Australia, Royce does not tell me. Tell me about Royce when you knew him in Australia. Tell me . . .'

I got to know Esther deeply.

One a.m. Two a.m. By the end I even phoned Esther. I would tell her about the Janacek opera or the Messiaen at the Carnegie Hall or my chance discovery of another musuem.

'Now you have a son,' Royce once wrote me, 'you will have to learn to care, to love, to distance, to renounce. *Coraggio.'*

'The Frick! Two months and you have not been to the Frick already? How careless of me, I am a fool, I am foolish not to direct you to the Frick. Suppers I have had in the private rooms. You must go to the Frick immediately, there is the Fragonard Room, but also, ah, there is the Library. And in the West Gallery, the Rembrandt *Polish Rider*. Not to have discovered the *Polish Rider!'*

'*Coraggio!* One day you will not think of the burden in responsibility, you will remember vision – will it hurt you then? Will it wound you deeper than fatherhood? than love? Do we have any choice in who we love, or how, or why? You at least have a son. Courage.'

In New York Royce constantly evaded me. After three months I was due to move to Boston for the next stage of my research. Royce often phoned. We had once spent a drunken night together; he had once taken me to visit one of Esther's salon friends; we had once walked up Third Avenue, gesticulating and remembering. He never spoke of the London years; we talked music, or poetry or the Sydney that had vanished with the 1950s. I had never seen Esther.

Her voice, though, told me more than did Royce's. Our long talks created a whole landscape of her features: hypersensitive, attuned to the delicacy of relationships where the things unsaid cast white smoke, like the ash of bushfires. A city moonlight person, in whose tutelage I had learned to move the entire cycle of my living from office-hour regularity to nocturnal alertness, later and later. In our phone conversations she had etched in the calamitous war damage in Europe, the craters of California and the moneyed gulches of Manhattan: her voice was a face that looked past them and grew from them. She would have an orchid pinned to her black dress, there would be heavy gold rings on many of her fingers, crooked teeth but not too crooked, a scrawny neck now but still a definite air, birdlike and quick, stiff-backed, brown eyes luminous. She would reach out a hand, impulsively, and if we did meet, I would be formal at first, but on departure I would peck her on both cheeks (paper dry, and sweet smelling) and we would gaze long. The agony of separation.

Perhaps, in his room at the Pickwick Arms, Royce had a wardrobe crammed with manuscripts: stories based on his long London years, his Italian interlude, and plays rich with cosmopolitan frisson and complexity, a many-layered novel based on the long, tortuous dialogue with Esther, Proust-like and haunting . . .

Coraggio.

Well, I would have met her and I did not.

Instead, after Royce did phone to arrange the meeting on the eve of my departure I said yes and then spent the afternoon seeing Fellini, *Satyricon,* being drenched with the carnal, the excessive, and the pathos of earthly wishes.

When I shuffled out, into grey rain and darkness, it was well past cocktail hour. The moment was over.

I knew I was returning to New York months ago. I wrote to Royce, care of Esther, noting the new address.

Another mutual friend had told me Esther was reunited with her ex-husband but that Royce was still constantly there in attendance. 'He services them both now, in a manner of speaking.'

I remembered Esther speaking: 'Like a son. I will see Royce is looked after like a son.'

My own son is at university, bearded and independent.

Royce's migration papers have been straightened out. I was one of the referees.

When I wrote I had no reply. But I knew Esther's name, her address. I determined to phone her. It was Esther, in a sense, I must return to.

I could not believe the number unlisted. I walked up to 1110 Fifth Avenue. I did not go in. What would I say to the doorman? It was a penthouse apartment. Would Esther even remember me?

The Manhattan telephone directory is published by Nynex Information Resources. Perhaps I should have contacted them. Perhaps there had been a mistake, an omission. They might have Esther's name on a supplementary listing.

Who was I kidding?

In the end I gave up. Perhaps it was not necessary. It might be best to remember and not to reinvent acquaintances.

I shrugged my shoulders and desultorily skimmed through the telephone pages.

> Shannon
> Shapelly
> Shapiro

I looked closer. No, in a city of so many millions there was not one person bearing my own name. We do not exist, you and I, Esther. We are unlisted. There are whole pages that bear Royce's surname. Columns of people with his initials. He is somewhere out there, one of the multitudes. You are both at this moment uncontactable.

A Real Little Marriage-wrecker

GERARD WINDSOR

I have no trouble now understanding his behaviour then. Which is no great boast. I've had twelve years to dissect it. Though in fairness to myself I think I could say I only took half that time. I had the list of his excuses made out years back. I had to compile it myself; he left, and left me without providing any. But it's a respectable list. I mean it's lengthy and plausible enough. It does me credit. I juggle the order occasionally, depending on my mood – which might range from the sardonic as far even as the tender.

I was on home ground. He wasn't. That fact had numerous ramifications. In the first place he was more lonely and hence more on the prowl than men even normally are. And he was as much a prey himself – not so much to me as to the courting rituals of Ireland. A lone, quite charming young man blundering onto the whirligig of pub and dance hall. From one to the other, one to the other – two, three nights a week. And from there to the carseat-inhibited courts proceeding to their messy consummations. He couldn't turn away from the group, or from the woman in it who had picked him up. There was nowhere else to go. The progression was inevitable. And, irresponsible as men might be, he could hardly be blamed for being unready for this country's contraception laws. Prohibited imports, and nowhere available, and him sticking out anyway with his voice – he couldn't be expected to be scouting for condoms in a country town. So it happens.

He was not on home ground; he was just passing through.

41

He never had any intention of settling here. His life was rooted elsewhere. So irremovable a fact was this that it never presented itself to him as a question. To be pulled up short, and stranded here, with an instant wife and child, *by* them in fact, would have done terrible violence to his outlook and all his expectations. Maybe the psyche could have yanked itself into the new mould, but God knows what the legacy of all that would have been. A woman would have been investing in trouble.

And then again, he had no family here. I had. A mixed blessing of course, in such circumstances. But the worst of it is over soon. Once the child is born, benevolence forces its way to the surface. There may not be forgiveness, but a child of their own blood cannot be resisted; the family rallies round. But he had no one. He would imagine and feel the long-range condemnation from his own home, and it would never fade because he was the source of it himself. And the child, never seen or caressed or spoken to, would remain distant to any family of his, merely a symbol of shame and exile and blighted hopes.

It's a fair case for the defence isn't it? It admits of further riders and allows itself to be proclaimed in a variety of voices. I can shift from one to another so that no one is quite sure of my lasting attitude to the man. Even a fact apparently in his favour can be enunciated so scathingly that he is quite crucified on my irony. He is capable of playing so many roles – resident whipping boy for his sex one moment, my tragic romance the next – that he is of immense use to me.

I am fantasising of course, practising the gestures for a great act of bravado. I really can't say whether I have worked through his desertion or not. I always wonder about people who affirm they have managed such feats.

So she is eleven now and we are in the cocoon of the shortest, darkest days of the year. And he turns up. There had been no trailer of any kind: no contact, no rumours, no anonymous messages or donations. He rings from Dublin and says he is coming down. There is no stopping him. And I am curious. So I say he can come, but I do nothing more positive. I do not go to meet him nor give him directions. I merely make sure that he will arrive when the child is at school.

He is solemn when he arrives. That seems correct. There is no bonhomie, no large gestures of emotion. We do not touch, though I notice that his hands are held ready to shake mine. But I do not invite them. Hence I find that I tend to avoid his eyes. If I met them, it would be hard to avoid some kind of emotional statement, and that would be premature. As a result my manner is a little too much the aggrieved and stern elder silently letting in the delinquent for his dressing-down. But better to err this way than to gush or be frivolous. That might relax him for a moment, but he would turn uneasy, and wonder.

The conversation goes like this. (I try to keep a neutral tone.) 'This is an unexpected surprise.' I wonder whether he is going to suggest that he just happened to be in the area.

'I've been thinking about it for a long time,' he says.

I wait. The running is all his to make.

'I owe you an apology. Saying that is totally inadequate, I know. But to go on and on, explaining and repeating myself, would be useless. And messy. I am very sorry. I really am. I panicked. And I felt helpless. I'm sorry.' That is clearly the end of his set speech. I can actually see him relax in the chair after he has made it. His strategy is obvious, but sensible enough. A comprehensive apology, no attempt at excuse. And so my guns are all spiked. But I am not thrown off balance. If I want to come back to the point, I can do so, and thereby take the upper hand, at any time.

'Well . . .' he begins, now that he feels set free, 'tell me all about yourself.'

I shrug. I still feel just too cool, and no one can launch cold into a lively, revealing response to that kind of invitation. 'What would you like to know?' Superficially the question sounds like an invitation to intimacy, but of course it is quite the opposite. I am refusing to be carefreely open with him. Let him specify what he wants to know, and I will see about accommodating him.

'Well, what are you doing? Are you working?' he tries.

I know what he means. I will ignore the gaucherie in the question. I tell him about the advantages of being a school library assistant, and how you have just enough and no more to do with the children, and how the hours suit. And he nods, and says yes, and smiles, and all the time I can see him waiting for what I don't mention. His eyes wander. But in fact there is no obvious evidence of a child. She is at that age, just past toys and not into the chaos of adolescence, where things identifiably hers are not left lying around. He seems anxious when he doesn't see anything. I realise he may hardly know a thing – whether the child was a boy or a girl, whether it's still alive, whether it lives with me or is in a home or a boarding school. He may know. He may be in touch with other people around here. But he looks anxious. I can even see him juggling and formulating his approach.

And eventually, at a moment when I am reaching down merely to scratch my ankle, he says, with a nicely calculated ambiguity, 'And the child? How are you coping with that?'

He's not really interested in my coping, I warn myself. He just wants to know about the child. So I tell him. 'She's a gas little woman, really she is. We get along famously. I can't see anything other than the Irishwoman in her.' I pause and perhaps I raise my eyebrows in just the faintest smile. 'Maybe that's a compliment to you. After all you were at home here. You seemed to acclimatise very well.' But going that far is a mistake. Referring to the old days, and then to his paternity, especially so casually, is holding out a hand far too readily. 'We're very close. Naturally enough. Not that she's spoiled. But you can go and ask other people that. She's a good child. I know I can say that. My balanced outlook is well known to everyone.' I purse my mouth and give a brief nod of the head as though defying him to contradict me. He does not know whether it is a joke or not.

'You're very lucky,' is all he says. He's uneasy, and his glances slip to the window, and try to edge round corners and penetrate outside this room, the only one he has been in. And, once, there is a sudden noise of young, running feet on the footpath outside, and far from looking round he seizes up. He adjusts, even taps his tie and moves his hand through his hair, and concentrates on controlling himself. His own child is to walk in, never before seen, eleven years of age, knowing nothing. He holds his breath in trembling and in concentration. The steps pass on down the street.

I say to him, 'She's at school now of course.'

'Oh yes, of course,' he echoes me.

'Do you have any children yourself?' I ask.

'No, I'm afraid not,' he tells me.

'But you're married now, aren't you?'

'Yes, I'm married now, but I'm afraid I've got no children.'

He controls the tone of his voice carefully, so that I pick up the note of regret. I don't see any point, or even any place for a comment. I don't want to encourage domestic or marital intimacies. If he must come on his mission of curiosity, I'll make sure we remain distant animals for him to stare at briefly and then pass on.

Then he throws me. 'I'd like to stay here,' he says.

Gentle, gentle, I tell myself. 'That might involve just a few too many explanations. She's at the age where she's more than got her wits about her. And I've only got the two bedrooms. I'm sorry.'

'Don't be sorry,' he says. 'It's my fault. I don't make myself clear. I mean that I don't intend to go home, to Australia I mean. I want to stay here with you, with you both.'

Of course I am stunned. There was no foreseeing that one. Mostly I am angered. The presumption of it! And yet the tardiness of it! But because I have kept myself under such restraint throughout the meeting, I can be fair to him even now. And there is no suggestion in his voice or his manner at all that he is doing us a favour. I can admit that. And I even notice somewhere inside me, a spurt of exhilaration that I have no power over. There is something in the prospect that excites me. I could nurse that feeling. The idea of sharing the burden, and allowing the child her . . . let's call it her inheritance, there's something seductive about that. But that's not fair to the idea, to call it seductive. If I embraced it, I would not be a victim, a prey. But I stay cool. 'And why would you want to do that?'

He looks at me boldly, for the first time. 'You two are the nearest . . .' and he stops himself, and starts again. 'You two are my real family. What I have at home, in Australia, is not even half the real thing.' The cynical ghost must have passed across my face. He waves his hand. 'I'm not after sympathy. There's no one who doesn't understand me.' He smiles. 'I'm not complaining, I'm not criticising, I'm not trying to jump again into the same stream. Just that this is where my child is, my only child, and this is where her mother is.'

Again I must flinch, although it is very low-key. He is aware enough to pick it up. 'That means what it says. I'm not putting you down. You don't want any declaration from me, at least not now. And there's certainly no place for mere flirtatious flattery.'

I wonder if he is goading me into some kind of romantic mood by this dismissal of any thought of it. Maybe semi-consciously, but no more than that, I decide.

'It seems to me unarguable,' he continues, 'that I should be anywhere else. Doesn't it to you?' He pauses, but thankfully he doesn't wait to force me into an answer. 'Don't get me wrong. The last thing I want to do is to force myself on you. I'll get my own place. And we'll take it from there.' He opens out his left hand in one of those gestures that seems more a shrug than anything else. 'I'm being direct, and maybe over-simplifying things,' he decides to say. 'But then the funda-mental issue is very simple.'

'But your life is not your children,' I try to tell him, 'any more than they should be a woman's life.'

He frowns, impatiently. 'Who said she would be?'

'But you can't just throw up all your work at home.'

'Please, please,' he says, 'I've thought about all that, I've looked after it – and, besides, it's irrelevant to you.' He looks at me, quite searchingly, and must be confirmed in his notions, for he adds, 'I know what I'm doing. I don't want you to be feeling any of that sort of responsibility towards me. As I said, I don't want to put a burden or a pressure on you at all. Lord save us, the whole idea is to be a source of help, not the opposite.'

I am in at least two minds about all this. I am bemused by this odd species of conversion or repentance that seems to have overtaken him. And he shows too much of the fanatic's humourlessness about his whole plan. But then again, the sincerity, and the apparently unselfish terms of the offer, are attractive. What would I have to lose by accepting it? His dull earnestness would pass in time – that was never part of his personality – but the solicitude and usefulness, and maybe more, would remain.

So I make him tea while I think about this. And he comes out to the kitchen with me, and stands in the doorway easily but not over-familiarly. Yes, I think, you do the balancing trick well enough, a style of reticent charm. I'll wear that.

Then he sees the napkin ring, the christening present. With the child's name and the date of the ceremony on it. And the napkin, untidily, only just pushed into it. He puts out his hand to touch it, to pick it up, to play with it. And he sees the egg stains, and the smudges, and the long-unpolished dullness of the silver. And I can't help noticing that his mind, betrayed rather than veiled by his eyes, becomes a playground, resounding with children's business, and skips, and wayward-ness, and high-pitched insistent cries. But there is only one child in it, and she is doing everything for *him*. And calling to *him*. I turn away; the noise is embarrassing. I forget to warm the pot, and spoon the tea straight in. For the first time since he arrived I am upset, I have lost control. He is in love with that child, I tell myself.

'Who are the godparents?' he says. 'What second name did you give her?' He hardly pauses. 'Does she come home for lunch?'

No, I correct myself, why don't I listen to what the man is really saying? He's not in love with this daughter of mine. He's in love with a child all right, but the child has still to materialise. I can't risk its being this child of mine. I look through the kitchen window into the grey, grey day. I lower my eyes into the sink and upend the teapot. Then I turn round, and I have to hold hard behind me to the cold metal of the sink to restrain myself from rushing over and throwing my arms around him. But I look straight at him, and I feel for him, and he must be able to see it in my eyes. 'I'm sorry,' I say, 'I really am. But go home to your wife. You're not needed anywhere else.' And again I say I'm sorry, and it's really for speaking so harshly. But I make no further concession. I stay anchored to the sink. And, whatever else he understands, he understands that's final. And he goes.

And the warm feeling of righteous triumph leaves me glowing but quite weak. By the time she arrives home from school and I pull myself out of the chair I can admit that it was a self-indulgent exercise. But I suspect that it was a useful one for all that.

Through Road

JEAN BEDFORD

It starts the minute we get into the car. The kids are in the back seat complaining because they're missing 'Laverne and Shirley' or some shit and I can tell Robert's wishing he could have stayed at home himself.

Then the car won't go. I yank on the key and push the accelerator as hard as I can and it just moans a bit and won't catch at all.

'Have you tried the choke?' he says.

'No, I haven't tried the choke. It's automatic.'

'Did you give it some revs when you turned the key then?'

'Yes, I gave it revs. Just leave it a minute.' I think I've flooded it and want to give it time to settle. I can smell petrol.

'You've probably flooded it.'

'Mmmm. . .'

We sit and wait a few minutes. The kids are getting on our nerves but neither of us is going to be the first to yell at them. Finally I sit up again and reach for the key. This time the motor catches and starts. We grin at each other and Robert tells the kids he'll whack them both if they don't shut up. We're already ten minutes late and we're still in the parking lot.

I drive off, concentrating on staying on the right side of the road, with all the bulk of the car on *my* right side, which disturbs the habit reactions of twenty years. The roads are very dark, and narrow, and I get a surprise every time a car passes me from the other direction. At the first intersection we have to turn up a slight hill and the car dies as soon as I take my foot off the accelerator.

'What's the matter?' he says anxiously.

'It's OK. I just don't want to roll backwards when the lights change.'

The lights do change and I manage to let go the handbrake, turn the ignition key and put the semi-automatic shift into first, then quickly shove my foot on the gas pedal. I'm sitting hunched forward holding the wheel tightly, trying to work out the shape of the road ahead. I know we've got another two or three intersections, one where I have to cut across the traffic and make a left turn, something I haven't done here yet. The first part is easy, just bends in the road and no traffic coming, but then we get to the major crossing and, I hope, the road my friend lives on. I don't know which way to go and the street numbers aren't indicated. The kids are quarrelling in low voices and Robert's starting to tell me about some book review he read in the *TLS*.

'You've got a green light,' he says.

'Yes, I know. But I don't know which way to turn.'

'Are you sure this is the road?'

'Well, it says so on the sign. Unless they're lying.' I know I'm being unfair – his poor night vision precludes him from reading the signs.

'Who's fucking this duck?' I say, and he laughs.

'Didn't what's her name? Ellis? Didn't she tell you which way to turn?'

'She *said* right. But on the map her road doesn't go to the right here – it's called something else entirely.' While I'm talking the light has turned amber and I decide to take the left turn.

'Shit! Look out!'

He grabs the wheel just as I start to turn into three lanes of oncoming cars. I make a wobbly recovery and somehow get to the correct side of the road. I pull into the next byway and study the map again. The house numbers here are nothing like the one written on my scrap of paper.

This goes on for another half an hour. We do U-turns and end up back at Palo Alto. We look at the map again in the grounds of an old people's home. We go up and down the road, and every time I take my foot off the gas the motor dies and I have to do my no-hands, four-feet juggling act with the brake and gears and accelerator. We get back to the original crossing and I turn right.

'Are you OK now?'

'No. I'm heading home. At least I know where that is.' The oil light has begun to flicker on and off. 'We'll have an omelette at home, kids, and visit Ellis some other day. All right?'

They don't care, they're just mad they've missed their TV show.

'Oh, bugger it.' I pull over to the side of the road about a mile from home. 'I can't bear to admit defeat. What if we have one more go? We'll ignore the map and believe Ellis. What do you reckon?'

'Sure, mom.' The kids' accents are so good now I don't know whether they're still putting them on or if they've really acquired a California voice. I know Robert would rather go home, but he agrees too.

We go back, make a new turn and end up outside I. Magnin's in a shopping complex. We approach from a different angle and I spot a house number very close to the one Ellis has given me and I pull up immediately. We're almost there. An hour and a half late, and we still have to walk a hundred yards or so along a dark road, throwing ourselves into the hedge with each passing car, but we are really there. Even the children are silent and grateful by now. We see lights in the windows, I recognise Jolly's bike, we stumble across the unlit lawn and ring the bell.

The party is OK. Everyone has given us up and started eating but as soon as I have a couple of fast beers and a bowl of spaghetti I feel fine. I serve Robert his pasta, making sure I give him plenty, knowing that that sort of car tension can lower his sugar radically. I intend to remind him to have an extra serving of fruit or icecream, but I get talking and I forget. It's the first time he has met these people, my fellow post-doctoral students, and I don't want to nag him in front of them.

I look over at him from time to time; he seems to be getting on well, talking about Australia and Barry Humphries with Joe, who has spent some time in England. The kids are a great hit,

Sally shimmying away to the music and Rosa curling up on an oversize cushion, sleeping like a rosy cherub through all the noise and people stumbling over her. I smoke a lot and Robert makes smart-arsed remarks about it, but good-humouredly.

For the last half hour we sit together in the big rocking chair and stroke each other's arms. When we leave, the kids sleep-stunned in the back seat under a quilt, we get home without any problems at all. Ellis turns out to live about seven minutes away.

We put the kids to bed and come downstairs to drink tea. We gossip a while, aimlessly, about the other people at the party, sorting them into who we really like, don't mind, who reminds us of friends back home. Robert admits he's had a good time. Then we go to bed. After he puts out the lights I turn to him. Things are not always this relaxed between us.

'I'm sorry,' he says. 'I'm too tired. Is that OK?'

'Sure,' I say in a broad American voice. 'It'll keep.'

Then I lie awake for a while thinking about everything: what we are doing here, thousands of miles from home, what we are still doing together; sorting out all the things that make life worth going on with. Apart from the children there don't seem to be many. . .

. . . When I was still living in New Guinea, Annie Minsen warned me, at a cricket match. It was a blue, pellucid day during the Dry and we were playing on a pitch set into a grassy promontory – if the ball fell into the sea it was automatically a six.

'I've nursed diabetics,' Annie said. 'Really, you don't want to get involved with one. He's OK now, maybe, but with age comes complications. It's hard on their families.'

We were sitting in the shade of a gnarled, creamily flowering frangipani, eating sweet orange quarters. I was thinking of *goin pinis*; going finish. Home for good. I wondered if Annie was getting her revenge for my asking if she was Eurasian when we first met. She was angrily proud of her pure Chinese lineage. I thought idly that she might have ideas of racial purity, or euthanasia for the genetically unsound.

'Of course,' she said, as if hearing my thoughts, 'there would be some danger in having children too. It could be hereditary, no one knows.'

Later, Robert and I often referred, joking, to this conversation. 'Perhaps you should have listened,' he always said. 'Can't say I wasn't warned,' I always replied.

But warnings often come too late. It was not possible, then, for me to weigh potential failure against the languid joy of those early months; the hot Port Moresby nights; the seeming cornucopia of mango, paw-paw, avocado; gin-and-tonics so cold and strong they shone blue in their frosted glasses. It was a sexual love then, of frantic, earnest experiment, our two bodies seeming to share the one parameter of skin. There were the dawn walks along the grey-sand beach with small crabs plopping dirty holes at our feet; there were the late-night, early-morning, sweaty lovemakings, in my narrow bed, Creedence Clearwater blaring from the stereo bought cheap from the strange Russian in Engineering. There were my arrivals at morning classes still trembling in the aftermath of orgasm, sure that my language students could smell him on me, understood my shaking hands. So that sex became irretrievably associated with the diagrams of Transformational Grammar, which I never thought to apply to my own life as Chomsky might have advised. The deep meaning of any sentence always there, programmed into our synapses, discoverable under the most convoluted spider-web of syntax: the most sophisticated, intricate, evolving, cunningly spun love affair reducible, perhaps, to girl meets boy.

And so, tonight, in another foreign country, thinking all this, I fall asleep, waking before dawn with the familiar apprehension already prickling at my skin, the old coldness in the bowels. I put my hand out, tentatively, to feel the soaked sheets, his cool, clammy flesh.

'Bobby. Are you OK?' If he can answer it's not too bad.

'Love. Are you all right?' My voice is soft, friendly, I keep it steady. I don't want to startle him awake. That can trigger deep shock, leads to ambulances, straitjackets, the messy jabbing at veins with syringes like horseneedles.

I touch him gently on the shoulder. His eyes open but his whole body is stiff, extended. I know the cramps have started. He is awake but he cannot speak. Sweat is still breaking out all over him, even his feet are covered in tiny droplets.

'Bobby? It's OK. I'll get some sugar milk. It's OK.'

I tremble, going down the stairs, and my palms are moist, but I am fast and efficient, spooning sugar into milk until it is barely liquid. My body does not panic, but my mind is racing, racing. Back in the bedroom it is clear that he cannot take the milk himself. I run downstairs again for more sugar until the glass is full of a sweet paste. This has happened before, I tell myself repeatedly as I go back up, it will be all right. I dip my finger into the mixture and place it on his tongue. I do this many times. I know it will be absorbed eventually but I hope it will be before he goes into real insulin shock. His eyes roll, but he is swallowing. Now I can put my arm behind the pillow to prop his head and spoon the sugar into his mouth. Finally he begins to lick it from the spoon himself. When that glass is finished I go quietly down for more, this time drinkable. I wait beside the stove for five minutes exactly by the clock, to give the first sugar time to work a little. I don't want to go back upstairs until he is out of it but I can't risk waiting longer.

He is muttering when I come in, about boxing. He is counting himself out '. . . One . . . two . . . three . . . you bastard . . . I can get up . . . four . . . five . . . you rotten cunt . . . all right . . . six . . . seven . . . I'm getting up . . .' I know this is the tricky stage, when he is conscious but not really aware of where he is. I have to become part of the delirium myself if I want him to drink.

'Here's your milk, champ,' I say. I keep my voice light and dry. He refuses it. He begins to recite dirty verse and reaches for my breast.

'Only if you have some of this first,' I say.

He laughs, and I laugh too. He goes on with Abdul el Bulbul Emir . . . 'The harlots turned green, the men shouted "Quean!", It was laughed at for years by the Tsar. For Abdul the fool, left half of his tool, Up Ivan Skivinsky Skivar . . .'

He laughs again, softly. I try to hand him the milk but he knocks it away and some spills on the bed.

'I haven't finished,' he says. 'There are ten more verses at least.'

'No,' I say. 'That was the last verse, now you must drink the milk.'

He raises his head and looks at me and then he groans.

'Oh Jesus, Jesus. My love, I'm sorry. Oh Christ you bastard.'

'It's OK,' I say and I try to smile. 'Here, drink this.'

'I hate it. What is it?'

'Just finish it, there's not much more.'

When he has drunk it all I put the glass down in a puddle of sticky syrup and then I get my dressing gown on and sit on the bed. This is the time when I must not recriminate, as I have too often before, must not ask how or why or whether he over-injected or had too little carbohydrate at dinner. This is the time when he is remorseful, apologetic, sometimes begs to die. I stroke his damp hair, gently, holding in my anger. He has stopped sweating, he is out of it. His eyes close and I let him sleep for a little while. When I am sure his breathing is normal I wake him up so that we can change the sheets. He goes to shower and then makes a pot of tea which we drink, sitting up, in the fresh bed. The sky is grey outside the window, it is morning. Suddenly the digital alarm sounds and I switch it off.

'You're not going to run this morning are you?' I ask. I can't help it.

'Not now. Perhaps later.' His voice is obstinate, he knows what I think about running after a bad reaction. He puts his hand on my thigh. 'I'm sorry. I don't know how you put up with me.'

'Well,' I say, 'I was warned, and I took no notice.'

I take the cups downstairs, with the sticky glass, and I wash them at the sink. I stand with my hands in the warm water trying to fight down my anger, and the tears come. I think that I hate him but that I can't leave him because he needs me. I think that it is his fault I was not with my mother when she died and that I might not forgive that. I think about how we drank and smoked dope and went to parties and Chinese restaurants when we first lived together, about how if I met him now, teetotal, non-smoking, jogging ascetic, I would not be attracted. I think that I would like a word-processor and about his contempt for technology. I think about how he never acts on the notes the children bring home from school, that it is always me who arranges the cakes for the fete, the presents for birthdays and Christmas. I think that I always buy his underwear and socks. Then I find myself laughing, at the sink, the water turning cold around my wrists. I am reminded of my mother, rouged, permed, the cigarette tongued to the corner of her mouth, who always said when things were at their worst, 'Well, you have to laugh, don't you? If you don't laugh, you cry.'

When I go back to bed he is getting up. He dresses in his running gear, turns the light off and pulls down the blind against the morning noise. I can hear the children stirring in the next room.

'Hey,' I say, 'come here.'

We kiss, affectionately, like a very old couple. He tucks the blankets around me, closes the bedroom door and goes to organise the kids' breakfast, dressing, school, as he usually does.

I know that he won't wake me until he gets back from running. I think of him, pushing himself panting round and round the track until he has done his five miles, while I sleep. I hope, closing my eyes, that I am smiling.

The Voyage of Their Life

GLENDA ADAMS

The rooster was crowing, at 2 in the afternoon, and the cicadas had started up again after their lunchtime quiet.

'It's a case of too much noise,' said Henry Watter, the father of Lark. 'Far too much noise.' He seized the hammer and rushed into the backyard. He thrust the rooster into a wooden crate and hammered it shut, the sun glinting on the hammerhead and on the lenses of his metal-rimmed glasses. The Bakers' dog next door started barking. The rooster continued crowing. From further off came the buzz of a lawnmower.

Lark looked through the old seventy-eights and the sheet music stacked near the pianola – Caruso singing 'Vesti La Giubba', a silly song called 'I Lift up My Finger and I Say Tweet, Tweet'. She had already saved a hundred pounds, almost enough for a one-way passage to somewhere, Singapore or Ceylon perhaps, or even Kansas, and she had arranged for an interview with Qantas to be an air hostess, after her exams. That was one way to get away.

Lark's father rushed into the house, then returned to the backyard with several army blankets and an old Belgian flag, which he draped over the crate, layer on layer, creating night for the confused bird.

'Sits there like a stunned mullet,' said Henry Watter.

'Do you think that's wise, Henry?' asked Lark's mother from under her pink cloth sun hat. Her hands, in white gloves, were pegging clothes on the line with such alacrity that she could have been playing a scherzo on the pianola. The gloves protected her hands from the sun. The sun hat, in addition to performing its intended function, protected her head from the kookaburras and magpies which liked to swoop down to take strands of hair for their nests.

'Like bombers,' said Henry Watter. 'It's a case of World War II in our own backyard. This country's a joke. One big joke.'

The crowing continued, muted, while he lobbed stones at the yelping dog next door. Every now and then he threw a stone into the trees to silence the cicadas. And he stood, waiting for the next noise, in his singlet and khaki shorts, which were held up by a piece of rope tied around his waist in a reef knot. His feet, in black nylon ankle socks and lace-up shoes, looked as if they had been planted and had sprouted those white legs now trembling with rage.

The lorikeets, fifty or sixty of them, started lining up on the veranda rail, jostling and squawking, peering in the window, arranged in a multicoloured tableau vivant, waiting for the daily bread that Lark's mother put out for them. Taking care of Australia's natural heritage, she called it.

Lark's father took a mop and waved it at the birds on the veranda rail. 'Heritage be damned,' he said. 'In this flaming country it's a case of too much nature. Far too much nature.'

'Henry, please, no language,' whispered Lark's mother.

'Where's the cat when it's needed?' Henry Watter muttered. He swung at the birds. 'William the First,' he said and swung again. 'William the Second,' and he swung again. 'Henry the First, Stephen.'

'Watch my windows,' called Lark's mother from under her hat. 'They'll cost the earth to replace.'

'Henry the Second, Richard Lionheart, John.' Lark's father threw the mop down beside the back steps and stamped inside.

'Mind my parsley and my mint,' said Lark's mother.

'William and Mary,' said Lark's father. 'Far, far too much nature.'

Lark had always planned to run away. When she was four, she had packed her little cardboard sewing case with her supplies for the journey – a swimsuit, an umbrella, her money box, and a little bottle of water – and kept it under the bed, next to the large black umbrella that could also be used as a walking stick. She wanted to wander around and around the world, until she found some kind of island to settle on.

'I'm going now,' she often said, taking the suitcase and the umbrella, standing at the front door.

'She's going now,' they said, if they said anything at all.

And sometimes she went along the cliff road, above the Pacific Ocean, past the school, as far as the corner.

In that house in Park Avenue on the cliff in Sydney, Henry Watter sat memorising *Bartlett's Familiar Quotations*.

Lark was dumping her books in a canvas bag.

'Test me,' Lark's father said.

The lorikeets were at the window, nudging the glass, tapping it with their beaks, chattering.

'I was just going down to the beach to study,' said Lark.

'Test me first,' said her father. He, too, had been preparing to run away for years.

Lark sighed. 'Kings of England? Shakespeare? Definitions?'

Henry Watter pointed at the street map of London pinned across the bookshelves.

'Streets of London, then,' said Lark.

The muffled cries of the rooster still reached them.

'God love a duck,' said Henry Watter. And then, 'God stiffen the crows.'

The Bakers' dog was still yelping.

'How do you get from Regent's Park Zoo to,' Lark searched for somewhere for him to go, 'to the Tower of London.'

When Lark was young, Henry Watter had taken her to the zoo, the Sydney zoo, and at the end of the day had said, 'Let us catch the ferry now and go home.' Lark thought he had said he was going to catch a *fairy,* and she was in some state of excitement as they walked down the path to the harbour. At the wharf, when he asked, 'Is this the ferry to the Quay?,' the boat hand nodded and they boarded. 'Where's the fairy?' Lark asked, and her father said, 'You're on it.' It felt like a cruel joke. Lark ran onto the wharf and refused to get back on the ferry. Her father had to get off, too, and the ferry left without them. That particular ferry caught fire in the middle of the harbour and the passengers had to take to the lifeboats. Several of them drowned. They all said it was Lark's sense of impending doom that had saved them.

Henry Watter settled in his chair, turning his back on the map. He pushed his glasses on top of his head. His voice became soft and slow. 'Turn left on Marylebone Road, then south on Tottenham Court Road, which turns into Charing Cross Road, to Trafalgar Square. Then turn left on The Strand. Keep going.' And he kept going, until he ended up at the Tower. 'Of course,' he added, 'you could go out the northern end of the park, near Primrose Hill, and walk along the footpath beside the canal to Camden Town, then take the tube.' He took care to explode the 't' in tube. 'You see, Larkie, I'll get along there, when I go. I can say tube like an aristocrat, instead of chube like a pleb.'

'I'm going to the beach now,' said Lark. 'I have to study my French.'

'Just one more, Larkie, please,' pleaded Henry Watter.

'But I'll really need my French, when I go,' said Lark.

'And I'll need to know my England.'

Lark sighed. 'Name three of Shakespeare's clowns,' she said, 'not including poor Yorick.'

The lorikeets were calling out. The tableau had broken formation and the birds were falling over one another in anticipation.

Henry Watter placed *Bartlett's Familiar Quotations* in Lark's hands. 'Test me, Larkie.'

She let the book fall open. ' "There is a tide in the affairs of men, which, taken at the flood, leads on to fortune." '

Henry Watter sat up straight. ' "Omitted, all the voyage of their life is bound in shallows and in miseries." W. Shakespeare, J. Caesar. Act four, scene three.'

Mrs Watter was putting out the bread soaked in milk and honey. The beaks of the lorikeets hit the tin pans like gravel falling on a tin roof.

'Get the cat,' cried Henry Watter. 'Set it on those birds.' He fell back into his chair. He shook his head for a while, then picked up the dictionary and continued to memorise it. 'Martello tower,' he said. 'A circular, masonry fort.'

'But you'll note,' said Lark's mother, 'that sometimes he holds the book upside down. I do believe he thinks he is a writer or something. He keeps scribbling things in an exercise book. I find it under the mattress when I turn the bed.'

With her books under her arm and the beach umbrella over her shoulder, Lark walked along Park Avenue to the path that led to the beach. She hoped to find Solomon White there. They had started doing things together, going out. The night before, they had seen *'Cat on a Hot Tin Roof'* and Solomon had asked Lark if she could put on her nylons the way Elizabeth Taylor had in the movie, a kind of peeling-on motion. Lark had said she thought she could. And they were to go to the Recovery Ball together, after Lark's exams. Solomon had graduated and no longer had final exams, only his research, and he was waiting to hear from the dozens of universities abroad, where he had applied to do his doctoral research.

Solomon's younger brother, Marshall, was in the schoolyard, mowing the lawn, earning his pocket money. That was a good sign. It seemed to mean that the Whites were around, not off at their country house or at a luncheon in the eastern suburbs.

The three White boys were named after islands in the South Pacific – Gilbert, Solomon and Marshall.

'Better than Guam,' Solomon said, 'or Nauru.'

'I wish I were named after an island,' cried Lark, 'or that an island were named after me.'

'You'd have to own one,' said Solomon, who had already travelled a lot. 'Then you could name it what you wanted.'

The Whites were the most exotic family in Park Avenue. Mr and Mrs White had even taken their three sons to England for a year, for the culture, when they were all very young. Solomon's great-grandfather, Charles White, and his great-grandmother were said to have Christianised the entire South Pacific. It had been ascertained that Charles White had drunk with Robert Louis Stevenson. And he would have conducted the service in 1914 when the ashes of the storyteller's wife were brought to Samoa, if a storm had not prevented his boat from leaving the island where he was proselytising at the time.

Lark pushed hard on the rusty metal catch of the old canvas

umbrella. Another year and she should have enough money to go away. She lay on the sand and started with *L'etranger,* trusting that sentences like, 'I was almost blinded by the blaze of light,' 'the sand was hot as fire,' and 'now and then a longer wave wet our canvas shoes' would be useful during her future adventures, away. Two flies buzzed around her, alighting on her lips and nostrils, and, as she read, she had to keep brushing her hand against her face.

Solomon White threw his car keys on the pages of Lark's book. She had not sensed his walking toward her across the sand. *'La campagne bourdonnait du chant des insectes,'* she said to Solomon. 'The countryside was throbbing with the hum of insects. I'll be needing that, when I go away.'

Solomon was shaking his head to get rid of the two flies, which had transferred their attention to him. He sat on the sand beside her and rubbed suntan oil on her back.

'Can you justify the following being regarded as a short story?' Lark asked, looking out to sea. 'What does the author achieve within the severe limits he has set himself? That's the kind of question I'm going to have to answer.' She continued, quoting, ' "To die like Joan of Arc," said Terbaud, from the top of a pyre built with his furniture. The Saint Owen fire brigade hindered him." '

Solomon laughed. 'That's not a story.'

'Why not? You have plot, character, a protagonist who wants something urgently, in this case, a death like Joan of Arc's, an antagonist, in this case the fire brigade, you have a sense of time and place,' said Lark. 'That's all a story needs. Three lines. Less.'

And then Mrs Baker came huffing past, since it was Saturday and not a sign of turpitude to be on the beach, and stopped to shout that it was a hot day, like a furnace. Solomon continued to rub the oil on Lark's back, Lark agreed that it was a hot day, and Mrs Baker passed on to pitch her umbrella a little further along the sand next to a friend, and her chattering began again. 'Like a parakeet in a cage,' Lark said.

Lark's mother remarked that Mrs Baker had seen Lark on the beach with a young man.

'I was with Solomon White,' said Lark.

Lark's mother asked what he had been doing.

Lark frowned and thought. 'Possibly he was helping me put up the umbrella.'

'Mrs Baker said that Solomon White was rubbing oil on your body.'

'That's right,' said Lark. 'That's what he was doing.'

'Then why didn't you say so?'

From his chair Henry Watter called, 'Get thee to a nunnery.'

And Lark thought it would not be long now before she left.

'I'm leaving,' Solomon White had told Lark as he smoothed the oil over her back and arms. 'I have the fellowship. Champaign-Urbana. I am going forever.'

Lark had hunched over her book. She wished that Solomon would fail at something. *'Rester ici ou partir, cela revenait au même,'* she'd said, surly. 'To stay here or to leave, it comes to the same thing.'

'Sour grapes,' said Solomon. 'You'll be going soon, too. Everyone does.'

They went down to the water's edge and walked along the bright sand to the sandstone rock platform at the base of the weathered cliff. The sun glinted on the mica and quartzite fragments in the stone. The sea gulls picked at the bits and pieces of oysters and periwinkles. The sea was calm. The waves welled up, rose, like a loaf of bread, and spilled gently across the rock shelf, wetting their feet. They lay down together on the rocks. The water, tepid from its journey across the warm rock shelf, slid under their backs. Lark's head rested on Solomon's shoulder.

'You're giving me a golden shoulder,' he said, and kissed her. 'Perhaps you'll end up with me in Champaign-Urbana. Who knows?'

'End up?' said Lark. 'We would just be beginning.' She sat up and watched the sea gulls. 'I want to go to Paris. You'd like living in Paris too,' she quoted. 'And of course we could travel about France for some months in the year.'

'Paris?' said Solomon, puzzled, sitting up. 'I have to go to America. Sometimes I have absolutely no idea what you're talking about.'

'Camus,' said Lark.

Very far out a ship was gliding past, a freighter heading north, for Newcastle or Gladstone, and then possibly further, across the Pacific to America.

'Could I come with you now?' Lark had asked into Solomon's shoulder.

'I'll write,' Solomon had said. 'I'll tell you what it's like, away. We'll see what happens. I'll miss you, you know.'

'Can you justify the following being regarded as a short story?' "Silot, a valet, established an attractive woman in the home of his absent master at Neuilly, then disappeared carrying away everything but her." '

'You didn't go around the rocks, did you?' asked Lark's mother.

'I don't remember,' said Lark.

'Mrs Baker said you went around the rocks with him,' said Lark's mother. 'You know what happens around the rocks. It's not nice, for one thing, and for another the waves can be dangerous. They can kill.'

'He's leaving,' Lark said. 'You don't have to worry about him and me any more. He's off, lucky devil.'

'Please, Lark, no language,' said Mrs Watter.

Lark walked slowly along the clifftop road from the house to the little school with the iron fence. Solomon White had flown off to America.

'We'll have to fly,' Mrs Watter had said once, when Lark was very young and they were running late for the bus into town. Mrs Watter had seized Lark's hand and run down the front path, hauling Lark along, who expected that at any moment they were to rise into the air and fly to the bus.

Lark stopped at the school gates, leaning her forehead against the bars, her eyes closed. The cicadas were shouting, like a male chorus, causing the air to throb, the sound waves almost palpable. She heard again those mouth organs, the recorders, triangles, tambourines, little drums and the sound of spoons beating against saucepans and saw those children, some fifty of them, parading in a circle around the school lawn, looking neither happy nor sad. The older ones, Solomon White among them, were playing the musical instruments, the younger were banging the spoons and saucepans. Lark was crying because she had only two spoons to beat together. The headmistress stood on the school veranda and announced several times, wringing her hands, 'We have won the war in Europe, children. God was on our side. The Germans have been brought to their knees. We have cut them down.'

A girl who was a celebrity in the school because she had been in England when the war broke out was allowed to plant a tree in a special ceremony.

'VE Day will be our May Day forever more,' said the headmistress. 'And now there remains only the Pacific to be won.'

In the cloakroom Lark stole the woollen beret of the girl who had planted the tree. She crammed her own panama hat on her head, trying to tuck the beret under it, out of sight. When the girl cried that she could not find her beret, the teacher seized Lark's panama and reclaimed the beret. Her face leant down into Lark's.

'Two hats?' the teacher said, sarcastic, dangling both in Lark's face, humiliating her in front of all the children. 'Get your own beret, if you want one.'

But with wartime rationing, only the rich had woollen berets.

'What is May Day?' Lark had asked her father.

'Mayda?' He sat up, his book face down on his knees, delighted with the question. 'Mayda is a legendary island southwest of Ireland, and west of Brittany.'

'May Day?'

'Oh, you mean Mayday! That's an international distress call. Do you want me to teach it to you?'

'No,' said Lark.

Then she remembered leaning against the mulberry tree and watching her mother chop the head off a chicken. The body ran around the yard. The Pacific war was over and they were celebrating with a chicken dinner. The Bakers took down the flags of the allies, which they had flown every day of the war. They offered the Belgian flag to Lark, the little girl next door. Lark was surprised that the black, yellow and red cloth was woollen and extremely rough to the touch. She wrapped the flag around her, like a cloak. She put on her father's gas mask and crept to the fence and peered over at the Bakers' boy. He ran to his mother, screaming that there was a monster on the back fence, and Mrs Baker told him that the Watters were a strange lot.

'Ask me the stops on the air route from Sydney to London,' Henry Watter said to little Lark. 'It won't be long now, before I go.' Then he continued, without waiting for her to form the question, 'Sydney, Brisbane, Gladstone, Townsville, Karumba, Groote Eylandt, Darwin, Kupang, Bima, Surabaja, Batavia, Klabat Bay, Singapore, Penang, Bangkok, Rangoon, Akyab, Calcutta, Allahabad, Gwalior, Karachi, Gwador, Dubai, Bahrein, Basra, Tiberias, Athens, Brindisi, Rome, Marseilles, Macon, Southampton, London.'

Lark lifted her head from the fence rail. The cicadas, accompanied by lawnmowers, were still at it.

To her Qantas interview Lark wore a floral blouse buttoned to the neck and a dark-green linen skirt with four buttons at the back, forming the four points of a square, like the buttons on a man's double-breasted jacket. She thought she looked rather like an air hostess already. 'With those buttons, I hope you don't have to sit down,' Lark's father said. In her coat pocket she carried Solomon White's first letter.

The secretary told her to take off her coat before she went in to the personnel officer. 'He has to check your deportment,' she said. So Lark abandoned her coat and entered the huge office, where a man in a brown suit sat behind a desk at the far end and watched her deportment as she walked to him.

'Why,' he asked, 'do you want to be a Qantas air hostess?' He tapped a pencil against his finger, as if he had asked a riddle about the meaning of life.

Lark hesitated. She thought of saying she had always admired Qantas and had wanted to serve that particular company ever since she was little.

'I want to leave Australia,' she said. 'I want to go away.'

She had to walk out again, across that vast floor, with that personnel officer watching those four buttons and judging.

'The bermuda season has arrived here and both men and women are gaily decked in the new season's colours and subtle variations of cut and style,' Solomon White wrote. 'And here is a piece of one-upmanship you might like to have at your fingertips. The word is "rain check." I called a girl to ask her for a date – you have to go out on dates in America, it's the done thing, it doesn't mean anything – and she said she was very sorry, she couldn't make it but would I give her a rain check please. I said, yes of course, but being a cautious soul I inquired what it was I had just given her.' Solomon White seemed to be in the most exciting place in the northern hemisphere. And while he had not mentioned again that Lark might join him, he had said that he remembered her head resting against his shoulder and that he missed her.

'I feel now that it is time for me to attend to other matters,' Solomon had ended his letter. 'So if you will excuse me I will just pour myself another bourbon and squirt from the cocktail bar and make a graceful exit through the kitchen, where the pretzels and beer nuts are kept.'

Lark was informed that she was not the right material for an air hostess.

She searched through the Saturday *Herald* for jobs abroad, governesses wanted, anywhere, fares paid.

'We had an air raid today according to the radio,' Solomon had written. 'But since I didn't see any aeroplanes or bombs I can only assume that it was a hoax, a failure on somebody's part, or perhaps, a civil defense effort. I was in Washington, D.C., with a friend during our semester break and viewed the Constitution, the Bill of Rights, and the Declaration of Independence in their bombproof, shockproof, fireproof, helium-filled vault. The traditions of America are very obvious to one and all and, quite seriously, I came away very impressed. I can now think of America as something more than a plastic hot dog, a huge imperalist financial machine and the home of the Midwest.'

And then he had added, 'Summer in Champaign-Urbana is a time for socialising in a capitalistic sort of way, and I am drastically short of money. Yesterday a young lady and I went out stealing peaches and tomatoes from the university orchard. It doesn't mean what you think. In America it's just a social necessity to date.'

In the library among the many books written by various

Charles Whites, Lark found one by a Charles White who was the first man to ride a single horse across the North American continent, from Catalina Island in California to Coney Island in New York. She copied this information out and sent it to Solomon White, in the middle of the North American continent. 'Why don't we do something inventive like your ancestor?' she wrote. 'We could write a book about it. Together.'

Solomon White wrote and told Lark that he was facing a long, hot, lonely summer and could no longer do without the steady companionship of a female. He had succeeded in meeting a tall, fairly attractive, fairly blonde American. They had been to New York together. 'It's the most exciting place I've been to,' he wrote. 'You should see the real Park Avenue.' And some weeks later Solomon White's mother conveyed to Lark the good news that Solomon was getting married to a fairly tall, really beautiful American blonde. And Solomon's letters to Lark stopped altogether.

Lark dreamt she was waiting for a New York subway to whisk her off to an unknown destination. When the train hurtled into the station, it bore the sign, 'Beware the deadly gases of Atmium and Thomium.' It was definitely her train. She had to board it, although she had no gas mask.

At dinner Lark said, 'I'm going now.'

'This bird is tough,' said Henry Watter. He looked up. 'She's finally going?'

'To Paris,' said Lark. 'Or New York.'

'What do you want to go there for?' Henry Watter asked. 'England's the only place.' He chewed at his food, looking at each piece on his fork before he put it in his mouth. 'Tough old bird. Just like your mother.'

'It's that Solomon, isn't it?' said Mrs Watter.

Lark shook her head. 'I always meant to go.'

'Well, at least we finally got rid of that rooster,' said Henry Watter, chewing.

'And you'll get married of course.'

Lark shrugged.

'Just like a war bride,' said Lark's mother. 'I remember them after the war, so excited to be going away. I wanted to go, too.'

'No more crowing in the middle of the flaming day,' said

Henry Watter. He looked at Lark. 'I chopped its damned head off, you know. We're eating it.'

'Please, Henry, language,' said Lark's mother.

'Throw me the gravy,' said Henry Watter.

'Please, Henry, pass,' said Mrs Watter, handing him the gravy boat. She stared out the window. 'I used to go down to Pyrmont to see the boats off and throw streamers to all those soldiers and their war brides, sailing off across the Pacific at the end of the war. We'd hold onto the streamers as if we might be taken along, too.'

Henry Watter held the gravy in the air, making it sail along, up and down, like a toy boat on the sea. 'Take the current when it serves,' he said.

'Henry, please, manners.'

'J. Caesar. A self-made man. Like N. Bonaparte. Self-made men,' said Henry Watter. He stood up. 'And so to bed.'

Lark's mother stayed a moment longer at the table before clearing away the dishes. 'We even thought the men going off to war were lucky to be travelling,' she said softly. 'When I was a little girl, I was taken down to the Quay to wave them off to Gallipoli, as if they were going on a holiday. It was very jolly. And only much later did we learn what Gallipoli really was, that Churchill and our own government had betrayed us.'

Lark's earliest memory was a picture in the Sydney newspaper. An Australian soldier, a prisoner in the Changi camp in Singapore, was about to be beheaded by a Japanese holding a sword. He was kneeling, his arms tied behind his back, his head bowed. To spare his family at home, the soldier's face had been blacked out.

'A good thing we got the bomb first,' shouted Henry Watter from the bathroom.

'So much noise.' Lark's mother shook her head. 'Sometimes,' she whispered, 'I have absolutely no idea what he's talking about.'

Lark helped with the dishes, then went to her room to pack her things for the voyage.

Framed

SUSAN POINTON

I wake from uneasy dreams to find myself on a beach at night somewhere on the coast of northern New South Wales. For a moment I cannot conceive of how I came to be here, but when I lift my head I can see the silhouette of my companion who is going about the ritual of washing and cleaning with a methodicalness that stifles me. For a little while I watch him, blithely oblivious of how much he is suffocating me with his precise and predictable actions. I throw back the blanket and stumble out into the darkness away from him. I stand on the edge of the black water and look up to see the moon suddenly break through a silver-lined formation of pitch-black cloud.

In Paris there lives a man with hair like fire who crossed the space between me and the outside world. In Paris there lives a man with courage that makes me contemptuous of these sleepy streets, these dull-voiced people, these shapeless lives. He danced in my sunbeam – he trapped the Australian sun in his hair. In a few weeks I will get on to an aeroplane and fly, like a bird, like a god, across continents and oceans, across summer and winter, across night and day, across the world so that I can see his face again. Because in my bedroom the sunbeam remains empty, my heart remains cold.

Make yourself at home the concierge says. So I am burning incense to veil the smells of decay and hanging pictures of Krishna over the peeling paint. My own familiar things stand

69

out like islands in the unknown ocean of this room. And my face in the mirror – it is familiar and yet different. Somehow the senses have been quickened, the head is held higher, the eyes shine brighter. How strange and yet not strange, to behold the reflection of a woman who is in love.

The incense smoke curls slowly in the currents from the hot water pipes and makes an unhurried escape through the open window. We are playing in the sanctuary of my room while the Paris morning bustles in the street below. He tells me fairy stories about Samurai and princesses while he makes my body tremble with his smiles and with his kisses. We fight and wrestle like children, laughing and tumbling on the floor. We poke out our tongues at each other and compete to make the silliest faces. We begin with tea and conversation and end up all wound up in each other's legs and arms and hair.

We regard each other, breathless, staring bright-eyed as children into each other's faces. I bury my face in the hair on his chest and beat my fists against his protesting hands.

'You are Orc,' I explain, 'the fiery child, the redheaded spirit of the imagination come to lead me back to Eden.'

Drunk with love, I laugh at his puzzled face.

We walk in the Jewish quarter along echoing cobbled streets and try a little of all the different fish roes in the cafe. We plunge over the Pont Marie, cutting up the medieval morning with our noisy passage while barges carrying artists with their easels set up on the deck glide silently below. I catch our reflection in a mirror in the street. I think our image will be framed for ever in the narrow glass panel in that street, long after we are gone and forgotten. I think those grey stone walls will preserve our laughter like the song in a music box.

'Where is your wife now?'

'I expect she is sleeping. It is very late.'

'Does she ever wait up for you?'

'She used to. When we were first married. Now she knows I am always late.'

'She doesn't mind.'

'What?'

'That you're always late home. She doesn't mind it?'

'Sometimes.'

'Does she go out late too at night?'

'Sometimes. It is harder for her. Because of our daughter.'

'Did she want to have a child?'

'Yes. She wanted this.'

'Does she still want to?'

'We will have many children. I want sons. Many sons. To do the work for me when I am old.'

'Does your wife know about me?'

'Let us play some music. Do you want to dance the tango?'

'I don't know how to dance the tango.'

'I will show you. Come with me. We will go to a little place near here where I know the man. I will teach you to dance the tango.'

'Don't be stupid. It's 2 o'clock in the morning!'

'We will dance the tango all night. And in the morning we will go to Fontainebleau.'

We climbed to the highest point of Fontainebleau and stood looking out over the valley. I closed my eyes and I could hear nothing except one single persistent bird. I opened my eyes and you were looking at me so I asked you what the big house was whose towers were just poking through above the line of the distant trees. You took my hand in the difficult places and led the way through a carpet of soft red leaves and springy bracken that crackled and sprang back under our feet. You are the same colour as the forest I said and you laughed but it was true; this is your forest, this ancient elegant place so different from my birthplace, here where you prance so easily bright-eyed like a child, leaping from rock to rock while I follow you perfectly happily through a day which I secretly hope will never end.

'What do you call it in French – when a woman is in love with a man who is married?'

'We call him a lucky man.'

'Don't be stupid. You're such an arrogant pig sometimes.'

'We call it Life. That's all it is. It is Life.'

'No, there is a word. A special word. I've heard it before.'

'Well, you tell me then.'

'I can't remember. It's an old word. A historical word. I read

it in a book by Flaubert.'
    'It is an old French tradition. All people do this.'
    'I wish I could remember it.'
    'It's not important. To always have words for everything. Is better just to feel. Now. Immediately.'
    'In a minute. When I think of this word . . .'
    'Demi-monde. The word is *demi-monde.'*
    'That's right! That's it. The word for mistress. *Demi-monde.* Half-world.'

In this most elegant and dignified of cities young men with rocker haircuts and stovepipe jeans stamp angrily past the gilded cathedrals, turning up the volume on their transistors to drown out the sound of an organ drifting from the open doorway of a Gothic eglise. And I, my eyes shining, career down the Champs Elysées with you in your old car, pretending we are flying a war aeroplane and shooting down the hapless pedestrians on the same streets where the tumbrels rolled towards the guillotine.

And in this gracious monument to a time of arrogant imperialism and artistic endeavour who is this crazy person beside me, this fiery, strutting young man who is making the noise of machine guns, of cowboys, of aeroplanes, of kookaburras to make me laugh, who is screaming his love for me out of the windows at the disapproving crowd, who charms me with his beauty and his energy and his complete conviction in himself.

Like gangsters we speed down the slippery cobbled streets in the rain, past the cafes and the palaces and the churches, over the ancient bridges on the Seine, past Our Holy Mother and the disco queues to come to a stop outside the synagogue at Le Marais. There in the alley, hidden from the past, the future and the present by the misty veil on the rain-streaked windows, duped into a belief in security by the darkness of the night and the beating of the rain on the car roof we regard each other with great happiness. What is happening here? Why do you keep smiling at me and making my heart melt over and over again? You are the fire.

    'Why did you come here?' he whispers to me.
    'I came to retrieve my heart.'

He smiles at me arrogantly in the rain.

'Do you have it?'

'Yes,' he says.

'Well at least I have come to the right place.'

I know this as I hold him and we burn together in the cold of a northern winter.

What do you want from this man anyway? Joan asks me with customary New York directness, regarding me from behind her glasses which she has pushed down to the tip of her nose. I uncurl from the floor where I have been doing yoga to make me strong and calm. Nothing I answer. I only want to know him. I read those same words yesterday on a plaque in the vestibule of the Gothic eglise at Les Halles.

She watches me suspiciously and I fall into pashimattanasana to hide my mischievous smile. But what if you become pregnant? she persists, as if she was reading my mind. He would never know, I counter her, enjoying the sound of the phrase. But that would be a tragedy in your life. I think it would be a gift from God.

I love Joan – I love her passion and her hunger for life – I love the immediacy of her response and how openly and bravely she displays her rollercoaster emotions. I don't mean to be flippant – I really mean what I say to her, but in my heart there is always a catch of guilt and uncertainty. The doubt of self-delusion, and the two wounds of betrayal and rejection. The inability to remove myself from this situation, from this unknown woman's life, countered with the barren way I feel as I walk childless and homeless through these streets, holding my love like a flame I shield inside me.

'I am leaving here in a few days.'

'I know that.'

'Will I ever see you again?'

'I don't know.'

'Maybe if you come to Australia . . .?'

'I don't know. It is so far . . .'

Where are we going? I venture in the middle of our laughter, as I notice that he is steering the car through unfamiliar streets, a district I have never had occasion to visit before. It's a secret he says and I clap my hands and jump about in the seat like a child. A secret! A secret! How exciting! What an exciting man to make games for me like a child. So much better than the stifling intercourse of restaurants to career like maniacs in his car through the empty streets in the middle of the night, making faces into the windows of other cars and yelling our private jokes to the passers-by. Maybe it was merely superstition – that feeling of foreboding that has pervaded my last few days here – that feeling of something building – that shift of colours in a prism slowly revolving. We are here and we are laughing; I can feel the warmth of him beside me and I only have to turn my head to see him smiling at me, seeing me and making me feel alive.

But suddenly there is a sign illuminated on a post; a street sign that is unfamiliar and yet known – known as if in a nightmare one watches in horror the materialisation of one's previously undefined fear. I am trapped. The car stops and we are silent – the only sound is the cooling of the motor. I am poised in my seat like an animal wanting to flee and he is looking at me although I will not meet his eyes. Wild thoughts rush into my head – what is the danger? I have walked into a trap and for what purpose? What is he trying to do to me? I look around me at the unfamiliar street, the foreign houses, the man who is opening the door to guide me from the car. I want to run but as in a nightmare I am drawn in fascination to what lies behind that door.

Welcome to my home he says.

I see the horse. The wooden horse that he told me he had carved himself for his little girl. In quick succession I see the bed they sleep in, the clothes strewn around, a bottle of perfume and a child's toy. I see the crib with rumpled blankets, as if a child was hastily taken from it maybe only minutes before my arrival. I am sure that if I laid my hand on the soft pink cover it would be warm, that I could lean over and bend my head and smell the warm milky smell of a child. Whisky? A voice is coming from somewhere – a voice I think I recognise – a glass is put into my hand and I can see gold liquid shaking about in the light from a Christmas tree. A tree,

standing in the corner of the room with its lights winking at
me in a sequence of party colours and some strange foreign
man standing next to it smiling at me and gesturing widely
with his arms. There is a little table with two chairs and I let
myself slide into one and stare with manic intensity at a piece
of paper lying in front of me – a piece of paper with words on
it – what does it say? I don't know. I can't read it – my eyes are
not clear – I can't see clearly. I look up and there on the wall is
the tapestry we bought together one sunny day twelve
thousand miles away and so long ago that I can hardly
remember. Did we catch a cab and what did we eat for
breakfast on that day? Ah, there is the tape deck he told me
about – and the shirt he wore that day we went to the beach
and he found a blue flower growing half-way up a mountain.
And there is the tree with its pretty coloured lights – the gifts
and sweets still scattered on the floor – the remnants of an
interrupted fete.

What is he doing? I see him cross the room and kneel down
over something on the floor. Is it a gun? No – it's his answering
machine. I watch the changing lights he must have rigged on
the tree while he plays through his messages – they are all in a
foreign language – I don't understand a word of what they
mean and the voices are alien and disembodied – the voices of
strangers I have never met.

But what is this on the wall above me? A photo of a child, a
child with his face, naked and laughing at me, reaching out
her arms towards me, towards the camera, towards him. A
naked child in the arms of a naked woman who is smiling at
me, smiling at the camera, smiling at him, holding up the
child who has his face. I am trying to read what is written on
the piece of paper that is before me, blonde and naked, but the
goddammed lights from the tree keep getting in my eyes and I
can't understand a word, not a single word and what the hell
are those foreign people talking about through all that static
and beeping?

He is going about his business unconcerned, tidying and
moving through the apartment with an ease which shows that
he is home. I am in black, crouched at his kitchen table with a
glass of whisky in my hand and tears in my eyes, some dark
intruder, an emotional thief in this blonde and sunny circle;

this family Christmas scene in which the two principal characters are missing for some reason that I can't understand. A voice comes on the tape – a woman's voice – calmly making arrangements with him – details of travel and a rendezvous. If I am very still here at the table maybe I will cease to be here at all and there will be only this foreign man moving about his lounge room with a glass of whisky in his hand, tidying away his daughter's scattered gifts while he listens to his wife on the answering machine telling him to pick her up in the car from the station early the next day.

But he turns to me and sees me – we watch each other's eyes even as the voice on the tape continues and ends with a term of endearment that is replaced by a beep and an amplified hiss. For the first time I look at him across the room and I can see that he is not really the enemy, that I need not be afraid, so I let him help me on with my coat and take the half-full glass from my hands and empty the contents down the sink and wash the glass and replace it in the shelf and put the bottle back in the cupboard and turn off the answering machine, reset it, and turn off the lights on the tree, and find the car keys that he had thrown on the bed when we came in and usher me out the door and onto the street and open the door of the car for me to get in and slide into the driver's seat beside me and turn the key and start the engine and drive me away from there into the night.

An old car, a long black road in the middle of the night – nothing outside the windows except a string of yellow lights on either side and the silhouette of some isolated house where everybody is asleep. Then suddenly a semi-trailer sealed with a tarpaulin – just one loud roar – and then silence again. I am holding onto the hand of the man sitting next to me. I am playing with something hard on his finger, idly toying, it is his wedding ring. He turns to look at me and I see the reflection of my face in his – wild, frightened, like a child who has just confronted something he never knew existed until this moment. A bright sign appears above us with a pointing arrow – PARIS – THIS WAY. 'Do you want to go to Paris?' he asks me. I nod. We hang tightly onto each other's hands as we sail on into the darkness.

I must go. Don't go he said to me – you must stay here until you feel better. If you leave now you will only regret it later. But what is better? Is it better to learn how not to love him? Better to maybe learn how to hate him, or even not to care at all?

The road goes on and on into the darkness.
   Well I say I have learned many things today.
   Brightly.
   What have you learned he asks me.
   I have learned how stupid I am.
   Bitterly.
   Then you have learned nothing today he says.
   I am frightened. Very frightened.
   I am dark and cold.
   The road goes on and on. There is nothing. Except a man beside me who takes my hand when I start to cry.
   I suppose this is what I came for I think remembering T. S. Eliot and the snow falling on the forest.
   Listen to me he says.
   I stare ahead at the road.
   I love you he says.
   I try to pull my hand away.
   You must not be ashamed of love he says. It is the most beautiful thing in life and you must not deny it. Life is becoming very difficult for people now because there are not many things left around them that affirm life. These things have become precious now. You are not stupid. But it is also better to know what is real than to continue to have these fantasies in your head.

But today – *mais aujourd, hui je suis très forte* – it is the last conjunction of the stars Joan says. We sing and eat the last of the chocolates and the fruit. Joan beats time to her guitar with one foot in a lurex sock as we raise our voices in a ragged harmony. It is a New Year and I am completely free. I will return to the South Pacific and make lots of money. No more sacrifices, no more illusions – no more heroes I scream from the windows of the car. I write my New Year's resolutions in the front of a brand new journal – it is one line repeated again and again like a mantra or the punishment of a guilty schoolchild – no heroes, no heroes, no heroes . . .

Islands

ANGELO LOUKAKIS

All this has come about because of my wanting to be useful, wanting to play my part. The Committee made me the offer, and I responded. The Committee said I could help us put it all together. I sincerely believe it was their fault that I fell from grace.

We want to know about Our Heritage, they said. Can you help? Sure, fine, I said. No problems. Just tell me what you want to know about, give me some money, and send me out. I'll come back with the goods.

Islands, for instance. We discover that we are surrounded by Islands. Should we not consider them? Aren't they part of the picture too? Of course they are. We ought to know about all our Islands – from A to Z.

I was told that X and Y had never been done. I'll do them, I said. Just give me the money and no worries – I'll have the info in no time at all.

In the above I am describing the behaviour of a well-meaning but at the same time corrupt fool. This fool, me, has become the world's foremost authority on these Islands. Bearing in mind I have in my time studied many Islands, X and Y are the ones I have covered in the greatest detail.

Why? Because they asked me to do it. This was at a time when I thought it was impossible to refuse a sacred task. In those days I could never be accused of not doing my bit for the New Society.

I turn now to address you, the individuals on the Committee, the men who sent me to these places, to Islands X and Y. Please try to listen. To you I have this to say —

Thanks a lot, pals.

You've given me some terrible nightmares.

Not for the prosy reasons you might be contemplating — like the actual work of getting to these places and gathering the material. That was nothing. That was no trouble at all. I'm talking about the real nightmares, the ones I've had ever since I first visited, you guessed it, Islands X and Y.

The nightmares started after I got back home from these places. Which was after I had discovered they had offshore Islands of their own. *They* are what continue to fill my dreams at night. *They* are the real problem.

As you well know, Island X is in the Pacific, and Island Y is in the Mediterranean. We agreed before I set out on these capers a decade ago, that they were both significant because they were both, in different ways, part of Our Experience. Our first settlers colonised X in the early days, but then forgot about the place, more or less left it to its own devices. On the other hand, many of our later settlers came from Y after the War. In the intervening period, Y has also been forgotten.

They were really easy to do, you know. Camera, notepads, a few interviews with the locals, an amount of research in libraries and so on, and hey presto! We are ready to go into print! The books will remind everyone, will make them think about Who We Are, will make them all aware of their cultural traditions. That's what you said to me.

But what you didn't know, indeed nobody here knew, was that Island X had its own tiny little rocky outcrop a few hundred metres off its northern coast — in other words its own Island! I have since named this one Island X(i). And Island Y, the same thing, a little island further out — only in this case off the southern tip. This one I call Island Y(i).

These are the places I have been trying to forget. All the years since I 'did' them, they have been plaguing me. I wish I could go back to the days before I ever knew they existed. I think I was probably happier then.

I hope you anonymous gentlemen are paying attention. There is nothing difficult about what I am saying. This isn't fiction. I don't write fiction, as you above all must be aware. This is not some story, trading off 'mysteries' and 'enigmas', busily developing the felicitous ambiguities one sees in certain kinds of literary prose. I will lay it all out for you, you bastards, plain and simple. So that (a) you can see what you've done to me, and (b) you might finally understand something about the nature of knowledge about ourselves, and (c) as a result, leave me alone.

I must tell you, by the way, that in the critical phase of this last psychic upheaval I had an idea that if I sat down and wrote out all the details about these extra Islands, these unexpected accessories to X and Y, I might be able to purge myself.

I never got around to doing that because I realised there was no point. All was permanently etched in my brain anyway, like you might brand a piece of leather. I really have no need to write anything about these places, these rocks which have become such features in the geography of my dreams. If you'd like to know, I can reel it all off by heart anyway.

But at one stage I did stupidly think that fully detailed, then fully analysed, these places might just disappear, and be replaced by sleep, sleep of the kind I haven't had for years. It hasn't proved possible.

I do have a full tape of the analysis in my head, if you are curious. In fact I think I will tell you whether you are or your aren't.

We can pass over X and Y themselves very briefly, for they are clichés. Y is a typical impoverished Mediterranean island of the sort which has been sending us its children for decades. This place is really part of a foreign country where the system of inheritance puts such pressure on land, the plots then become too small to support anybody, and emigration follows. X was a place we used to help with our social hygiene – this was where we once upon a time sent all those people who broke Our Laws, who never seemed to be able to fit in happily.

Anyway, you've got all this – I delivered it all up to you when you wanted it, didn't I?

No, let's get to the guts of it.

Island X(i)?

This is a volcanic remnant, two kilometres from X, and itself about two kilometres wide. Unlike the main Island, it has no history of human habitation. You can see it from X; it rises sheer from the water and is quite high. It is apparently barren – although no one knows why that is so. It is also spectacular to look at. From X it looks like a series of slashes of colour; the rock formations are in red, purple, crimson, yellow, orange. Perhaps this is what the planet Mars looks like.

I wanted to get over to see that Island from up close, but I never made it. Why? Because no one would help me. I asked the natives whether there was a boat. No, they said. There is no reason to go there. Nobody goes there, nobody has ever been there. There's nothing to see . . . that's what the ones who were willing to talk at all said – the others just shrugged or shook their heads. There was an awful lot of shrugging and head-shaking on X, I'll tell you.

In the dream I am standing inside the collapsed walls of the old gaol by the sea. I am not really imprisoned – in real life I walked in, in real life I walked out – but I am standing there holding some kind of plant and looking across the water to X(i) and crying because I want to get over there, I want to be there but I can't. I desperately want to be there, but there is no way. Not only because there are no boats, but because I can't move. I am immobilised. My legs refuse to take me anywhere, no matter how hard I try to get them moving.

Over and over again, I have this blasted dream.

It alternates with the island Y(i) dream.

Island Y(i)?

This is a small outcrop of limestone in the sea less than five hundred metres from the main coastal town of Y. Unlike at X, the locals here had a least a few things to tell me about this outcrop. It had never had a name, as far as anyone could tell, but the man who ran the cafe told me that in the sixteenth century it was a marine fortress belonging to one or other of the maritime Dukes of Venice. What looked like the remains of an old fort could still be distinguished from Y.

What was left of this structure, they told me, was used a hundred years ago as a shelter for lepers, and an infirmary. They didn't know how much of this usage could still be seen as no one had been across since it closed down over fifty years ago.

It was late afternoon of a winter's day ten years ago when I went down to the port and hired a caique powered by a small petrol engine. Here I would not be thwarted.

The boat was moored at a little wooden wharf. Walking along that wharf I looked down and saw an ancient, submerged pier running right alongside. I stood and stared down through the clear water lapping over the top of it. It was still more or less intact and seemed to be made of marble blocks. I remember wondering why storms or tides have never washed it all away.

The stretch of water between Y and Y(i) was so quiet, and one couldn't but believe it had always been like this, and always would be. I set off across an oil-flat clam, with the sound of the two-stroke engine for company.

The dream always starts with this vivid component of going across the water. I have to tell you, however, in some versions I wade across by walking along the old pier.

The next bit is always the same as it was in reality.

I run the boat up a shingle beach where I tie it up by throwing a rope around a large rock. I walk over the beach and get to an old track which seems to lead up to the ruins, and does so. Once at the top, I walk onto what looks like a parade ground with the object of getting to what's left of an old archway or entrance on the far side. Centuries ago, this was probably used as a place for assembling the soldiery. But now it was paved with concrete, concrete which couldn't have been more than seventy or eighty years old, and marked out in little squares, about a metre by a metre.

I walk across this ground where, at one point, in the middle of these small squares, the concrete gives way. There is a crack and my leg goes through and down into a hole as far as my knee. I pull up one of the bits of broken concrete to free my leg. I get it out again, then get on my hands and knees to look down. A cranium and arm and leg bones. A grave, a grave was what I had fallen into. I had been traversing what must have been the graveyard from the abandoned leper colony.

After this, there is really nothing to see as far as I am concerned. I go down to the beach and take the boat back to Y.

That's not how it goes when I'm dreaming about it. That's *never* how it goes when I am dreaming about it. Want to know the rest? Nothing to it. You are no doubt thinking that in the dream, when I fall partially into the grave, my legs gets caught and I can't get out or something equally gothic.

No way. In this thing that's been pestering me all these years, I invariably get out of the grave all right, even get back to the beach all right, just as I did in life. But when I get back to the beach, I always find the boat is gone. There is no getting off this Hell.

Until I wake up.

Do you see all the gaps, friends? People on X and Y were unable to tell me enough to help me complete the picture. I have never blamed them though; they didn't have all the details or the wherewithal to help me anyway. They were unaware. Besides in the end, I was the one who was supposed to be in charge of getting the facts. They are not at fault, that much I realise and accept.

If I could have got across to X(i) all would have been well, I am sure. If the people at Y had known more about Y(i) they would have told me about that stupid cemetery and I could have avoided it easily enough.

But there you are. People don't know enough, it seems. Imagine if they took more responsibility for knowing about things, what good would flow as a consequence.

But to the Committee, I say this – you were fully congnisant of the fact that I would only ever be able to glean part of the story in these places. I think you probably also know about these offshore Islands, and deliberately chose not to tell me about them, because you were only interested in using me to get what you wanted.

It's what *you* want really. You dress it up and talk about Our Experience, Our Culture, and how we have to record it and measure it and chart it and understand and all that bullshit. But it's all simply to do with your own aggrandisement.

In addition to being corrupt you know, I as an innocent idiot who thought knowledge mattered. What a laugh! Of course it doesn't matter when it is controlled by people like you.

Know what I intend doing? I'm going to give it all away. I'm going to resign from any further duties of this sort. I have some money, you know. Money which I intend to spend on buying a boat, something big enough to take me to any island anywhere. I'm going to get in this boat, fill it full of provisions and things to write with and on, and then sail off.

My first destination will be X(i), because that one is really quite close. There, I will do it all over again, I will do the job properly – I will find out everything. I will get all the facts first hand and I will set them down. But for my benefit only, just mine, and nobody else's.

Unless there are other people I might discover in my travels who genuinely want to know. I will gladly share my knowledge with such people.

Later, of course, I will have to do the same at Y(i). This is the only way I can see by which I might lift the curse of these Islands. Nightmares, I sincerely believe, will become things of the past.

The only thing that's worrying me is this – I know there are many small Islands in the seas of the earth. I'm not sure I will ever be able to get to them all. I suppose the only thing one can do is try. I fervently hope that these Islands exist as single entities. Islands with Islands of their own, I have found, are very difficult to do.

The Sun in Winter

DAVID MALOUF

It was dark in the church, even at noon. Diagonals of chill
sunlight were stacked between the piers, sifting down
luminous dust, and so thick with it that they seemed more
substantial almost than stone. He had a sense of two churches,
one raised vertically on Gothic arches and a thousand years
old, the other compounded of light and dust, at an angle to the
first and newly created in the moment of his looking. At the
end of the nave, set far back on a platform, like a miraculous
vision that the arctic air had immediately snap-frozen, was a
Virgin with a child at her knee. The Michael-angelo. So this
church he was in must be the Onze Vrouw.

'Excuse me.'

The voice came from a pew two rows away, behind him: a
plain woman of maybe forty, with the stolid look and close-
pored waxy skin of those wives of donors he had been looking
at earlier in the side panels of local altars. She was buttoned to
the neck in a square-shouldered raincoat and wore a scarf
rather than a wimple, but behind her as she knelt might have
been two or three miniatures of herself – infant daughters
with their hands strictly clasped – and if he peeped under her
shoes, he thought, there would be a monster of the deep, a
sad-eyed amorphous creature with a hump to its back,
gloomily committed to evil but sick with love for the world it
glimpsed, all angels, beyond the hem of her skirt.

'You're not Flemish, are you,' she was saying, half in
question (that was her politeness) and half as fact.

'No,' he admitted. 'Australian.'

They were whispering – this was after all a church – but her 'Ah, the *New* World' was no more than a breath. She made it sound so romantic, so much more of a venture than he had ever seen it, that he laughed outright, then checked himself; but not before his laughter came back to him, oddly transformed, from the hollow vault. No Australian in those days thought of himself as coming under so grand a term. Things are different now.

'You see,' she told him in a delighted whisper, 'I guessed! I knew you were not Flemish – that, if you don't mind, is obvious – so I thought, I'll speak to him in English, or maybe on this occasion I'll try Esperanto. Do you by any chance know Esperanto?' He shook his head. 'Well, never mind,' she said, 'there's plenty of time.' She did not say for what. 'But you *are* Catholic.'

Wrong again. Well, not exactly, but his 'No' was emphatic, she was taken aback. She refrained from putting the further question and looked for a moment as if she did not know how to proceed. Then following the turn of his head she found the Madonna. 'Ah,' she said, 'you are interested in art. You have come for the Madonna.' Relieved at last to have comprehended him she regarded the figure with a proprietary air. Silently, and with a certain old world grandeur and largesse, she presented it to him.

He should, to be honest, have informed her then that he had been a Catholic once (he was just twenty) and still wasn't so far gone as to be lapsed – though too far to claim communion; and that for today he had rather exhausted his interest in art at the little hospital full of Memlings and over their splendid van Eycks. Which left no reason for his being here but the crude one: his need to find sanctuary for a time from their killing cold.

Out there, blades of ice slicing in off the North Sea had found no obstacle, it seemed, in more than twenty miles of flat lands crawling with fog, till they found *him,* the one vertical (given a belltower or two) on the whole ring of the horizon. He had been, for long minutes out there, the assembly-point for forty-seven demons. His bones scraped like glaciers. Huge ice-plates ground in his skull. He had been afraid his eyeballs might freeze, contract, drop out, and go rolling away over the ancient flags. It seemed foolish after all that to say simply, 'I was cold.'

'Well, in that case,' she told him, 'you must allow me to make an appointment. I am an official guide of this town. I am working all day in a government office, motor-vehicle licences, but precisely at four we can meet and I will show you our dear sad Bruges – that is, of course, if you are agreeable. No, no – please – it is for my own pleasure, no fee is involved. Because I see that you are interested, I glimpsed it right off.' She turned up the collar of her coat and gave him an engaging smile, 'It is OK?' She produced the Americanism with a cluck of clear self-satisfaction, as proof that she was, though a guide of this old and impressively dead city, very much of his own century and not at all hoity-toity about the usages of the New World. It was a brief kick of the heels that promised fun as well as instruction in the splendours and miseries of the place.

'Well then,' she said when he made no protest, 'it is decided – till four. You will see that our Bruges is very beautiful, very *triste,* you understand French? *Bruges la Morte.* And German too maybe, a little? *Die tote Stadt.'* She pronounced this with a small shiver in her voice, a kind of silvery chill that made him think of the backs of mirrors. At the same time she gave him just the tips of her gloved fingers. 'So – I must be off now. We meet at four.'

Which is how, without especially wanting it, he came to know the whole history of the town. On a cold afternoon in the fifties, with fog swirling thick white in the polled avenues and lying in ghostly drifts above the canals, and the red-brick facades of palaces, convents, museums laid bare under the claws of ivy, he tramped with his guide over little hump-backed bridges, across sodden lawns, to see a window the size of a hand-mirror with a bloody history, a group of torture instruments (themselves twisted now and flaking rust), the site, almost too ordinary, of a minor miracle, a courtyard where five old ladies were making lace with fingers as knobbled and misshapen as twigs, and the statue of a man in a frock coat who had given birth to the decimal system.

The woman's story he caught in the gaps between centuries

and he got the two histories, her own and the city's, rather mixed, so that he could not recall later whether it was his lady or the daughter of a local duke who had suffered a fall in the woods, and her young man or some earlier one who had been shut up and tortured in one of the many towers. The building she pointed to as being the former Gestapo headquarters looked much like all the rest, though it might of course have been a late imitation.

She made light of things, including her own life, which had not, he gathered, been happy; but she could be serious as well as ironic. To see what all this really was, she insisted – beyond the relics and the old-fashioned horrors and shows – you needed a passion for the everyday. That was how she put it. And for that, mere looking got you nowhere. 'All you see then,' she told him, 'is what catches the eye, the odd thing, the unusual. But to see what is common, that is the difficult thing, don't you think? For that we need imagination, and there is never enough of it – never, never enough.'

She had spoken with feeling, and now that it was over, her own small show, there was an awkwardness. It had grown dark. The night, a block of solid ice with herrings in it, deep blue, was being cranked down over the plain; you could hear it creaking. He stamped a little, puffing clouds of white, and shyly, sheepishly grinned. 'Cold,' he sang, shuffling his feet, and when she laughed at the little dance he was doing he continued it, waving his arms about as well. Then they came, rather too quickly, to the end of his small show. She pulled at her gloves and stood waiting.

Something more was expected of him, he knew that. But what? Was he to name it? Should he perhaps, in spite of her earlier disclaimer, offer a tip? Was that it? Surely not. But money was just one of the things, here in Europe, that he hadn't got the hang of, the weight, the place, the meaning; one of the many – along with tones, looks, little movements of the hands and eyebrows, unspoken demands and the easy meeting of them – that more than galleries or torture chambers made up what he had come here to see, and to absorb too if he could manage it. He felt hopelessly young and raw. He ought to have known – he had known – from that invisible kick of the heels, that she had more to show him than this crumblingly haunted and picturesque corner of the past, where sadness, a mood of silvery reflection, had been turned into the high worship of death – a glory perhaps, but one that was too full of shadows to bear the sun. He felt suddenly a great wish for the sun in its full power as at home, and it burned up in him. He *was* the sun. It belonged to the world he had come from and to his youth.

The woman had taken his hand. 'My dear friend,' she was saying, with that soft tremor in her voice, '– I *can* call you that, can't I? I feel that we *are* friends. In such a short time we have grown close. I would like to show you one thing more – very beautiful but not of the past. Something personal.'

She led him along the edge of the canal and out into a street broader than the rest, its cobbles gleaming in the mist. Stone steps led up to classical porticoes, and in long, brightly-lit windows there were Christmas decorations, holly with red ribbons, and bells powdered with frost. They came to a halt in front of one of the largest and brightest of these displays, and he wondered why. Still at the antipodes, deep in his dream of sunlight and youth, he did not see at first that they had arrived.

'There,' the woman was saying. She put her nose to the glass and there was a ring of fog.

The window was full of funerary objects: ornamental wreaths in iridescent enamel, candles of all sizes like organ-pipes in carved and coloured wax, angels large and small, some in glass, some in plaster, some in honey-coloured wood in which you saw all the decades of growth; one of them was playing a lute; others had viols, pan pipes, primitive sidedrums; others again pointed a slender index finger as at a naughty child and were smiling in an ambiguous, un-other-worldly way. It was all so lively and colourful that he might have missed its meaning altogether without the coffin, which held a central place in the foreground and was tilted so that you saw the richness of the buttoned interior. Very comfortable it looked too – luxuriously inviting. Though the scene did not suggest repose. The heavy lid had been pushed strongly aside, as if what lay there just a moment ago had got up, shaken itself after long sleep, and gone striding off down the quay. The whole thing puzzled him. He wondered for a moment if she hadn't led him to the site of another and more recent miracle. But no.

'Such a coffin,' she was telling him softly, 'I have ordered for myself. – Oh, don't look surprised! – I am not planning to die so soon, not at all! I am paying it off. The same. Exactly.'

He swallowed, nodded, smiled, but was dismayed; he couldn't have been more so, or felt more exposed and naked, if she had climbed up into the window, among the plump and knowing angels, and got into the thing – lain right down on the buttoned blue satin, and with her skirt rucked up to show stockings rolled tight over snowy thighs, had crooked a finger and beckoned him with a leer to join her. He blushed for the grossness of the vision, which was all his own.

But his moment of incomprehension passed. His shock, he saw, was for an impropriety she took quite for granted and for an event that belonged, as she calmly surveyed it, to a world of exuberant and even vulgar life. The window was the brightest thing she had shown him, the brightest thing he had seen all day, the most lively, least doleful.

So he survived the experience. They both did. And he was glad to recall years after, that when she smiled and touched his hand in token of their secret sympathy, a kind of grace had come over him and he did not start as he might have done; he was relieved of awkwardness, and was moved, for all his raw youth, by an emotion he could not have named, not then – for her, but also for himself – and which he would catch up with only later, when sufficient time had passed to make them of an age.

As they already were for a second, before she let him go, and in a burst of whitened breath, said 'Now my dear, dear friend, I will exact my fee. You may buy me a cup of chocolate at one of our excellent cafés. OK?'

PASTA MOMA

SYLVIA LAWSON

– Wait till you leave the place then, said my father. That's
when you find out you're Australian. Probably be surprised to
find out how Australian you are.

He didn't say 'how bloody Australian,' because that's not
the kind of Australian he is. He spoke quite tentatively, with
the tolerant wisdom of a father who knows better than to seem
authoritative. But then – I was twenty-five, and quite clear-
headed in my anti-nationalism – it had the same sort of effect
as my mother's recurrent proposals that oh well, marriage and
babies will settle you down, dear, sooner or later. In each
case, it was the bad faith that counted.

Not long afterwards, I did leave. It was late 1973, just over
ten years ago. Now it's the end of 1983, and the beginning of
these curious weeks when I can actually let my work slide
away; I can lie in the sun, read, think or not think. Now, when
Nigel and I have to re-negotiate the whole deal yet again, I
remember crossing America, and how I didn't manage to lose
him. For want of real trying, if you like.

I was riding the Amtrak train from Los Angeles to New York,
watching the blank spaces of New Mexico slide backwards,
when my father's sentence came back, the words re-shaping
themselves like a pattern in smoke. I had just emerged from a
conversation with a too-friendly husband and wife, earnestly
evangelical members of some Christian commune. They had
professed surprise that I was a total unbeliever –

– we think of Australia as such an *unspoilt* place, and you young Australians are always so *hopeful*.

They offered me shelter should I ever pass their way; and thankfully, left the train at Albuquerque. Hopeful? perhaps yes; then, ten months into the first Whitlam government, there was still that sense of breakthrough. And I – sneakily changing my mind here and there, not telling my friends too quickly – even I was beginning to wonder if Australia might become a place to return to, if it might cease to be the far outer edge of everything. For me, that is, a Euro-centred fine arts worker, and people like me. That argument with my father had been mainly about my right to work on European objects and ignore Australian ones, if I so chose, absolutely. He'd found it hard to take.

Now I was on my way to New York, where I was to look at the films of Jean Vigo in the Museum of Modern Art, and then to Europe, to consider for higher-degree purposes the relations of anarchism and the early European avant-garde. I had just off-loaded Nigel in Berkeley – and I mean off-loaded, because I couldn't think of it any other way.

It was *my* scholarship trip, damn it; my travelling allowance, my opportunity; and he had absolutely insisted on coming too. He had his fare, and his own Ph.D. work supplied a multitude of excuses for work – which, being Nigel, he would of course most assiduously *do* – in the newspaper files of the entire Western world. The influence of English and Irish newspapers on the colonial Australian press; the influence of late 19th century American newspapers on the late-colonial Australian press; and – lucky for me – the influence of Californian newspapers on the *Bulletin*. The last would be good for a whole chapter, and the library he needed was the Bancroft in Berkeley.

Drawn in by its treasures, Nigel emerged from the general sulkiness he'd worn, like a blanket, the whole flight from Sydney to San Francisco; and with freedom ahead, I could be more generous myself. So we had those two days wandering Berkeley, in September weather that felt disconcertingly like Sydney's, buying more than we could afford in the second-hand bookshops, enjoying the way the campus and the town flowed into each other; enjoying our own at-homeness in a Berkeley that was still, palpably, living after '68. The flower

people, or their slightly younger siblings, still sold
leathercraft and beads all over the pavements; people still
greeted us merely because they liked the look of us, and
assumed we were their political-generational kin.

Several times in the heat of the day, we came back to the bar-
row near the campus gates where they sold orange juice;
FRESH SQUOZEN, said the notice, and it was. I watched Nigel
drinking his slowly, with control – he was mostly controlled,
like that – after I'd finished mine; and took pleasure again in
all that was darkly fine-tuned and civilised about him.

– Don't *gulp*, he said, taking my paper cup. You always
gulp.

We agreed to meet, two weeks on, in New York. There could
be no protracting the interval; Nigel's excuse for New York
was only too good, the historical resources of the Columbia
School of Journalism. But two weeks alone was – for me then –
a dizzy and daring prospect; in five years, I'd hardly had a
night away from him. I knew dismally – though he refused to
know – that we had, by our mid-twenties, arrived at the full
banality of the habituated couple; Nigel-and-Shane, Shane-
and-Nigel are coming. We still challenged, and therefore still
enjoyed each other. But too much irritation patterned the
nights and weekends, and the conflicts were far more mine
than his. Two months before leaving, and against his will, I'd
had an abortion; the hostility and hurt were still palpable
between us. In fact I also wanted a child, even children – but
not yet; more immediately, I needed to go exploring, the sort
of exploration which has to be done untrammelled, which
could not be done while I had to concern myself at every turn
with his nervy reactions and over-reactions.

– God, I broke out at him once, the sort of travelling
together *you* want makes me think of retired couples on
cruises, with mum always watching out for dad's indigestion.

– Come off it, Shane. He'd refuse to quarrel, disappearing
back into notes and microfilm. He'd point out sometimes that
after all we each worked alone, most of the time anyhow.
– Shane, when I've finished working I *need* you.

I left him in Berkeley, refusing to delay any longer my own
moment of setting forth. Scrupulously, I gave him my share of
the money for posting books back to Sydney; and we parted in

the friendly dimness of a bookshop where he'd found a long-dead editor's memoirs, and was happy. – Look, I said, I don't want to wait round for lunch; I'll dash now.

I kissed him. – Take it easy, Shane. I said I'm coming, I'll come to the train with you. – Don't be silly, that's too many taxis. You've got the New York numbers, right? See you when you get there.

He put down the book, held me gently and gravely. – All right then, Shane. Be careful.

I kissed him again, and ran. In my elation, I kicked a spread of bright ceramic dolls into disarray on the pavement; stopped to apologise to the seller, a calm-eyed girl in plaits and sari; then went overboard and bought one. Peace, she said as I left.

Deliberately, I was taking trains all the way; to LA, to talk to people in cinema studies at UCLA and get some addresses; then right across to New York. It was some notion I had of real travelling, something about covering the ground and seeing things, meeting people.

Before the train left that afternoon, I had time to ride the cable car and explore Fishermen's Wharf; jaunts which exposed nationality when someone said – Where you from, young lady, London? I'm Australian, I'd say, and the response was *Far out, f'real?* from a black boy selling coffee; it *is* far out, I couldn't help joking back. The porter said – I guess you'd play a lotta tennis, then? Along the north Californian coast, the sea looked grey and oily. I caught myself feeling complacent.

Things got a lot tougher in Westwood, Los Angeles. It wasn't that the film school people weren't helpful; I was laden with letters of introduction to people teaching avant-garde cinema/film theory/European art history/film history, anything I liked. It was their acute curiosity. I was chauffeured, taken to lunch and dinner, and presented with whole shopping lists of questions on the Labor government's film and media policies, on the new national film and TV school, on the plans for reviving an Australian film industry. I couldn't answer any of it.

In a moderately agreeable Hamburger Hamlet, a particularly nice, black associate-professor named Dexter quizzed me over his mound of chopped rare beef. I had to be honest. I told him I hadn't seen a single recent Australian film – had, in fact, energetically refused to see them; and that for years I'd been contending that all the cultural-nationalist stuff was thoroughly misguided. I had several elaborate reasons for this. They were about aggressive provincialism, and (in other conversations) the anxieties of the post-colonial state. That phrase had just come in at the time. Anyhow, I asked Dexter, why are you people all so interested in what goes on down under?

He seemed astounded. – We're interested, he said – slowly and patiently, quite like Nigel – because teaching here we're virtually part of imperial Hollywood, we're feeding off it all the time, and we think it's fascinating that one of the colonies gets up off its butt and makes a declaration of independence.

He ate, and thought. – That is, if that's what's happening, but it's hard to tell.

He annoyed me, not just because he knew more about the Australian end than I did, but because I felt coerced. He was holding out this jacket labelled Australian. It was rough, homespun, nationalist, and it didn't fit; but he was telling me I really ought to wear it.

Driving me back to the cheap hotel on the edge of the Westwood campus, he made it clear, with a bit of relieving humour, that he did think I was a snob. But – he said, pulling up – it was really great meeting me. Maybe we could catch up in New York, since he had to go there next week himself. He didn't so much as put a hand out, and that commended him. Feeling splendidly unfaithful, I gave him the New York numbers.

Thus Los Angeles was my first foreign city, and I did not make friends with it. From the Amtrak window, the culverts, canals and freeways made images from old gangster films; this place was never real. The car was empty but for myself and the Christians, who began our conversation by offering me some of their coffee. They were replaced at Albuquerque by a harassed mother and a small, unhappy female child, whom I was able to console a little, as we went north-east, with the doll from Berkeley. In fading light we crossed the south-eastern tip of Colorado, and I saw one perfect, dreaming silver peak.

After Chicago, late next day, everything changed. The car was full, agitated, anxious, the stewards brusque. I swapped stories with my neighbour, a girl who seemed to be in flight from both upper-middle Pittsburgh and a husband. We talked, and read intermittently, under dim spots; then a head steward came to tell us that if we didn't stop disturbing the other passengers – who were all asleep, so far as we would tell – he'd turn off the master switch and deprive us of light completely. We murmured on a little, and he carried out the threat. This, Mailer had said, was the freest and most authoritarian country in the world.

I was frightened of New York, and especially frightened of arriving there. All the more important, therefore, to do it alone. Still inept with nickels and dimes and push-button telephones, I messed up my first contact with Ellen Barstow, the graduate film student whose apartment I was to share for the next fortnight. My second attempt and the second reply from a highly irritated older female voice, showed that indeed I had the wrong number; I had mis-heard, or mis-transcribed. The directory didn't help; a graduate student, probably a subtenant, would not be listed under her own name. I felt I was losing round one with New York already; then thought of ringing her workplace, although she wouldn't be there, and carefully explaining the position. In the George Amberg Memorial Institute of Cinema Studies at New York University, the secretary was meticulously helpful.

Out of the cab, through the security system and out of the creaking elevator into Ellen's cramped little segment of East Fifteenth Street, I could afford to exhale my panic. She was very nice and very fat, with that funny mix of nerviness and placidity which fat people often have; smocked and spectacled, and it took a while to decide that she wasn't, in fact, pregnant.

– Don't worry, stop apologising, just relax, you've made a long trip, and you have to understand that coming to New York City just freaks everyone, just *everyone*.

It was a litany I grew used to. I heard it on the buses, on the subway, on my solitary ride on the Staten Island ferry, on my walk over the Verrizzano bridge; as though the repetition itself (don't worry so much, just relax, this city's fixed to drive you *bananas*) was a charm, a panacea.

Over heaped tuna salad, with chips on the side, Ellen heard my plans for next week.

– For crying out loud, didn't they tell you about what's going on at MOMA?

I was blank.

– Sorry, the Museum of Modern Art. I guess you could get there and look at the movies, but I mean, I wouldn't.

I had the fleeting impression that a stack of unexploded wartime bombs had been found in the institutional vaults. Then Ellen managed to spell it out. Most of the lower-rung professional and administrative staff – PASTA – of the Museum were on strike, bravely and scandalously so. They wanted pay, and parts in decision-making, to match their responsibilities. In this area, industrial action was unheard of; working in the Museum was supposed to be a calling, a privilege, even for a junior assistant curator.

They knew of my impending arrival; the appropriate letters had come, memos had circulated. Other visiting researchers were involved, but an Australian was unusual, particularly one researching film. They knew it was a lot to ask of people on hard-won excursions they mightn't be able to repeat. But when the predicted call came for me in the morning, I agreed, without the slightest sense of sacrifice, not to cross their picket line.

I could look at the Vigo films later, maybe in London; I could even go on to the cinemathèque in Paris. Without missing a strike, I consigned the thesis to a deep freeze somewhere across the Atlantic – salut, Jean Vigo, with your comprehension of chaos – and resolved on the instant that my New York chapter could be differently composed. The strike would be much more fun than sitting for all those days in front of the Steenbeck viewer. I was not only unfaithful (well, potentially); I was positively frivolous.

And a shameless fraud. At home, I'd never really supported a strike or stood on a picket line in my life. Vietnam marches – that was different. And a couple of anti-censorship demos outside art-house cinemas. Now, on the instant, I appropriated convict rebellions, the Eureka Stockade, the shearers' strikes

of the nineties (or what I'd gathered up of them from Nigel),
and the Kelly gang facing the final shoot-out.

I helped make posters, handed leaflets, harangued the
customers. I answered questions, from all directions, about
Australia (and grew nonchalant, making up the answers when
I didn't know them: of course the Labor government will co-
operate with the CIA – they're politicians, aren't they?) I wore
my own black and yellow badge, PASTA MOMA. I said it
sounded like a particularly ample Italian dinner.

For ten marvellous days, I gravitated between the picket
line and NYU. On the telephone, among the students, in the
street I heard myself spelling out the words like some hyper-
articulate New Yorker: Australians *do not* break strikes – at
least, not any Australians you *would want* to know about.
Australians *do not cross* picket lines.

One day, with PASTA's agreement, I went inside the place,
and travelled to a high, carpeted office to explain to a silver-
haired dignitary, who had received the letter of introduction,
why I would not after all be using the Museum's distinguished
resources. He wanted to apologise, he talked of incon-
venience and disappointment, said that of course those young
people had his sympathy, but this was not the most productive
way, etcetera. I smiled, and left him without shaking hands.
But then the elevator took me to a level below the street, and I
cheated. Before going back to the line, I bought a dozen
extremely beautiful postcards.

Every morning, I woke to the grey and gritty daylight.
Through Ellen's courageous ferns, the dirty glass, the iron
grille, and the tall adjoining walls, I looked up from the divan
to a square of white sky, and heard the radio announcing that
today's pollution levels were 'unacceptable'. (What were we
supposed to do, go out into the stale air with gasmasks?) I
woke also, every morning, to the knowledge that today, no
later, I must send Nigel a card with the right phone number.
Those I had given him were the scrambled home number and a
contact in the MOMA film archive. No one answering the latter
would have a clue; and Nigel, having only the vaguest idea
about Ellen, wouldn't think of ringing NYU.

Every morning I woke knowing I had to do it. Every day, flying around, having my piece of the action, I didn't get around

to it. (There was Dexter too. But I bet myself that he'd know enough to work it out, if he wanted to.) The strike was my daily work; diversion was the avant-garde film seminar at NYU (Rene Clair's *Entr'acte*, slowed down to two frames a second on the Athena analyser-projector); and the real, all-stops-out entertainment was Watergate, running practically all night, every night on CBS as Nixon fired one Special Prosecutor after another and informants were smoked out of the woodwork. On the second Sunday, I walked with Ellen down through the Village to the docks; every few yards somebody handed us a petition for Nixon's impeachment. I signed them all happily, adding 'Australian visitor'.

Talking on the picket line, I heard a camera click almost in my ear. There was Dexter, shaking hands and laughing: I see you're picking up on that Australian radical tradition? The taunt was irresistibly precise. I walked with him that evening in Central Park; and in enveloping dark, a little cold in a grove of plane trees, we managed the nearest thing in my own records to the legendary zipless encounter. I did go to his hotel, but somehow felt that taking a cab back to Fifteenth Street not too long after midnight was less adulterous than if I'd stayed all night.

Ships-that-pass, no complications. Dexter (it's-been-great-being-with-you) was returning to wife and children in Santa Monica.

– Dexter, what's it really like having kids?

– Great. Why don't you and that historical guy of yours get it together and find out?

– Because I've got to get a thesis written, and I want my own job. (Those, anyhow, were the reasons I could talk about; there might be others.)

– Baby, baby. He laughed richly, a hand playing around my back, but he was still saying it: You're a real ball-cutter, baby.

I managed, not long after that, to get out of bed. Next day I was back on the line, in the pale, dirty sunshine. A tall, extraordinary female figure emerged, out of the Museum's great glass doors and off a *Harper's* cover: blonde hair swinging, of no determinable age, dressed head to foot in next year's as though it hadn't taken her a second's thought. One of the PASTA leaders sought to detain her, and I caught her end of their exchange. – You're employed here in art, and you're using the tactics of steelworkers or auto workers in some yard in Detroit. I just cannot understand how you can apply these methods . . . the Board *is* prepared to talk about your grievances . . . Blonde mane, caramel cashmere, grey Italian leather swept away.

– That, Ellen explained, is a Rockefeller.

– F. Scott Fitz. had a point there, I said. – Yeah? – You know, when he said the very rich *are* different from you and me, and Hemingway put him down. He said, Yes, Scott, they have more money.

But then I was arguing with this fat painter, who wasn't so different from the Rockefeller lady. In check shirt and spotted bow tie, he looked like the caricature of an artist out of Hemingway's Paris. He too claimed that strikes were strictly for the real proletariat, and that artworkers should never strike anyhow; it was a betrayal of their vocational commitment.

I was floundering round among the issues when Ellen came panting down the line.

– Shane, there's this Australian up there. He wants to cross. I said look, right-thinking Australians do not cross picket lines, and I said to him we've got one Australian right here helping us –

With deathly dread and certain knowledge, I paced back with her.

– Shane, thank Christ to find you. He was about to enfold me; I flung his arms back in a fury I couldn't have imagined.

– Nigel. What the hell do you think you're doing? These people here are on a real strike. Don't you understand anything?

– Shane. He stepped back, totally incredulous. – I can't believe you. Have you got the very slightest bloody idea what I've been through trying to find you? The character on the phone in there hadn't a clue, the other number was wrong – Jesus, he flashed bitterly, did you do this to me on purpose?

Yes, cried a voice in my mind. *Yes, I did indeed.*

I stepped to his left, so that the line could ignore us, and our drama was its own island in the stream.

– Look, you just can't have imagined that I'd be beavering away in there while –

– Why the bloody hell not? You've got a job to do and you came a long way to do it – what's this lot got to do with you? It's not a damn peace campaign or something, it's a potty little squabble about wages for people who've got better deals than anyone you'll ever know in art jobs in Australia, what the devil do you think?

– And what the hell would you know?

We ran out of steam, of course; but I wouldn't go off with him. I gave him Ellen's address, and the right number, and he went to check his Columbia contacts. I had never felt more resentfully married. A re-arrested escapee, I resumed my place, chose to go on to a strike meeting in an uptown apartment, and then to the Bleecker Street cinema.

Penitence, of a sort, set in. I re-entered at 10.30, with a bag of hamburgers. Ellen, justly self-protective, had managed not to hear too much of us.

– Your guy called. He's been eating with some Columbia professor, but he'll show up soon. Hey, he's really nice. If you've got some more like that in Australia I'll be over on the next plane.

– They've all got their problems, I said. Ellen, I think I'll crash. I can get up to let him in.

– Well, you want to pull out the sofa bed? It means you're a little bit public, but there's only me around.

– Don't worry about it for now. We'll manage later.

In her loft-bed, she snored a little. I lay staring at that cut of sky. Since the cloud and smog reflected the lights of Manhattan, it never really darkened. I felt protective and defensive about Ellen, and all the others like her.

The buzzer went, twice, uncertainly. – Hello? I spoke into the grille. His voice came thickly. – Please, Shane, please.

He was drunker than he'd ever been; he was wrecked. There was nothing to do but pull him through the doorway, into the elevator, into the apartment. I undressed him, propelled him to the bathroom, and finally, in the small divan bed, could only hold him and stroke him indefinitely.

Through the next five years, through my time in Europe, the four-year-trek through my thesis, the struggle for a job, the deeper struggle went on. He was more easily successful, a senior lecturer in Australian history by thirty-one, with the whole field of press history his own preserve. In Sydney at the end of 1975, we fought bitterly; he actually believed there was a case for the dismissal of the prime minister. – There's got to be an umpire, said Nigel.

We lived apart, together, apart. We tried weekends together. I came back in 1980 from a European conference trip, where I'd given papers on the relations of province and metropolis in art, and on post-colonial avant-gardes. I discussed matters a bit more easily these days with my father, whose dictum had long since tailed off, a kind of skywriting trailing and crumbling away. Now, returned again, I faced Nigel. He had now, for others at least, the teasing glamour of mature male success.

– I'm playing the field, he told me.

– You do that, mate. Only I'm not playmate number three, four or five, right? I'm not playmate number anything.

There could be no humble pie. My tutorship was finished, my money too. I shared a house with three others, went on the dole and wrote. At the end of that year I was offered a lectureship two states away. We've taken turns to fly back and forth. Not quite equally; I've been going to Sydney more often, although I'm paid less.

I am there now, at the beginning of my twelve weeks' maternity leave. Genevieve, our daughter, will be born in a fortnight or so. (When you're pushing thirty-seven, you've got to have amniocentesis.) She will come back to Adelaide with me; and – because of her? because of us, not me? – Nigel is applying for a job there.

I kept track through Ellen, for a while, of events inside the Museum. They didn't get much out of the Rockefellers; a few lousy dollars, a few points of status. But they'd made trouble, they kept that strike up for sixteen weeks – as the Rockefeller lady said, like so many steel or auto workers.

So the PASTA MOMA badge, which I found again lately going through my papers, doesn't exactly signify a victory for the people. I pinned it on to a very worn old teddy bear, who wears all the badges I've got for yesterday's causes; mine, others', no one's. PASTA MOMA is there beside PEACE, SMILE, and A Woman Needs A Man Like A Fish Needs A Bicycle. Bullshit; but the teddy bear can wear them. The teddy bear is

Genevieve's inheritance.

Note

This story is based in part on a real event, the strike action taken late in 1973 by professional and administrative staff (PASTA) of the Museum of Modern Art in New York City. Nevertheless all the characters in the story are fictitious, and no reference whatever is intended here to any historical person.

The Absolutely Ordinary Family

ANDREW TAYLOR

She should have brought the guidebook with her, she realised.
It would have been something to hold, even to read, to take
her mind off herself while she waited for her lunch. Instead,
she tried to take an interest in her surroundings.

The restaurant where she sat was in a little square, not far
from the Roman amphitheatre, and shaded by plane trees. A
fountain in the middle formed a kind of traffic island, though
in this sleepy lunchtime there was little traffic. The tables
were mostly occupied by tourists; some perhaps, like herself,
school teachers on long service leave. Or simply touring.
Several tables of Germans, an English family, a group of young
Spaniards or South Americans, she couldn't say which. Next to
her was a couple with two young children, one still a toddler
in a stroller, the other, a boy, older, maybe seven or eight. Even
though they were at the table closest to her she couldn't work
out their nationality as they were speaking so quietly, though
it might have been German. The woman seemed to speak
German to the baby, but she thought she heard the boy say
something in English. The table on the other side of hers was
empty. She wondered how much longer before her pizza was
ready.

Even before she left Melbourne she should have known it
was a mistake to travel Europe with Terry. And it had been her
idea, which made it worse. After so many years of transience,
shifting, making do, incompleteness – at her worst moments
she called it loneliness, at her best self-sufficiency – this

chance to travel Europe with Terry seemed to hold out promises she had never known existed. Or some long need in her, she began to admit, had dreamed up promises of a fulfilment Terry was going to provide, whether he knew it or not. It was too dramatic to call it a last chance: she was still too young for that. But it seemed too good to miss, and there were no guarantees that there would be many more like it.

Their long service leaves had coincided. As a history teacher, he wanted to see Europe. As a French and German teacher, she was going there to. It would be her third visit, so she knew her way around. But she was quite ignorant of European history, apart from the fragments she had to purvey along with the language and literature. On the other hand, Terry could speak only English. Each had a need the other could fulfil, each had something to offer as well as gain. In the clear hot Gallic afternoon, she hardly dared to think of what further fulfilments she had only semi-consciously planned to build on such a slight foundation.

She was interrupted by the waiter bringing her pizza. She ordered a second beer and looked around her. The empty table beside her had been taken by a couple in orange, photos of their guru hanging from leather cords around their necks. They seemed to be discussing salads. On the other side, the baby in the stroller was playing up. She – it might be a boy, but to her mind it was almost definitely a she – was obviously very tired, but filled with perverse and irritable energy. The father took her out of the stroller and placed her in a chair, from which she kept reaching up onto the table for glasses, knives, forks, throwing napkins on the ground, smearing sunglasses with grime, almost wrecking a camera.

'Nein! Nein!' went the boy, snatching breakables from her grasp. The parents, with that automatic, unconscious watchfulness some people have when they are worn out, constantly moved things out of her reach. The table was like a chessboard, saved by these endless and exhausted movements from sudden and irreversible disaster.

It had to be her fault, she admitted. If she had been content with Terry merely as a travelling companion it might have worked. But sharing cheap hotel rooms, even double beds, night after night, made that impossible. After all, they were adults, not children. And, let's admit it, he was attractive, and people looked at him. Also, he knew where they were walking. She could speak the language, order the hotel rooms, sort out the supplements they had to pay on their Eurail passes and explain the menus. But it was Terry who knew when and under which Emperor Provence was colonised, which Roman governor built the theatre in Orange, why – probably – the Popes came to Avignon. It was all useless knowledge in Australia, required by a curriculum and meaning nothing to the students. But in Europe it shaped the streets just as surely as the language she spoke guided them through them. She realised that he seemed to represent a kind of continuity, and that she had a longing for it.

Even the fact that he was about ten years her junior, she acknowledged, represented a kind of continuity that her own age was depriving her of. Not that it made her panic. She had never wanted children, and didn't want them now. But she knew that her body would change soon and his would not. He was like the history he taught and over which they walked – an accomplished fact, visible if not wholly learnable, something one never got 100 per cent for, but could get close to. Whereas she . . . well, she would change.

Experienced as she was in sex, she knew that their first night was more than unsatisfactory. It had been hesitant, awkward, lacking any real rhythm. They were two dancers moving to different tunes. She had encouraged Terry afterwards, had tried to show him that despite everything she had enjoyed it. But it didn't work. She could hear him lying quietly in the bed beside her, in the dark, drinking a whole bottle of wine. She knew enough not to interfere.

But she did four days later. Last night, in fact. In their hotel in Orange. She had asked him if he were sorry for what they had done. No. Did he feel that she was too old? He laughed briefly. If he was gay, of course, he should have said something. No. For Christ's sake, she said, nobody today has to worry about being gay. She'd been with a few women herself. No.

'Am I too old?' she asked him again. For a reply, he had turned towards her, kissed her and caressed her breasts. And so they made love for the second time. But it was no better. In fact it was far worse, because they knew now it would never be better. Whatever languages her body had learned couldn't summon what she needed from him. And whatever knowledge his body had acquired was locked within it. Afterwards, he went out on the town, apparently to the English Bar. He stumbled into their room around 1.30 dead drunk, collapsing halfway across his bed. She took his shoes off and went back to her own bed, hoping that he wouldn't snore.

When she had dressed, that morning, and was ready to go out, Terry was still asleep. He had dragged off his clothes at some stage during the night, and hunched himself under a sheet. He smiled at her as she said she was going out, and she had leant down and kissed him. She saw that under the sheet his penis was erect – he had been dreaming and was still mostly asleep. Half under his bed was an almost full bottle of anise.

The Roman theatre at Orange struck her as very much what it should have been: very hard to climb and very old looking. Workmen had erected a stage of piping and pineboard over the old stones, and others were stringing wires and adjusting brackets for lights. Posters told her that in six days time a season of *Antigone, Aida* and a choral work by someone whose name meant nothing to her was about to begin. A young boy rushed past her.

'I want to take a photo of Julius Caesar,' the boy said.

'That's not Julius Caesar, that's Augustus Caesar,' a man's voice had replied. 'Augustus Caesar lived after Julius Caesar, but not much later . . .'

They passed out of earshot. She looked up then and saw what they were talking about. High above the stage area of the ancient Roman theatre, isolated by the whiteness of its marble against the greenish-brown stone of the rest, was the statue of a Roman emperor. Augustus, in whose time the theatre had been built, gazed down still in imperial white on the stage empty of all but a couple of technicians laying wires, and on the rows of empty stone seats. He seemed so small, so much above it all, so difficult even to photograph properly; he was so far away, that for a moment she felt sorry for him. He had outlived his theatre and its audience – not that he ever visited it. He had outlived his empire even. He was a white fossil in a changing world, visible indeed, and gazing with Augustan, truly Augustan, aplomb on a world that he couldn't see.

A noise in the restaurant brought her back to the present. There was a kind of excited yet hushed babble of voices, mostly female, and she looked around to see what had caused it.

The boy from the table next to her was pushing his baby sister in her stroller along the street away from the restaurant, about fifteen metres off. At least, he was trying to push her. But the baby had got upright in the stroller and was standing, one foot tangled in the strap that was meant to keep her sitting, facing the way they were going. One hand held the aluminium frame of the stroller, while the other was stretched imperiously before her. 'Onwards!' she seemed to be commanding, the outstretched arm and finger poised in the same gesture as Augustus in his theatre. The parents had been trying to eat their lunch, but the mother had half-risen from her chair.

It was clear that the boy was about to make a terrible mistake. As he pushed the baby across the rough cobbles he held closely, almost desperately, not to the baby but to the stroller, as though by doing so he would smooth the baby's passage and help her to balance. But the baby was too young to balance. She leant forward, pointing at something, and in her eagerness let go of the stroller's frame and brought her left arm around to point as well. The boy saw what was happening and despairingly clutched the stroller, trying to keep it steady. As a result the stroller stopped dead, and the baby, anchored at the foot by the straps on the seat, cascaded forward in a semicircle. There was a gasp from the people in the restaurant, then a clearly audible thud as the baby's head hit the cobbles.

The mother was halfway there before the baby started to yell. She pushed the boy roughly away, caught up the baby and the stroller together – the baby's foot was still caught in its straps – and started to disentangle them. She walked the screaming baby up and down, then went across to the fountain where she wet her hand and cooled the baby, which was a livid red with yelling. Slowly its crying gave way to intermittent whimpering, and the people in the restaurant went back to their lunches.

She noticed though that the husband appeared to take no active part in the drama. He sat at his place, knife and fork in his hand, watching. The boy walked towards him, looking utterly devastated, very upright, very scared, very small. He stopped about two metres away, looking straight at the father. Who put his knife and fork down, took a long and slow sip of his wine, then stretched his arm out to the boy. When the boy came up to him the father put his arm gently around his shoulder, held him close and talked to him quietly for a while. Then the boy went round to his own chair and started to eat his pizza again.

Meanwhile the baby had stopped whimpering. As the mother carried it back to the table, the boy put down his knife and fork and stared at her. He was very still, and very white.

'You're hopeless, absolutely hopeless!' It was a hiss, a private abuse, but from the next table she could hear the mother clearly. 'How hopeless can you get? You can't even take the baby for a walk! Why did you take her over there? Christ, what a useless, hopeless kid! Look at him! Would you like me now, yes, how about this? – you get in the stroller and I'll push you across the street so that you can fall out and hit your head on the ground like she has. Come on! Get in the stroller – you're no brighter than a one-year-old baby – get in the stroller and I'll push you around so that you fall out and hit your head. How would you like that, eh? Come on, get in the stroller!'

The boy sat rigid, his hands at his sides, as her tirade continued. His white face stared up at her, yet also through her, unblinking, perhaps too terrified to blink. The father was now holding the baby, who was chewing a crust of his pizza and no longer involved in the scene.

'Will you please shut up!' the husband said in such a low voice that only she, at the next table, could hear it. 'We all know how fucking wonderful you are, how terrific you are with kids, what a perfect mother you are, how you understand everything, how as a child you'd never make any mistakes, the Great Only Child, the expert in everything . . . Just leave him alone. You told him to take the baby for a walk, he was only doing what you asked him to do, and all your fucking knowledge, your brilliant . . .' His voice went on and on, but too quietly now for her to hear what he said. The wife didn't interrupt, and he didn't pause. The boy watched them, looking at times from face to face. Then the man stopped. The wife said something and he replied. They were quiet. They began to eat what was left of their lunch.

At her table next to them, she ordered a coffee. She knew she should go back to the hotel at some stage and find out what Terry was doing. But she put it off. Terry could look after himself.

As soon as she said it, thought it, she realised that she didn't know whether she'd meant it as an expression of a truth that she had witnessed (Terry could look after himself) or a way of wiping him off her conscience (let Terry, history teacher, get lost in his history and she could forget his sexual problems etc.) She thought she ought to go.

Beside her, the baby had been let loose on the ground. The boy was throwing a toy monkey at her, which she would nuzzle and thrust back at him, giggling. The man and the woman were studying a road map. Now and then their hands would touch, apparently accidentally, and then their fingers would loiter a little, with unobtrusive but unmistakable purpose. The wife ordered an icecream for the boy. When it came, he sat on his seat to eat it, chatting cheerfully to them as they made their plans for the rest of the day, it seemed. The father would borrow a spoon occasionally and feed bits of the icecream to the baby. Then they paid and left.

She sat on at her table, with her empty coffee cup, watching them as they walked away. The man was still carrying the baby, while the boy pushed the empty stroller. As they turned the corner and disappeared, the wife was rummaging for something, possibly sunglasses, in her shoulder-bag. An absolutely ordinary family on holiday. They would go back home with their photos of France, and of the too small, too remote Roman emperor gazing over the empty theatre in his vanished empire, and would tell their friends about the sights they'd seen and the meals they'd eaten. Such was family life.

She felt that she should despise them – their frazzled tempers, the violence of their anger towards each other, the abuse they could fling so readily, without stint, so nakedly, so visibly, it seemed so careless of the consequences, of each other's feelings, of what used to be called the proprieties. If that was family life, then she should be glad she'd escaped it. Perhaps even evaded it, not altogether unconsciously either, she admitted to herself.

Yet that wasn't the whole picture. She thought of the quietness with which the woman had listened to the man's abuse, and how readily the boy had started playing again with the baby, the source, she would have thought, of all his trouble. So cheerfully too. And there was the man's curious inactivity as the crisis approached, almost as if he were watching a performance of something he had directed. And the way he had comforted the boy. It was like a private play publicly performed in a language whose meanings had been subtly altered, even deliberately falsified, by the actors, to preserve the privacy of its meaning. Witness as she was to their drama, which by any canon of good behaviour should have disgusted her, she felt not repelled, but excluded. Yes, even a little envious.

So that when she found Terry's note on her return to the hotel, she felt more disappointment, more loneliness even, than she was prepared for.

'I've gone to Paris to be alone for a week. Perhaps more,' he had written. 'You can contact me there via American Express, and then we must work out whether to travel on together or go separate ways. It's not that you're not a good person to travel with – quite the opposite, nobody could be better. But . . .' He faltered. She looked up from the letter at the cheap hotel bedroom suddenly so empty. 'But there are things I don't know how to express,' the letter continued. 'Perhaps I don't even really know yet, myself, what they are. I need to be alone for a while, to work them out. To get things clear. You must have been like that yourself, at times, surely? And you'll understand, won't you?'

She supposed she understood. Or she understood now that she understood as much as anyone in the audience could. Because that, she saw, was where she would always be, watching the drama in other people's lives. Poor Terry, though.

One thing she did know for certain, from her own past experience, was that she needed a stiff strong drink. Perhaps a lot of them. She went out to a bar to get one.

Holy Mackerel

ALISON BROINOWSKI

Through most of Indian airspace it was dark. So that seven hundred million people down there, growing by a million a month, could be better imagined than in daylight, when views of open country, not visibly crawling with humanity, maimed beggars or sacred cows, might be misleading. Besides, on the Calcutta to London leg they served steak, at least to passengers who could stomach it.

Delegates from a world food conference were flying back, I could tell. What they weren't good at doing they were good at talking about, across aisles and between seats. Their conference had finished, it seemed, without electing the next president. Some man, I gathered, had been expected to get the job, but he had outraged the international baby food industry.

'When as everyone knows, it's dirty bottles and unboiled water that makes bad formulas,' said the man across the aisle.

'But nobody dares say it,' the one behind said.

There had been another contender, apparently, whose country had this year achieved self-sufficiency in rice production and had good third world credentials as a result. 'Unless you count the upper class there, who get imported Californian rice on the black market,' the delegate by the window seat said. 'It's middle class self-sufficiency, that's all. The lower class can't afford even the local stuff, so they don't show up as demand statistics.'

'Notice how their statistics got better in presidential election year?'

As with Caesar, so with airlines. Planes cut people, like Gaul, into three classes, by capacity to pay. The many are those who pay for themselves, the few are those for whom someone else pays, and the fewest are those to whom it doesn't matter. Other dividing lines meander less predictably lengthwise: subsets of non-smokers, headphone wearers, criers, vomiters, boozers, sleepers and talkers. An aircraft is a social matrix: you can get both less and more than you paid for, and what you win on one axis you can lose on another.

The delegates were having trouble talking international food politics over the port, across rows and around seats. One, an Indian, was having influence with the airline. So it was done: I was upgraded from their midst, bag and baggage, to first class, through the curtains, into the wide open spaces, where you could hear a martini pick drop, where one hadn't spoken to another since Honolulu, where dinner was only just beginning, and where even the headphones had superior earfittings, an aid to business class digestion.

But the social matrix had me next to a talker.

It was the pink smoked salmon that got him going. 'Contradiction in terms,' he accused me, as much as the inflight menu, I and the hors d'oeuvres having arrived at the same time. 'Never smoke anything but red.'

He looked the wrong side of fifty to smoke anything unconventional.

'People see pink salmon, or king salmon even, and think they're getting the best. Don't know nearly enough about classes of salmon. What it is they're paying for. People who write these wretched menus have no idea.'

He wasn't fooled by my headphones, and kept talking until my defences had to come down. Perhaps I could get them back on for the main course. 'I doubt if I do either,' I said.

'Red, half red, pink, chum, and king, in that order.'

'Chum?'

'Chimbote – American Indian word. There's a world of difference. Quality *and* price.'

'Really.'

'Price can triple as you go up the line. Only top of the market red is smoked. Stupidity on the airline's part to say pink and serve red.'

'Is it all right to eat?'

'Red's *very* all right. But heavens, if we mixed the classes we'd soon hear about it from our customers. Take crab.'

He took, in fact, the *entrecôte poivrade,* in preference to the *murgh tandoori,* and a change of wines.

'Crab. When my company put Thai crab on the UK market under our label, we got hundreds, even thousands, of letters complaining about the taste. We used to sell Canadian crab, d'you see, and before that Japanese. Then they priced themselves out of the market, and we moved into canning in Thailand. We were careful, extremely so. No blue meat used, all white or pink, legs on the top and bottom, body meat in the middle, parchment lining, no mains water in the brine. But still we got letters wanting the old class of product back. That's the sort of customer we're catering to. Discriminating.'

'What did you do?'

'There was nothing we could do. We had to sell the high-priced Japanese crab in the UK and the Thai crab in Belgium.'

'Belgium?'

'Well, d'you see, they don't really know the difference over there. It's the escalator effect, as they say these days.'

'Rising expectations?'

'More like social class, actually, only worldwide. Countries move up, is what happens. Get more fastidious about what they eat. I've been in this business for thirty-odd years. Seen it happen. Mackerel's the same. Extraordinary, really, when you come to think about it. Some people can hardly tell a mackerel from a sardine. They've got something called mackerel in a can in Manila, I saw it, with a sauce made of bananas and red colouring. In the UK we'd go out of business if we touched it. You can't get people to move back down the escalator.'

'Really.'

'Well, we want to keep the top product reaching our best customers, so we have to find markets in countries that are more – more flexible. Will take a lower quality product, a lower grade of fish, buy from the countries at the bottom.'

'And bigger fish have bigger fish and so ad infinitum.'

'Eh? Look, this is serious. Seafood's a multimillion dollar business.'

'I'm sure.'

The trolley came. A choice between four dressings for the salad was required.

'Salmon technology is very advanced. To keep that Canadian salmon competitive, I was telling you about, here's an example, they have an artificial breeding cycle. Here, say your wine glass is the breeding pond and mine is the open sea, all right? There's an endless cycle of salmon going from one to another.'

I looked, but he was quite serious. 'Imagine that.'

'Yes. Salmon swim upstream to here to spawn, see, to the breeding station. Workers here take the eggs out of the females and mix them up in big vats with the sperm, and then when the fish hatch they put the fingerlings back into the stream and the salmon swim down to the rivers, there, and it begins again. Now, this is the fascinating part, to my mind, next season, salmon are a returning species, you see, they come back to the breeding station to spawn. Even though they were bred there artificially in the first place.'

'Amazing.'

'Yes. Thank you, the mango sherbet. So you can see how important it is.'

'What, feeding ourselves, or feeding the world?'

He heh-heh'd a bit. 'Well, it's a big business, as I said, but it's not world scale yet, not the quality trade. May never be.'

'Feeding the five thousand, then?'

'In a manner of speaking, yes.'

'You only need the loaves to go with the fishes and you could take over from Macdonald's.'

'Eh? I'm glad to say I've never been inside one of those places.'

Cheeses were brought on a board. Tropical fruit from distant plantations could be selected or, for the conventional, just desserts.

'What were you doing in Delhi?'

'Inspecting one of their canneries. Not good, not good enough, I'm afraid. Had to let them go. Good mackerel, mind you, well enough packed, but the autoclave procedure left much to be desired. They were hurrying up the cooling process by running cold water over the expanded cans. Caught them at it. Slightest leak at that stage and we'd be importing Delhi water into the UK. Could lose your By Appointment for that sort of thing.'

'So what happens to India, to their industry?'

'They go down the escalator, as I said, find other markets. Burma, on the black, China, perhaps, Eastern Europe, land-locked countries. Food aid shipments, paid for by some international agency. Pet food. Australia, New Zealand; places where some people will eat anything if it's cheap.'

'I thought the world was short of food.'

He pushed away his plate to make room for the cognac glass. It was his sixth airline meal in eight hours. 'Don't believe a word of it. World produces enough for everyone. No shortage. What the world is short of is people who know good food and have the money to buy it.'

Conversation had to pause for digestion of that, as much as of dinner. Somewhere to the south of our flight path was Ethiopia, the spreading Sahara, Mozambique.

Gazing into the crystal ball of brandy, he fished out his best one of the flight. 'Two sorts of people, seems to me, d'you know? Ourselves' – a gesture around near-empty first class ' – and those who actually eat to stay *alive*.'

A Thousand Miles from the Ocean

HELEN GARNER

At Karachi they were not allowed off the plane. She went and stood at the open back door. Everything outside was dust-coloured, and shimmered. Two men in khaki uniforms squatted on the tarmac in the shadow of the plane's tail. They spoke quietly together, with eloquent gestures of the wrist and hands. Behind her, in the cool, the other passengers waited in silence.

The Lufthansa DC10 flew on up the Persian Gulf. Some people were bored and struck up conversations with neighbouring strangers. The Australian beside her opened his briefcase and showed her a plastic album. It contained photographs of the neon lighting systems he sold. He turned the pages slowly, and told her in detail about each picture. *I should never have come. I knew this before I got on the plane. Before I bought the ticket.* 'Now this one here,' said the Australian under his moustache, 'is a real goer.' His shoes were pale grey slip-ons with a heel and a very small gold buckle. She found it necessary to keep her eyes off his shoes, which were new, so while she listened she watched another young man, a German, turn and kneel in his seat, lay his arms along the head-rest, and address the person behind him. He looked as if the words he spoke were made of soft, unresisting matter, as if he were chewing air. While she waited for the lavatory she stopped and peered out through a round, distorting window the size of a hubcap. Halfway between her window and the long straight coastline a little white plane, a sheik's plane, spanked along smartly in the opposite direction. If I were on that plane I would be on my way home. I am going the wrong way.

She woke in the hotel. Her watch said 8.30. It was light outside. She went to the window and saw people walking about. The jackhammer stopped. She picked up the phone.

'Excuse me,' she said. 'Is it day or night?'

The receptionist laughed. 'Night,' he said.

She hung up.

In the Hauptbahnhof across the road she bought four oranges, and walked away with them hanging from her hand in a white plastic bag. I will be all right: I can buy. *Ich kann kaufen*. I should not be here. I can hardly pronounce his name. I am making a very expensive mistake.

In her room she began to dial a number.

On the way up the stairs he kept his hand on the back of her head. He laughed quietly, as if at a private joke.

'I am so tired,' he said. 'I must rest for one hour.'

'I'll read,' she said.

He threw himself face down, straight-legged, fully dressed, on his bed. She wandered away to the white shelves in the hallway. There were hundreds and hundreds of books. The floor was of blond wood laid in a herringbone pattern. The walls were white. The brass doorknobs were polished. The windows were covered with unbleached calico curtains. She took down *Dubliners* and sat at the kitchen table. She sat still. She heard his breathing slow down.

The coffee pot, the strainer, the bread knife still had price stickers on them. In the shelves there were no plates, but several small, odd objects: a green mug with yellow flowers and no handle, a white egg cup with a blue pattern. The kitchen windows opened on to a balcony which was stuffed with empty cardboard cartons stacked inside each other. Beyond the balcony, in someone else's yard, stood a large and leafy tree.

She sat at the table for an hour. Every now and then she turned a page. The sun, which had been shining, went behind a cloud. It did not appear to be any more one season than another.

He came to the kitchen doorway. 'I wish I could have gone

to sleep,' he said.

'You were asleep,' she said. 'I heard you breathing.'

Without looking at her he said rapidly, 'I went very deep inside myself.'

She stood up.

'Do you want to see my bicycle?' he said. 'That is mine. Down there.'

'The black one?'

'Ja.'

He stopped the car at a bend in the road. It seemed to be evening but the air was full of light. Flies hovered round the cows' faces. These are the first living creatures, except pigeons and humans, I have seen since I left home.

Frogs creaked. Darkness swam down. They walked. They walked into a wood. While they were in there, night came. The paths were wet. Dots of light flickered, went out, rekindled. Under the heavy trees a deer, hip-deep in grass, moved silently away.

They came out of the wood and walked along a road. The road ran beside a body of water. The road was lined with huge trees that touched far overhead. Wind off the water hissed through the trees. Behind them stood high, closed villas with shuttered windows and decorated wooden balconies.

'Beautiful. Beautiful,' he said.

Shutup. On the dark water a pleasure boat passed. Its rails were strung with fairy lights. Broken phrases of music bounced across the cold ripples. Couples danced with their whole fronts touching, out on the deck.

'Is that . . . the ocean?' she said.

He looked at her, and laughed. 'But we are a souzand *miles* from the ocean!'

They walked by the lake.

'Have you ever had a boat?' she said.

'A boat?'

'Yes.'

'A paddle boat, yes. My father used to take me out in his paddle boat.'

'Do you mean a canoe?' she said. 'A kayak?'

'Something. I hated it. Because my father was a very good . . . paddler. And he was trying to make me . . .'

'Tough?'

'Not tough. I was very small and I hated everything. I hated living with my family. I hated my brothers and sisters. He was only trying to make me like something. But I was so small, and sitting in front of this great, strong giant made me feel like a dwarf. And out on the sea – on the lake – he would say "which way is Peking? Which way is New York?" And I would be so nervous that I couldn't even think. I would guess. And he would say "No!" and hit me, bang, on the head with the paddle.

There was only one bed. It was narrow. It was his. He sat in the kitchen drinking with his friend. The friend said to her, 'Two main things have changed in this country over the past twenty years. The upbringing of children has become less authoritarian. And there is less militarism.' After midnight, while the two men talked to each other in the kitchen, she undressed and lay on the inside edge of the narrow mattress. At the hotel the sheet on my bed was firmly drawn, and the doona was folded like a wafer at the foot: I paid for comfort, and I got it. She slept till he came to bed, and then it was work all night to keep her back from touching his. Tomorrow I will feel better. Tomorrow I will be less the beaten dog. I will laugh, and be ordinary. His snoring was as loud as the jackhammer. The window was closed tight. Why did he sing to me, at the end of the summer on the other side of the world? Why did he hold me as I was falling asleep and sing me the song about the moon rising? I bled on the sheets and he laughed because the maid was angry. We stood on the cliff edge above an ocean of trees and he borrowed my nail clippers. As he clipped, the tiny sound expanded and rang in the clean air. 'Pik, pik, pik,' he said. Why did he make those phone calls? Why did he cry on the phone in the middle of the night?

He grumbled all the time. He laughed, to pretend it was a joke, but grumbling was his way of talking. Everything was *aw*-ful. His life was *aw*-ful.

'I'm sorry to keep laughing,' she said. 'Why don't you – no.'

'What? What?'

'I keep wanting to make useful suggestions. I know that's annoying.'

'No! No! Zey are good!'

'Why don't you have a massage every week?'

'Who? But who?'

'Why don't you do less of the same work?'

He laughed. 'Zat would be a very bad compromise.'

'You could live on less money, couldn't you?'

He looked distracted. 'But I have to pay for zis *apartment.*'

He went to work and the heavy door closed behind him. She tipped her coffee down the sink. The plughole was blocked by a frill of fried egg white.

She washed herself. She looked at the mirror and away again. She found the key and went down to the courtyard for the bike. An aproned woman on another balcony watched her unchain it, and did not respond to a raised hand.

The sky was clouded. The seat was high and when she wobbled across an intersection a smoothly pedalling blonde called out, 'Vorsicht!' She stopped and bought a cake of soap and an exercise book with square-ruled pages. She laboured over a map and found her way to a gallery. She passed between its tremendous pillars. It is my duty to look at something. I must drag my ignorance round on my back like a wet coat. He will ask me what I have seen and I must answer. Is there something the matter with me? The paintings look as vulgar as swap-cards, the objects in them as if made of plaster. *Grotte auf Malta 1806:* waves like boiled cauliflower. A heaven full of tumbling pink flabby things. Here is the famous Tintoretto: *Vulkan Überrascht Venus und Mars.* Venus has buds for breasts; a little dog hides under the table. 'The Nazis,' said a Frenchwoman behind her, 'got hold of that Tintoretto and never gave it back.' A small boy lay flat on his stomach on the floor, doing a pencil drawing of an ancient sculpture. His breathing was audible. His pencil made trenches in the paper. His father sat on a bench behind him, waiting and smiling.

In the lavatory she found her pants were black with blood.

The apartment was still empty. It was hard to guess the season or the time of day.

In his apartment there was no broom. There was no iron.

A narrow cupboard full of clothes: the belted raincoat, the Italian jumpers, the dozens of shirts still wrapped from the laundry, each one sporting its little cardboard bow-tie.

A Beethoven violin sonata on the turntable.

Under the bed, a copy of *Don Quixote* and a thermometer.

Through the double-glazed windows passed no sound.

Perhaps he has run away, left town, to get away from me and

my unwelcome visit.

On the kitchen wall, a sepia poster of a child, a little girl in romantic gypsy rags, whose glance expressed a precocious sexuality. I am in the wrong country, the wrong town. When I heard the empty hiss of the international call I should have put down the phone. In the middle of his night he took the pills that no longer worked. He cried on the phone. For me, though, it was bright day. I was on the day side of the planet where I had a garden, a house, creatures to care for. I should have hung up the phone. Man muss etwas *machen,* he said, gegen diese Traurigkeit: something has to be *done* about this sadness. Shutup. Oh, shutup. Is that the ocean? But we are a souzand *miles* from the ocean!

She walked closer to the furniture. She picked things up and examined them. She went into the cupboard again and pulled a jacket towards her face, then let it drop. That's better. Already making progress.

She went towards the window where his white desk stood. There was a little typewriter on it, and loose heaps of paper, books, envelopes. She twitched the curtain away from a framed picture it was hiding. It was a photo. She took it in her hand. It was herself. A small, dark face, an anxious look. And beneath the photo, under the glass, a torn scrap of paper, non-European paper with horizontal lines instead of squares. Her own handwriting said, *I'm sorry you had to sleep in my blood, but everything else I'm happy about.* She put it back on its hook, dropped the curtain over it, and began to go through the papers.

The apartment was full of letters from women. Barbara, Brigit, Emanuele, Els. Dozens of them. On his work desk. On top of the fridge. In the bedroom. He left the women's letters, single pages of them, scattered round the apartment like little land-mines to surprise himself: under a saucer, between the pages of a book. She read them. Their tone! Dry, clever, working hard at being amusing, at being light. Pathetic. A pathetic tone. Grown women, like herself. 'Capri, c'est pas fini,' wrote one on the back of a postcard. Si, c'est fini. I have spent thousands of dollars to come here and see myself on these pieces of paper. I am now a member of an honourable company.

The telephone began to ring: long, single, European blasts.

She dithered. She picked it up. It was not him. It was a young woman. They found a common language and spoke to each other.

'He has my poems,' said the young woman. She was shy, and light-voiced. 'He said that I could call him this weekend. He said we could have a drink together to discuss my poems.'

'I'll take a message.'

'My name is Jeanne. You know? In the French way of writing?'

'I'll tell him, I promise.'

The young woman laughed in her light, nervous voice. 'Thank you. You are very kind.'

Capri, c'est pas fini.

She picked up her bag and went out the door.

At the Hauptbahnhof a ragged dark-haired gypsy woman ran out of a door marked POLIZEI. Her shoes were broken, her teeth were broken. She ran with bent knees and bared teeth. She ran in a curving path across the station and out on to the street. Men looked at each other and laughed.

The train went south. South, and south. It stopped at every station. People got in and people got out. It ran along between mountains whose tops were crisp. People carried parcels and string bags, and sometimes children. They greeted each other in blurred dialects. The train crossed borders, it ran across a whole country. A grandmother ate yoghurt out of a plastic jar. She raised and dipped the spoon with a mechanical gesture. She licked the white rim off her lips and swallowed humbly. The train slid through a pass beside a jade river. Tremors rose from the river's depths and shuddered on its swollen surface. After the second border she opened the window. The train passed close to buildings the colour of old flowerpots, buildings set at random angles among dense foliage, buildings whose corners were softened with age. The shutters were green; they were fixed back against the walls to make room for washing and for red geraniums. The air had colour and texture. You could touch the air. It was yellow. It was almost pink. She turned back to the compartment and it was full of the scent of sleeping children.

Saint Kay's Day

BEVERLEY FARMER

How warm even a cold white room became when you turned
on the light! Any light would do the trick. Candlelight was
best of all, though, with its little shadowy fires. And a room
that faced the sunset was like a cave behind a waterfall, when
you lit candles in it and made shadows arch their wings like
bats on its walls and ceiling. With the shutters closed you
could be anywhere in the world. With them open, you were in
Greece: over the balcony rail was Mount Olympus, printed
indigo on the hot sky, and all the still gulf in between had little
boats pulling threads in the silk of it. What did it matter if the
room that faced the sunset was the only room you had, except
of course for a narrow kitchen, and a dark bathroom no bigger
than a telephone box? (And if little pale celluloid
cockroaches scurried into the air vent whenever you switched
the light on in that bathroom.) Even if the power did keep
failing. And her flat was small and dark and so icy – and this
was only November, late November – that she ached and
shuddered all day.

Sunset was when the lizard crept out and spread his sleek
bronze skin on the warm glow of one wall. He was company,
the rippling lizard.

'Aren't you lonely there, Kay?' Letters from home kept
asking that. 'When are you coming home? What's Thessaloniki
got that Sydney hasn't?'

Thessaloniki has Aleko, her letters never said in reply: Aleko
was still too new. Besides, was it only Aleko?

'We miss you, you know,' pleaded the letters.

'Well, I miss you,' she wrote back. 'But Thessaloniki is very beautiful and strange. More than Athens even. I've hardly begun to see the real Thessaloniki.'

'We're not getting any younger as you know.' Her father wrote as he spoke, flatly. 'Your Mum and I were hoping you'd be back this Christmas. First it was "my studies". Now it's "my working holiday". That's all very well, but you have to settle down sometime, don't you.'

'I've taken on students for English lessons. I can't let them down and just leave, can I?'

'But *aren't* you lonely, dear?' That was her mother.

'Well, you see, there's this lizard,' she wrote, 'and a sweet little Burmese cat . . .' The letters ignored that.

It *was* sweet, a spoilt coquette of a little cat, in this city of starved strays too. It came faithfully to her door every day after the siesta for its plate of warm milk. When she stroked it, it closed its eyes in its bat-eared black face and stretched itself in poses of pure lust. Its deep-furred bony little body vibrated warmly; it was just beautiful. It gave her hope that her own bony body would, when – *if* – the time came, be beautiful for Aleko. She told Aleko, in Greek, that she loved the cat because it spoke English: just as she hoped, he laughed aloud. He was at his most handsome then. His mouth, widening, lost its petulant droop. Because there was something petulant and spoilt about Aleko at times. He *was* selfish, he was vain. But he would grow out of it. He had a kind heart. Once he asked, looking down, looking at her hands as thin as dry leaves on the table: 'Why you are alone in your life, Kay?' So she told him about the man in Australia that she had loved and never really got over . . .

'It spik Greek too, this clever cat,' spluttered Aleko, in English. 'Ask it if it spik Burmese!' And, why she didn't know, but they collapsed at this and laughed together till they cried.

Aleko came for a lesson twice a week at around sunset. He always stayed on, though, drinking coffee in her chilly kitchen long after the hour was up. She was always free: in her two months in Thessaloniki Aleko was the only student she had found. The sixty drachmas that he paid her twice a week covered the rent; that was only five hundred a month. For everything else but the rent she had to withdraw savings. Any day now she hoped to find more students: it was hard without a telephone or a work permit. Her notices in English in the two libraries were still up:

ENGLISHWOMAN (because no one wanted an Australian accent): M.A. GRADUATE: SEEKS ADULT STUDENTS FOR ENGLISH LESSONS IN YOUR OWN HOME: 60 DRACHMAS PER HOUR (and her name and her address).

Aleko came to her place, his had no privacy. Aleko had written out notices in Greek for her. He might know someone who wanted lessons, or so he had hinted. He enjoyed hinting.

'Is your name's day next Thursday, you know thet,' he said after the last lesson, when they were waiting for the lift. 'We hev little party, okay, Kay? I bring a cake.'

'*My* name's day? Saint *Kay?*'

'Agia Aikaterini. Is the same. Aikaterini, Katerina, Katy, Kay.' With a quick smile as the lift bumped and opened: 'We be hev good time. Okay? Kay?' It amused him to say that.

'Okay, okay!' And the lift closed. When he comes, she decided, we mustn't fail, we must come to the point. Why have I been so prim all this time? (Who am I keeping it for?) I'll ask him to stay and we'll have dinner . . . No, not here, how can I?

How could she, when all she had to cook on was a portable Camping Gaz with one burner? On this she fried her eggs and vegetables and sardines, she boiled spaghetti and then sauce, she brewed Greek coffee in a copper *briki,* she cooked her morning porridge, having found oats here at last, imported from Holland and very dear, in a grocer's near the flower market. What a luxury, after so long, to stir the thickening mass of oats until it plopped and then add honey in a trickle like a brass wire and eat it out of the saucepan! She always ate at home. Even in Sydney she was too shy ever to eat out alone; here women just didn't. In the covered market she bought her quarter-kilo of leeks here; her quarter-kilo of split sardines rusty with blood there; here an eighth of a kilo of olives, there a half-litre of dry red – '*brousko',* she insisted – Cretan wine. Shopkeepers exchanged resigned smiles when they saw her coming. On the way home, she stared in the steamy windows of the restaurants along Odos Egnatias at the crusted golden beans in earthenware, at roast meats wrapped in their film of fat . . .

I'll ask him out to a restaurant, she decided. I'll pay. Aleko can choose where. And then – what?

Her life had never seemed so empty to her as it did now that Aleko was the centre of it. She went on the bus to a cinema sometimes. She shopped and window-shopped. The streets were windy and stank of diesel fumes. She read in the warmth of the two libraries, the British Council one on the sea front and the United States Information Service one on Aristotelous Square, which was where Aleko had seen her notice offering lessons. (But he never happened to come in again while she was in there.) She borrowed books to take home, and returned them mostly unread: she was too cold, too restless, to be bothered.

On grey days her room could have been a cube of air cut inside an iceberg.

Once or twice a week she did her washing in the sink and pegged it out on a rope along the balcony, or up on the *taratsa,* the flat roof, with everyone's else's, strung among dusty chimney pots and aerials; or even in the kitchen when it rained, and then her weak yellow bulb was screened by layers of washing that shed drips and shadows. She spread old newspapers – the *Times,* the airmail *Guardian,* bought for reading aloud with Aleko – over the powdery cement mosaic of her kitchen floor. She had a dream the morning of one washing day. She was hanging out a wet sheet in the wind when it became a sail, and a woman – who? – on a shore some- where was leaning forward to tell her reproachfully, 'Life is so *ephemeral.'* The word itself was like a puff of air: *ephemeral.* It stayed with her. She even looked it up in Greek: *efimero,* the same. Life was *efimero.* For days she was filled with a sense of urgency, of waste time. She was as housebound as an old widow, and she was all of twenty-eight.

She made herself go out for long walks. She sat on benches in the parks and ate the roast chestnuts or the corncobs that she bought on street corners, or a *souvlaki* in a paper bag. Men pestered her, gypsy women begged, gypsy boys smeared shoe polish on her suede boots and sneered in her protesting face. *'Raus!'* they called after her: all blond people were Germans.

One gypsy woman in particular, nursing a little red baby, worried Kay so much that she told Aleko about her: a gaunt woman whining out of a greasy scarf that let only her long brown teeth and nose show. Kay gave her ten drachmas. Aleko whistled at that. 'She'll remember *your* face,' he said. He believed the gypsy women took turns to hold the baby. But it really was a sick baby, it was yellow, with a crusted rash. Then there was the beggar woman at the Post Office counters, roaring with her hand stretched out at you, a tongueless and toothless giantess like a dead tree. She never failed to corner Kay. And sure enough, that gypsy with the sick baby ran into Kay all over the place as she photographed ruins – 'One earthquack do that,' Aleko explained – and huts and churches, and sculpted faces in the crowd. 'Tou*rist*?' furtive young men whispered behind her. 'Spik English, miss? Tou*rist*?'

No, she thought, never answering them though: I *live* in Thessaloniki. I live in Greece now.

The neighbours greeted her curtly when they met in the building. They shrieked at her when she swilled water on her balcony to wash the dust off and it piddled down the spout in a murky arc on to the footpath: though they all washed their balconies. They exchanged dark looks when they caught her seeing Aleko off at the lift. He was five years younger than she was, and looked younger still: their eyes said that this beautiful young man had undersold himself, because doubtless she was supporting him. How ludicrous she was, this lovesick broomstick, this *Anglida* of his! Kay took to not wearing her glasses, to make herself more worthy of Aleko. She knew her way in the blurred streets by now, and at home she could see everything except glasses and bottles, whose contents seemed to hang in mid-air in some disturbance of the light. During lessons – at the card table under her dim kitchen bulb – she sometimes had to bend in front of Aleko until her nose was on the page. She blushed. Could he see through her? If so, she thought, all he saw would be a burning scarlet flood of light . . .

On the morning of Saint Katerina's day Kay washed her hair, something she did less often now, it took so long to dry. She had what they called here a telephone shower, hand-held (but no bath or shower recess, so that it flooded the floor) and shivered in its lukewarm trickle every day. In September when she first came, she could squat on the *taratsa* and her hair ran like hot toffee over her bare knees, drying in minutes. Even on fine days now the sun had no warmth. That morning she dried her hair kneeling in front of the red bars of the radiator and pulling her fingers through the knots. With hours to fill in, on impulse she caught a throbbing blue bus to the city, to a tourist shop she knew, where she bought coloured candles and four hand-woven woollen *tagaria,* to use not as shoulder bags but as cushions. They made beautiful cushions with her summer clothes crammed in them, scattered on her bed – which was not ostentatiously her *bed,* since it was a rubber mat on the waxed planks of the bedroom floor with a *flokati* rug of tufted greasy wool over it instead of blankets. It wouldn't look too obvious, if they had their party there. *We hev little party*: that was sweet of him. She had coffee, sugar, brandy. The brandy was getting low, but a new bottle now would cut into the restaurant money. She stared in the mirror and spread over her velvet shoulders the polished stripes of her long hair. Would the sun never set? She lit the candles, switched on the radiator. Again and again, her heart jumping, she held her watch to her ear.

When at last the bell rang, she counted to ten first, before she opened the door. There stood Aleko, holding a large white box, red ribbons curled all over it. And beside him, a plump Greek girl. Gypsy-eyed, richly dark.

'Kay, hullo!' he shouted. *'Chronia polla!* Many heppy years!' He passed her the box, which automatically she took, her eyes fixed on his in her consternation. The girl, stepping forward, grabbed Kay's free hand in her warm brown one and shook it. *'Chronia polla,'* she said, 'Nitsa.'

'Nitsa?'

'. . . Yes. This is Nitsa,' Aleko said, his voice choked with self-consciousness and pride. 'Nitsa, this is my English teacher. This is Kay.'

They smiled, and Nitsa fluffed her tails of black hair loose with her hand. The corridor light clicked. They were in darkness. 'Well, come *in.*' Kay held the door open. 'Please, Nitsa, Aleko. Come in and sit down.' Who was it? Was she supposed to know? One of his sisters? She shut the door and

with an embarrassed laugh led them to the *flokati* in her
flickering room. They sat side by side on it, their backs to the
wall, stretching their legs out to the red bars. Kay hovered in
the doorway. 'May I open it?' She peeped, and did: in the box
were six cream sponge cakes of the kind called *pastes,* thickly
piped with cream and sanded with roast nuts. 'Oh look,
pastes!' she managed – she who loathed cream.

'You like it?'

'*Love* it, thank you. Both. They look de*lic*ious.'

'Is o*kay,* Kay.'

'You hev a goot view,' offered the girl, Nitsa. The lamps had
come on in the street, dripping and swaying at the water's
edge. The *volta* was beginning, shadows were shuffling past.
The whole sea was a dying fire. Beyond it the dark mountain
stood; white lights glittered on it like sparks astray in winds.

'Mount Olympus,' Kay said reverently.

'Yes, you know Olimbos? He hev a lot of snow nown.'

'Now,' smiled Kay.

'Yes, nown snow. Is winter nown.'

Aleko rewarded Nitsa with a dazed smile and took her hand.

'These beautiful *pastes*. Let's have them now.' Kay held up
the box and nodded to Nitsa. 'Nown?'

'No, no, Kay! Is all for you this one!'

'Aleko, I'd *die*. You have to help me. Well, excuse me, won't
you?' They would. They smiled ecstatically.

In the kitchen she was frantic to remember. Aleko had
mentioned sisters, hadn't he? Two sisters? Well, then! But no,
one's name was Maria and the other one's? – Toula. Nitsa must
be a cousin. Young men were expected to escort their cousins
too. Her hands quivering, Kay lit the Camping Gaz and stirred
coffee and water and sugar in the *briki*. She found plates and
forks for the *pastes*. Pouring two glasses of her dark brandy,
she drank one down, rinsed and refilled the glass. The coffee
frothed. She tipped it into the cups – at least she had three
cups. Please, Agia Aikaterini, Katerina, Katy, let Nitsa be a
cousin, she thought. They were very quiet in there on the
flokati.

Nitsa's hair was a shawl over Aleko, until they saw her and
sat bolt upright. And Nitsa was not a cousin.

'*Stin ygeia sou,* Kay,' they chanted, tossing down their

brandies. She served them a *pasta* each and, putting the tray of coffees on the floorboards near them, sat on a *tagari* cushion to munch her way through hers. They jabbed and licked and gulped. Once Aleko bent and stole a chunk off Nitsa's fork. 'Ach!' She squealed, delighted, and slapped his thigh. His teeth when he grinned were lathered with the cream. Kay smiled maternally.

'Aren't they de*li*cious!' She rinsed her mouth with coffee. 'Where did you get them?'

'From very goot shop. Terkenli, you know, Kay,' he boasted. 'Is near to the American library.'

'They must have cost a fortune. You shouldn't have.'

'You hev to eat!' He sucked his coffee. 'Look at you, all bones, is no goot for your healthy. Not *you*, you too fet.' He poked Nitsa's waist. *'Patata eisai esi.* One big fet patato.'

'Niata threfo,' Nitsa said loftily. Kay raised her brows.

'She hev to feed her youngness, she say. Young pipple need to eat *too much.'*

'Kala lei,' agreed Kay. Her tone was dry; not that they noticed.

'Ya!' Nitsa grinned at her and gave Aleko a triumphant shove that sent him sprawling. They giggled. How old was Nitsa? Kay could just make out their faces on the coppery wall, half lit among shadows and reflected in the glass door now that the sky was dark. Perhaps sixteen; eighteen at the most. She licked her white fork.

'Well, I'm still hungry.' She made her voice light. 'I'm going to bring the other *pastes* now.'

'No, no,' said Aleko feebly. She took their plates anyway and dished out the other three *pastes* in the kitchen. This time she remembered water, pouring them two glasses that turned the gold of beer when she brought them in.

'And now more coffee,' she said.

'No, no. No, really, Kay.'

'You always have two or three coffees!'

'Yes, but no, Kay, sorry. We carn stay nown.'

They couldn't stay. So that was that.

'I hev auntie in Melvourni,' mumbled Nitsa with her mouth full. 'You come from Melvourni?'

'No, Sydney.'

'Ach, Sydnayee.'

'Is nice place, Sydnayee, Kay?'

'Yes. It's like here in some ways. A city on the sea – '

'Like here? Is so cold?'

'Well, no – it's summer there now, of course.'

'*Po po!* Summer there nown!' Nitsa giggled with a great shudder. Aleko tugged the *flokati* up around her shoulders.

'You look like Eskimo,' he said happily, combing her back with dark fingers. 'One big fet Eskimo bear.'

Kay shut her eyes to remember Sydney and in what ways it was like here. But Sydney was a set of faded transparencies. What her parents wanted was their old Kay back. As for those of her old friends who were still there, what did she have to say to them? As much as she had to say to these two. *I zoii,* she thought she might say, as one who leans earnestly forward across widening water: *I zoi ieina toso efimeri –*

'We hev to visit another Katerinas, many Katerinas tonight,' Nitsa was explaining. Kay nodded.

'You lookink too sed, Kay.' He bent to help Nitsa up, brushing her crumbs off. 'I think so you hev nostalgear nown.'

'Oh a little bit. No, not really. I'm happy.' She scrambled up. 'It's been a lovely party, thank you both.'

'Well, I see you next lesson. Hey, silly me!' He glowed, all eagerness. 'I forgot to say you. Din I say I find you one new student? Well: Nitsa want to learn with me English!'

'. . . Oh. Yes, Nitsa? Oh, good.'

'We learnink together, okay? Is more funny.'

'Fun. Yes, I see.' Kay laughed indignantly, and he mistook her.

'We come together and both of us payink you sixty *drachmes,*' he said quickly. 'One hundred twenty. Okay – Kay?'

'Okay. That will be fun.' She smiled back at them. When they come next time, she thought, I can always say that my mother's sick and I have to go home. I don't have to stay in Thessaloniki or in Greece if I don't want to. Can I stay here now? How the neighbours would laugh if they knew! They laughed anyway.

She got rid of Aleko and Nitsa (who were more than anxious to be gone) and rinsed the dishes, leaving them to dry on the marble, the real marble, of the draining board. In her room she locked the balcony shutters and straightened the still-warm *flokati,* which smelled of Arpège. To think I hoped he could love *me,* she thought: it never even crossed his mind. (Though it must have crossed Nitsa's, clever little Nitsa's.) It seemed to Kay now that nothing more would ever happen to her; her life would never be any fuller than it was at this moment, in this lonely city or another.

Mewings, scratchings at the front door: wearily she let the cat in. It was greedy and luxurious, not lovable at all. It sniffed, peering round. She gave it its milk cold. It wet its nose, gazed up with a mew, backed away. When it was sure the milk wouldn't warm itself, it stalked to her cushion and curled up with its back to her. The lizard hadn't come out. Nitsa must have alarmed it: it knew Aleko. Maybe it was going torpid and would freeze stiff in this cold, not coming alive till spring. So might she, here. A moth, quivering loudly at her ear, stumbled away among the candle flames. Fire would eat the moth, or the cat would, or the lizard. *Efimero, efimero!* As for her, she had nothing to eat in the flat, not even a drop of *brousko* wine. She had to keep her strength up. How had Nitsa put it? *Niata threfo. Niata,* youth: well, hardly . . .

Kay took out her tin of oats and ran her fingers through the flakes. She could always have porridge for dinner, porridge with bright honey. But wasn't there something stringy in the oats? She stared. Webs of them clung to her fingers. Yes, the oats were strung on webs, like corks on a fishing net. She could have wailed aloud. Weevils had got into the oats!

No, it was too much. Biting her lips, she lit the Camping Gaz and put the tin of oats on the flame. Let them bake in it like silkworms in their cocoons: why should she throw her Dutch oats out? As she watched, though, a little horrified, a white grub broke the surface of the flakes and reared, waved itself at full length, hopped and hurled itself first on to the red-hot rim, then on to the floor. She knelt and peered. Where was it on the cement mosaic? What a heroic escape! She had read, in an American magazine at the library, about a man tied with ropes and thrown on to an anthill in a pit rearing like that: covered in red skeins of ants he reared to his feet, to his full height, in the agony of death. The grub had done that. But it was still alive, wasn't it? It had to be!

She turned the Camping Gaz off – there might be others still alive – and jammed on her glasses. In the thick yellow light she crouched down, slanting to throw her shadow aside, and felt with her fingertips every chip and speckle of the floor where the grub had fallen. But she found only dust.

Against her shoulder the Burmese cat came pushing its warm head, purring. Then it hunched, stared, danced around the table legs and, before Kay could move, patted something and licked it up. *'Pussy!'* she groaned. It closed blissful eyes, in its mincing delicacy like a furred brown spider. Pinching its scruff in her powdery fingers, she dropped it outside in the dark of the corridor and slammed the door. The flat reeked of singed oats.

'You blight on the earth,' she told her reflection in the pane. 'The futility of you!' Her face flashed, goggling back. She pulled off her glasses to wipe her eyes. And then: 'Crying over a dead grub! What would the neighbours think of the mad *Anglida* if they saw you now? Wouldn't they be right, too?' Because she could see the ludicrous side of it all, but only as if at a great distance . . . Saint Kay's day! Life is so *efimeri*! Oh dear, oh dear. I *will* go out, she thought suddenly, I'll go out for dinner anyway. At one of those restaurants with steamy panes in Odos Egnatias (but I'll take a book with me). I'll have Cretan *brousko* wine, blood-red in the copper measuring beaker, and crusty beans or meat out of an earthenware baking dish . . . She would go somewhere warm with fuzzy gold lights and an uproarious crowd, where you stayed as long as you wanted out there in the real Thessaloniki. And then? Then – come back here?

Besides, she wasn't hungry any more, not after the *pastes*, not after the oats.

In the cave of her bedroom she lay back with her hair spread out on the hot tufts of the *flokati*. The radiator hummed its one note. Veils of the candlelight began their frilling and soft unravelling on the whitewash. After a while the lizard came out and sunned himself. After a while, she could have been anywhere in the world. Saint Kay's day was as good as over. One month to Christmas Day, she thought; and knew that, wherever in the world she was at Christmas, she would be there among strangers. The shadows of small flames quivered over her. She was sleepy now. She lay, a log in a sinking fire.

Tourist

MARIAN ELDRIDGE

But which shower to choose? There are two on your floor of the *pensione*, each curtainless, one so small and steamy that you have to leave the door ajar and risk a stranger bursting in – a stranger, probably, who will squawk at you in Italian – the other so eccentric that water sprays all over the walls and your nearly new dressing gown and trickles into the passage. Which shower shall I try today? you would like to ask someone . . . Which shower shall I try today? you say in your head, jokey, so that whoever is listening can have no inkling of the small panic that underlies the silly question. Perhaps, after all, you should have played safe and booked into a hotel? But, as you put it to them back home in the tea room during one of those sessions when you examined your plans from every angle, hogging the tea break probably but that is a traveller's privilege; of course I can afford a hotel, you said, but a *pensione* in Rome sounds more *fun*. Well of course a *pensione* is more fun! came their prompt reply. More fun. More real. Let your hair down properly while you're about it – and you saw them exchange smiles. Be a devil! Take the plunge! Where's your sense of adventure?

So, when you are showered and dressed in your sensible dark blue, that gold ring from your Christmas bon-bon slipped onto your wedding finger, your handbag slung travel-wise over one shoulder and your camera over the other, all ready to plunge, you ask yourself what to look at today. They were full of advice, of course. The Forum. The fountains. The churches.

Yesterday, because it was close to your *pensione*, you looked through an ancient Basilica with a magnificent ceiling of plundered gold. Today you have a craving to be outdoors, to throw yourself into the Roman throng. The Via Veneto is a must! they told you. (They pronounced it Ven*ee*to, and so do you.) That's where the Beautiful People hang out, they said. You sit at a sidewalk cafe on the Via Ven*ee*to and you drink a leisurely cup of coffee and you watch the passing parade, imagine! an Italian film star straight off the set, or a fashion designer, or an oil baron just jetted in from the Gulf. If you don't see the Beautiful People you haven't seen Rome, they smiled. You look up 'Rome at Night' in your guide book and it is just as they said. It sounds so simple you almost believe it possible. 'On the Via Veneto spend a few evening hours simply sitting,' says the guide book. 'You'll be glad you did.' The Beautiful People beckon; they brush you with elegant eyelashes. You swan downstairs from the floor with the idiosyncratic showers and in the chair in the tiny reception room you practise sitting.

The manager, a young man less good-looking than your preconceived notions, is speaking on the telephone in rapid Italian. When he has finished he switches to English as easily as he clicks down the receiver. 'Good morning, Signora. Can I help you at all?' Thank you, I am just putting my courage together – 'I'm just checking my map' is what you actually say, unfolding the map and turning it this way and that. 'Let me know if you need any help, Signora,' he repeats, turning his attention to a young couple who have just arrived. Dropping rucksacks almost onto your feet, they begin '*Guten Morgen –*' then laugh tiredly and try in Italian. '*Guten Morgen. Ich spreche Deutsch*,' he says gently. An English-speaking guest you exchanged nods with at breakfast asks if there's anywhere close by to get a good, cheap lunch, dinner as well maybe. 'Turn right and right again and you'll find an excellent *locanda*,' says the manager, adding 'Tell Roberto that Giovanni sent you.' The guest hurries out, the Germans make their way upstairs, the manager busies himself with his books. You warm towards this Giovanni, so helpful, so reassuring, and you search your mind for some request of your own. On your map you can locate the Trevi Fountain (the most romantic in Rome, they swooned, teasing you about what to wish), but the Via Veneto isn't so easy. You are about to ask him to point it out when he suddenly looks up. 'Signora, your bag and your camera over your shoulder like that – *not* a good idea. In Rome unfortunately at this time of year we have many *scippatori*, young men on motorpeds on the lookout for women such as yourself, a tourist, that is, with valuable articles on straps which they seize as they ride by.' He leans towards you, his eyes like boiling black coffee. 'And if you imagine to hang on you will be dragged along the pavement and your knees smashed!' What are you to do? As you stare at him in perplexity he adds 'Only a suggestion, of course, but can you not carry what you need in a body belt? Then you are not quite such an obvious target.' Oh but you hate a body belt! It is so awkward and clumsy – so sweaty – unfeminine. How could he be so insensitive! You slump in your chair.

Somehow, finally your camera gets locked away in the *pensione* safe, someone whom in your fluster you forget to thank holds the lobby door open for you, and you pass out into the street, your shoulder-bag clamped to your stomach and your ears attuned to the put-put of the *scippatori*. Everyone rides a motorped, it seems, even a priest with flat black hat and swinging crucifix. In the streets is a babble of tongues. And you are part of it all! How you wish someone could take your photo to send them as proof! You keep away from the Metro, of course, because of the gypsies – those women, they warned you, their eyes lighting up at your consternation, those great dark women on the Metro stairways who will crowd you into a corner, thrust a plate of *cassata* into your face, and rob your pockets! Murmuring those phrases in capitals in the Berlitz guide: STOP! AIUTO! POLIZIA! and stepping carefully because of all the dog dirt, and the rank streams fanning out from the corners of buildings, you turn in the general direction of the Trevi Fountain.

In a small square you come unexpectedly upon the Fountain of Tortoises, four graceful naked youths each supporting a tortoise that is scrambling to drink at the upper basin. As you watch, one of them flips his tortoise right into the pool and, hopping down from his shell-shaped perch, says Come Signora, together you and I will see Rome. Upon which the second jumps down: Come with me, Signora ... then the third, and the fourth. What are you to do? Which one to choose? You twist and twist the gold bon-bon ring, trying to decide, and when they catch sight of it as it glints in the sun, each murmurs *Mi dispiace, Signora*, and leaps back onto the fountain. The water flows, the tortoises clamber, you walk on alone.

As for the Trevi – you feel a shock of disappointment. It is so grandiose, the water so sluggish and green, the marble youths twisting the necks of the seahorses so cruel. In the great pool at the foot of the fountain real youths, loud and suntanned, paddle and kick and grimace at cameras. Coins glitter. You shoo away a pigeon and sit down, feeling rather silly at having to push through all the families and couples just to toss away a good coin. In a dry grotto to one side of the fountain a man lies asleep, the full strength of the late summer sun beating down on his face. You sit for a long time, wondering what *they* would have you wish, and still he sleeps on.

At last deliberately not wishing, your heart beating because you have in a sense defied THEM, you turn back towards the centre of the city. There, somewhere, the Beautiful People are beginning to stir. You wonder about that red-faced sleeper – should you have wakened him? Although it is early September, autumn already, Rome surprises you with its heat. Soon, striding along the Via del Corso, the Via Quattro Novembre, the Via Nazionale, you feel as embarrassed as a schoolgirl as great dark patches spread under the arms of your dress. You would like to throw it away. Buy yourself something new! they groaned. Get a new image! they shrieked. But when you venture into one of the dozens of little shops with the dazzling window displays, all your carefully rehearsed Berlitz phrases desert you; at the assistant's courteous *'Posso aiutarla?'* you do not look up, you go on fingering the garments, you actually pretend to be deaf. The ease of this out-of-character dissembling so shocks you that you hurry away in search of some quiet place to collect yourself. You walk swiftly past several fountains, along a steep street and into the very bowels of a large dark church. And it is not a church at all, you discover, but a charnel house.

An old, old man in the brown robe of a religious order

welcomes you towards a gallery. Here, arresting as any fashion window, are grottoes of human bones, centuries of bones, skulls, ribs, pelvises, layers of arm bones, layers of leg bones, all painstakingly selected for length and shape and worked into exquisite designs. Electric light filters through a criss-crossing of fingers. An arrangement of pelvises clasped within a rectangle of arm bones suggests a motto that you puzzle to decipher. A hooded skeleton in brown, dusty garb grins at you over folded hands, inviting you to admire his artistry. From the wrinkled monk at the desk you buy a postcard picturing the soaring rose-patterned ceiling fashioned from vertebrae and thin, delicate ribs, and learn that you are in the *Cimitero dei Cappuccini*, the Capuchin Cemetery.

Outside, shivering a little although the sun is still powerful, you hurry into the first bar you come to and, thrusting thousands of *lire* at the cashier, order *un cappuccino*. 'Un cappuccino,' you repeat, and begin to laugh, remembering those old dusty men amongst the bones, *i cappuccini* – a woman laughing alone in a public place in a foreign country.

'Just a touch of the sun,' you say to the person standing next to you at the counter, a woman carrying an English-language guide book. The woman smiles. You like her face; she has good bones. She is about your age, a bit younger, five or ten years maybe. 'I've been out walking,' you explain. She too looks as though she has been walking; she is wearing blue-and-white running shoes with pink laces. 'There's more bite in the sun than you think,' and you continue, feeling terribly glad that you've met: two fellow travellers, sisters almost. 'For this time of year,' you add, noting with surprise that she doesn't bother with a protective ring on her finger. Unobtrusively you slip yours off and drop it into your half-empty cup.

'That's true,' says the woman.

She finishes her coffee. Hastily you say, 'I've been walking since daybreak and still there's so much to see!'

'There certainly is,' she agrees, pushing her cup across the counter.

'What have you seen today?' you demand before she can move away.

'Well!' She widens her eyes, remembering. 'I started with the Forum – '

'And the churches!, you take up. 'Have you seen the gold ceiling of Santa Maria Maggiore? No? Well, the Trevi Fountain, then? *Everyone* goes there! What about the Capuchin Cemetery – you haven't seen the Capuchin Cemetery? Why, you haven't seen anything!'

Into the little silence that follows this, you pour a wonderful idea that has been frothing up in your mind since you got rid of that ring. 'Listen, I know just the place to go at this time of day. The Via Veneto. You know about the Via Veneto? It's where people go with their friends to drink and eat dinner and then sit over coffee to watch the Beautiful People go by, the Aga Khan's grandson, Gucci, Sophia Loren, all that crowd. It's not expensive,' you add, glancing at her running shoes. 'All the tourists go there – all my friends – if you don't see the Via Veneto you haven't seen Rome!'

'Well!' she says again. 'It does sound rather fun, doesn't it? Where is it?'

'Oh it's quite nearby.' But when you spread out your map, and she spreads out hers, you can find the Via Veneto neither listed in the index nor on the map itself. 'Scusi, Signor,' you read carefully from your phrase book to the Italian standing on the other side of you. 'Dove Via Veneeto? Si Signor, Via Veneeto! . . . Never mind,' you say to your new friend. 'I'm sure it's this way.' In the Via Quattro Fontane you accost a young man, 'La Via Veneeto, please, per piacere?' but he shrugs and walks on. At the Piazza della Repubblica – where you are only a few minutes' walk from the Metro and your *pensione*, you realise – your friend says 'Well, these Beautiful People seem pretty elusive, don't they, and I'm just about whacked.'

'Of course, because you need to eat!' you encourage her. 'I know the very place, just a few steps from here. And Roberto will know all about it. And then we can go there together, you and I, for coffee.'

But the woman shakes her head. 'Some other time, maybe. But *you* go, the Via Veneto sounds fun.'

'Well of course it's fun!' you snap. 'But I can hardly go alone, can I?'

'Why not?' says the woman. *Why not?* How stupid this woman has become! You part then, and when you have had a second shower at the *pensione* (in the other one this time) and changed your dress and taken a headache powder, you turn right and right again and find Giovanni's *locanda*. It is, as you anticipate, a very ordinary place, clean, but with nothing notable about its lighting or ceiling or anything, an anonymous place. A waiter whom you assume is Roberto motions you to a table on the pavement with a grace that reminds you of the youths with the tortoises – except that he wears clothes, of course, and has a petulant mouth. He is so slow in bringing the menu that you decide to keep quiet about Giovanni's commendation. His manner becomes positively disdainful when you order the only familiar dish on the menu, *spaghetti bolognese*, instead of being adventurous and starting off with *soppressata* as he suggests. When he is not taking orders he is hanging around a table where a young woman is sitting alone. She has an American accent, and you overhear Roberto saying, 'I lika to practise, the Eenglish, when, the occasion, presents.' The *locanda* becomes busy, the young woman is joined by a young man, and Roberto moves away. At the table on the other side of you sit two girls, sixteen or eighteen perhaps, who do not eat but drink cup after cup of *caffè espresso*. The young woman talks earnestly in Italian to the young man, telling him her life story, you decide, telling him about the husband who isn't with her, the boss who won't promote her, her wedding ring flashing as the words pour. She has all his attention. An enormous motor bike roars past, turns, and stops opposite the table with the two girls. Roberto appears at the doorway and stands transfixed. At last he looks down at you, his eyes warm now, responsive, and murmurs, 'Is magnificent bike, is Ducati, can do more than two hundred and twenty!' The cyclist, leaning back with his feet propped on the ground, calls out. The girls exchange glances, then the one with her back to the street lights a cigarette, inhales and blows a smoke ring over her head. The cyclist waits. The young man on the other side of you is now holding the American woman's hand. The second of the two girls beckons Roberto and orders more coffee. Still the cyclist waits. And then the girl with her back to him jumps up, runs across to him, speaks, he guns the engine and is gone. The noise of it, even as it grows fainter, pierces the ordinary traffic. The two girls stare at each other.

At the first table the woman has retreated, the man is leaning towards her, she is shaking her head. And then you hear the familiar throb of that motor bike. The girls jump up as it circles, both of them climb onto the pillion seat and away they blast. The American woman has dropped her head, her body quiescent now, it is he who is talking, talking, still she shakes her head but now both hands are holding hers, his fingertips move along her arms.

The *locanda* has become crowded. A waiting couple fidgets near your table. Roberto makes it clear with an impatient swish of his serviette that he would like you to pay and go. Surely this day can not end so inconclusively? You make one last frantic effort. 'Scusi, Signora? Perhaps if the Signora writes –' and he hands you a pencil stub. 'Ah! Si, Via *Ven*eto, Signora! Via Vittorio *Ven*eto. You have the map, Signora?' And with a lofty smile he points to it at once, so obvious now, Via Vittorio Veneto (only your eye stopped at *Ve* in the index), Via Vittorio Veneto, the street of the Beautiful People, no more than a few minutes from where you actually were earlier, at the Capuchin Cemetery.

'Molto grazie! Una tazza di caffè, per piacere,' you say, deliberately using Italian so he can't practise his English. To drown your terrible disappointment you take out your souvenir postcard and using Roberto's pencil stub you write, very small so as to fit it all in: 'Hello back there! How's this! I'm at this very moment sitting amongst the Beautiful People at THE place to be. Name? *I Cappuccini*. You should see my shocking pink laces. My friend Roberto speaks English, German, Italian, he's so easy to talk to, he must have got my whole life story just over the *soppressata*. His hobby's Ducatis and he looks like –' You make a wild guess. ' – looks like Gucci.' As Roberto hovers, anxious for that table, you continue, 'He's *so* persuasive. So I'll have to stop now – Ciao!'

The New York Bell Captain

FRANK MOORHOUSE

Deposition One

In New York City, at the old Times Square Hotel, I place my six bottles of Heineken beer along the window sill to chill in snow, to save the 50-cent ice charge, to avoid filling the handbasin with ice and beer, and to spare myself the sight of the bell captain's outstretched palm. I then leave my room to push my way along the Manhattan streets through the muggers, but change my mind at the hotel door and the snow and return, instead, to drink my Heineken. Reaching the room I find the beer gone from the sill. Instantly, without a flicker of hesitation, I know that the bell captain has swiftly checked my room to find out if I am using the window sill to chill my beer instead of paying him 50 cents plus tip to bring up a plastic bag full of melting ice. Quick work on his part. I open out the window to look for clues and as I do the six bottles of Heineken are swept off the sill down fifteen stories into Fifty-Fourth Street – and the bad end of Fifty-Fourth. I am too apathetic to bother looking down. Already New York is dehumanising me. And I've lost my beer. At first I think it is all my mistake – that when I first looked for the beer I looked at the wrong window. That I then opened the right window in the wrong way and pushed them off. (May be a lot of the so-called muggings in New York are really head injuries from falling bottles from hotel window sills because hungry-handed bell captains charge too much for ice.) But as I sit

144

there bereft and brooding I arrive at a more convincing conclusion about the beer, the sill, the window. What the bell captain has done is to come into my room, find the bottles, steal one or two or even three and then switch them to where I will sweep the remaining bottles off. This way I will never know if he has been into my room to steal my beer. I will therefore be unable to bring substantiated allegations against him. All right. This round to the bell captain.

Deposition Two

I have proved that the bell captain provides ice which is at melting point. I suspected this from the start. The first time I ordered ice I paid him 50 cents, tipped him, checked my wallet, latched and locked the door and propped a chair against it, when I turned around all I had was a plastic bag of ice-water. So I did this. I bought a bag of ice from the drugstore next door to the hotel and sat there in my room and timed its melting against another bag of the bell captain's ice. The results were inconclusive but down in the bell captain's den, I am convinced that they leave the ice out of the freezer to bring it just to melting point and they give this ice to non-tippers or a person who doesn't tip 'enough' for bell captains. I have a frustrated urge to hand them my wallet, to put my wallet in the hand of the bell captain and ask him to take what he thinks is 'fair'. I was told of a man who had no hands and who kept his money in that unused outside breast pocket of his suit (which schoolboys, railway clerks, electricity-meter readers, and eccentrics use sensibly for pens and pencils) so that taxi drivers and so on could help themselves to the money. Poor bastard. Perhaps I should pull my hands into my sleeves and let New York help itself.

Deposition Three

Anyhow, what can they do to you if you don't tip? What they do in New York is they turn off the heat to your room. Can they do that? Is that mechanically possible – can they isolate one room out of six hundred and turn off its heat? Well they did it to my room. They must have a control panel down in the bell captain's den.

Deposition Four

Every afternoon I have a conversation through the keyhole with the maid who wants me to leave the room so that she can 'change the linen'. When am I going out, she inquires. For 'change the linen' read: Allow the bell captain to come in and prowl about my room and steal my Heineken beer. We come to an arrangement. I take my Heineken in my brief case and sit in the lobby while she 'changes the linen'.

Deposition Five

Oh, they know that Francois Blase is just a *nom de voyage*. I know I have not fooled them. The word has gone around too that we are exchange-rate millionaires. Bell captains study the exchange rate. In a ploy to extract larger tips the bell captain has told the doorman to stop opening the door for me, despite a tip of 75 cents the previous evening for bringing up half a dozen Heineken and a packet of crackerjack. When I didn't order ice they knew I was using the window sill.

When I suspect the doorman is not opening the door for me as a reprimand for using the window sill and not buying melted ice from them, I sit in the lobby and count the comings and goings and the times the doorman opens the door. To confirm my suspicions. He opens the door every time. I then rise from my chair in the lobby and go to the door, even saying something genial about the Miami Dolphins and the League to show my immersion in the life of the United States and to show that I bear no ideological or other objections and so on. The bell captain pretends not to hear and the doorman pretends to answer the telephone. I have to open the door myself. The first of twelve comings and goings that the doorman had not opened the door. I 'turn on my heel' and return to my room, deeply miffed.

Deposition Six

I eat, imprudently, in the lobby restaurant as I do not feel like
going out that much – things to do in my room and so on.
Obviously the waiter ignores me on the whisper from the bell
captain, despite my dollar tip to him for sending a cable home
for more money so that I could continue to tip the hotel staff. I
eventually have to lean from my chair and grab the waiter's
sleeve and jacket with both my hands pulling him to an
unsteady halt and me nearly out of my chair. With many
smiles, bowing and scrapings, I say that I am going to the
theatre and am therefore in a rush. He says what, at 5.45? But
anyhow I get some service. Except that what I ask for is off, he
says, although I think I see others being served it, and I think
he brings me something other than what I ordered, but it takes
so long I can't really remember what I ordered. At least I get
my Heineken. Of course, I am being penalised for some
breach of the hotel customs. I leave a 27 per cent tip as a gesture of my willingness to 'get along'.

Deposition Seven

I eat in the lobby restaurant again, not feeling like going out
because I see a blizzard hiding behind the clouds waiting to
lash out at me. This time the restaurant pulls a switch in
behaviour to throw me into anguish and confusion. On a
signal from the bell captain which I did not see, the waiter
serves me, this time, *too quickly*. A masquerade – uncivilised
haste masquerading as promptness. They want to get me out of
the restaurant, get me to rush my food. They don't like me
because I dawdle over my food with a book. Hah! They don't
like people who read books at dinner. They think, maybe, I am
'parading' my bookishness. So, it's the book-reading that
sticks in their gut.

Despite the rushed service, I tip heavily again. I do this for
three reasons: to preserve the good name of dinner-table
book-readers; to show that I am above pettiness; and to make
them think that maybe we are the world's fastest eaters as well
as being best at everything else. In short to repay confusion

with confusion.

I stand in the lobby picking my teeth, here it is only 6.15 and I've eaten a three-course dinner. I toy with the idea of going out and sparring with the people of New York, turning the table on a few muggers, but decide to go back to my room and have a quiet Heinie and watch colour TV. The bell captain and doorman smile, tip their caps, bow and so on – all unfelt gestures, a debasement of the body-language of service. I know they don't care. The doorman even goes through the motions of opening the lift door, which is automatic. I tip him without looking to see if he smiles or says thank you, and without consulting my Chamber of Commerce Guide to tipping in automatic lifts.

Deposition Eight

A stranger in the lobby asks me for change for the 'valet' slot machine. I at first pretend not to hear, a New York reflex, knowing that as soon as I reach for my money I will betray the amount that I carry, as soon as I speak he will know where I come from and am therefore rich and generous and foolish, and that Francois Blase is a cover, and that whatever I do will reveal me as naive and paranoiac. There is something else, I fear, which I call New York Sleight of Hand, which will make whatever I have disappear. He persists in what appears to be a civilised, middle-class way, so I give him a handful of change. He offers me a note. I wave it away. He thanks me wondrously and goes to the valet machine, looking back at me and back to his handful of money. At first I feel pleased with myself – it is this sort of gesture that gets us a good name. But when I glance over to the bell captain he appears to be scowling and refuses to meet my eyes. I enter the lift, troubled. In the lift it dawns on me. It is his job to give change and, anyhow, the valet machine is an automation of hotel employment and is probably declared black by the hotel staff. How stupid of me. I have robbed the bell captain of a quarter tip; diminished his role; and threatened his employment. I feel chilly. For these things I will have to pay.

Deposition Nine

When I get to my room the heat is off. Apart from the obvious offences like giving change in the lobby, using the window sill to chill beer, I must have done other offensive things. I rove over my dealings with the hotel staff and my mind recalls to me the automatic lift. One lift is automatic and the other is run by a one-armed black. I have preference for the automatic lift and this must count against me. Maybe I should use the one-armed black lift driver to keep him in employment, as an endorsement of the human element in mechanised society, and as a gesture against discrimination. Maybe I should tip the black lift driver too, although my information from the Chamber of Commerce is that lift drivers are not tipped. Next time, I go by the one-armed black's lift and I see that he is selling the Sunday *New York Times* and I buy a copy from him, although I worry about the newspaper seller in the lobby who is blind and what he will think. The one-armed lift driver charges me 75 cents for the 50-cent paper. With some sort of neurotic reversed response (like those who smile involuntarily when informed of tragedy), I apologise and thank the one-armed black lift driver. What about the blind paper seller?

Deposition Ten

I am, I tell myself, too passive before the minor oppressions. I am always virtuously assertive about the major oppressions of our times. Apartheid, you name it. But I remain timid before the accumulated indignities which sour the quality of life. I adopt a pretentious inner attitude of 'Pooh, I have not the mental time to worry about the miscellaneous petty injustices of the day-to-day world. My life is dedicated to a larger mission'. So I let waiters off.

I resolve to change this. I go down and confront the manager when my heat is off on the third afternoon. I begin by saying that I know all about Traveller Paranoia and that I have tested myself. I am not suffering from Traveller Paranoia. I want, I tell him, no accusations of that sort.

The depositions of my journal, which I produce as Exhibit A, and the whole heat business, clearly make a case against the bell captain and I call for his dismissal.

I refer the manager to the case of *Jackson* v. *Horizon Holidays Ltd.* A person who books a holiday at a hotel which falls short of the brochure description can claim damages for vexation and disappointment.

People throughout the world, I thunder, have for too long taken advantage of our open, relaxed, simplified, small-country responses to life. For too long now we have been known as 'easy going'. Because we inhabit a rich, technologically advanced, uncrowded, clean country we are resented and penalised.

I close my case.

'About the economics and geography of your country I know nothing, Mr Blase, but as for the heat – this is a fuel saving measure introduced because of the world fuel situation. Between 11 and 3, we turn off the heat. It is the warmest part of the day. Also, most people are usually out of their rooms at around these times.'

I stare at him.

I marvel at the ingenuity of his defence.

All right, I say, this time I'll accept what you say and, 'turning on my heel', I go back to my room.

I need time to pick apart this carefully prepared explanation.

Summing Up

Later, brooding in my cold room, the point of his last remark comes to me, 'most people are usually out of their rooms at around these times'.

What business is it of anyone that I have not left the hotel precincts for five days or so? Do I go out and be mugged on the streets of Manhattan so that the bell captain can have a free hand with the thieving of my Heineken? So they can pick over my luggage. I rent the room. I don't have to go out to see landmarks every day of my life. Anyhow, everything that happens

on a journey is 'experience'. It doesn't have to be all
landmarks and monuments. Maybe, for all they know, I am
exploring the inner spaces of my mind, the subterranean caves
of my personality, gazing with new understanding at the ruins
and monuments of my own archaeology. The seven wonders of
the heart. What would the staff of the old Times Square Hotel
know about that? Nothing. Nothing at all.

Rosalie's Folly

KATE GRENVILLE

The voice slides into her sleep like smoke into the last room of the house until she wakes up. My darling, he mumbles, my sweetheart. She lies feeling his warmth beside her and listening to his sleeping voice. She can almost see his face in the dark but not quite and slides her hand gently over until it's resting on his head against the thinning curls. He worries lately about losing his hair but she always tells him she loves him anyway. Flinging out a warm arm that strikes her shoulder he grunts, almost awake. He breathes deeply and evenly, falling back with a sigh into his dream. Anna, he murmurs, Anna, yes yes oh yes.

At 7.30 the alarm rings as it does every morning of the year except Saturdays Sundays and four weeks' annual leave. She gets out of bed and shivers as she does every morning of the year including Saturdays Sundays and four weeks' annual leave, and shakes Martin awake. He's a heavy sleeper. Seven thirty-three the kitchen. The kettle's on the stove and tea's in the teapot the toast's in the toaster all's right with the world. In the bathroom Martin shaves, always from left to right leaving the upper lip till last. The kettle boils toast leaps out of toaster the whole kitchen's jumping. Martin comes out of the bathroom with every trace of last night's stubble erased.

– Hi how are you this morning, he says rubbing a hand over his chin as if to check that every last hair is removed.

– Fine, she says, and you? Any good dreams?

He shakes his head and feels his lips as if they're swollen.

She puts the daily eggs in the water and watches the sand of the timer falling, first visibly then too fast to watch, into the bottom of the glass. She has a moment of panic as the last grains are sucked through the neck. Stop stop she wants to say, not yet!

– I think I had a dream . . . she says balancing the eggs in the egg-cups.

He taps the top of his egg too hard and the shell splinters down the side.

– Hmmm? Got the salt there?

He takes the salt and makes a neat pile on the side of the plate. She watches as he eats his egg, making sure the ratio of egg to toast is just right. She pours the milk into the cups before the tea, the way he likes it, and asks:

– Anything exciting going on at work?

She has to concentrate very hard on pouring the tea because of the way the lid of the teapot falls off.

– Exciting? Just the usual.

He spreads jam on his toast, going all the way to the crusts. He crunches loudly and stares at the tablecloth.

Her egg tastes sickly this morning and she pushes the plate away and drinks some tea. It's too hot and she scalds her lip. As she puts the mug down suddenly he looks up at her before going back to his breakfast. She watches him carefully redistributing a stray dab of butter. His voice seems very loud when he speaks through a mouthful of crumbs.

– This bread's not very good. Too brittle. Crumby.

She smiles at his face but it's turned away as he reaches for more jam.

– Okay, she says, I'll get rye next time.

She squeezes his hand which doesn't squeeze back.

– Hey, give us a smile . . .?

He glances at her and smiles briefly.

– Time to go, got to go.

He stands up and leans down to kiss her in the same movement.

– Have a good day. You feeling okay are you?

She stares at the debris of breakfast.

– Sure, I'm fine.

He shrugs into his coat and wraps the long scarf around his neck.

– Okay, he says. See you at 6 then.

She walks through the park on her way to the Tube, recognising the regulars who are there every morning at the same time. There's the old woman rocking from one bowed leg to the other with a snuffling clot of hair on its leash beside her. One day it'll snuffle itself into extinction and she'll stand broken-hearted beside the small stone that says FIDO MY ONLY FRIEND. There's the man with a face like an iron mask with his Alsatian sniffing the breeze for something to tear apart. And there's the corduroy couple with the bounding English Sheep Dog that will wonder, in a year's time (when they decide he's earning enough for them to have the baby now) why they don't love him any more. She can set her watch by the brisk old man who walks three times around the perimeter of the park, scrupulously resisting the temptation to cut off the corners. By the left, wheel.

However, these days in spite of himself he does have to cheat on one corner. It's only taken a week of garbage strike for one corner of the park to become a huge pile of rubbish. The heap thrives on the rich leavings of all those people who agree it's a scandal the government should do something. Terrible isn't it just terrible, says Mrs Laundromat, stretching the cardigan further over her huge behind. They didn't oughter allow it, says the greengrocer with one finger under the scales as he weighs her lunchtime apple. Is werry bad werry bad, says Mrs Ramachandran in the corner shop where the mice dart in and out between the boxes. The pile grows furtively. At night she's seen surreptitious figures cross the grass and as if by accident let their bag of rubbish drop. Who me? She and Martin have said nothing to each other, but any day now it'll be their turn to add to the shameful pile. How will she look the greengrocer in the eye then as they tut-tut a pound of carrots please yes they shouldn't allow it? Not in *our* street. Not in *my* life.

She's always hated the Tube and that silent crowd streaming through the tunnels towards another day. She queues behind the same dandruff-scattered shoulders as every other morning and gets into the same carriage. As usual all the seats are taken. She thinks of Martin, at work by now, unwinding the scarf and hanging it on the hatrack. Smiling hello to everyone, to all those welcoming morning faces in his office.

She glances around at the commuters and for a moment sees them with the clarity of nightmares. These faces, jammed close together, staring off aloofly as if over vast empty plains. These bodies swaying and bumping together and cringing from every touch. That woman there, with a face brutally blotched with a thousand dark freckles like a plague out of which she stares. This frozen pinstripe type reading his *Financial Times* with only the morsel of toilet paper stuck to a fresh shaving cut to show that blood flows in his veins. This whole silent rigid crowd, worrying about the pennies, the pension and job security. Being in love and wondering about those long blond hairs.

At Euston she changes trains and buys a paper as she does every morning from the old man who says the same thing every morning to her and to numberless nameless others, Cheers thanks love, as he takes the money and fumbles through his greasy pouch for change. He glances at her and says, Cheer up love it might never happen. She smiles weakly and takes the paper. MI5 DOUBLE AGENT TRAITOR says the headline. She crams her way through the crowds in the tunnel towards the other platform, driven by some urge to hurry hurry hurry. Arriving at the platform she finds herself panting but the compelling urgency doesn't lessen.

The faces in the carriage seem small and made of some waxy substance. All around her the headlines shout BETRAYAL I TRUSTED HIM COMPLETELY SAYS SPY BOSS. That bony yellow hand, it seems to be attached to my arm but none of it belongs to me. That sombre face outside the window why is it staring at me? IF THESE ALLEGATIONS ARE TRUE I AM ASTONISHED. No my dear, *you* are surprised, *I* am astonished.

In the tunnel the train slows and stops. The air is dense and suffocating like a weight on the head and the carriage bursts with silence while the waxwork commuters hold their breath. Beneath her, a man with a thin moustache is firmly unaware that the train has stopped, that the bomb has dropped, that we'll stay down here forever having to decide who'll eat whom because the rescue party will never come. He bites his lip and thinks hard about the crossword puzzle. Kind of mammal in five letters, last letter n. At the other end of the carriage someone says in a piercing whisper, Getting stuffy isn't it, and he coughs and makes a wild stab at the word. All around her, people read their newspapers as if Truth were engraved on them in letters of fire. Unfortunates without newspapers wind their watches or work out 764 multiplied by 375 in their heads.

The train jolts into motion and the commuters shuffle and cough. IF YOU CAN'T TRUST YOUR CLOSEST ASSOCIATE WHO CAN YOU TRUST? The train thunders into the station and the commuters thrust each other aside to get out as quickly as possible.

In her office the puny plants droop towards the window trying to remember what sunlight looks like. The fluorescent lights shrill their subliminal needle-hum through the air and the typewriter sits up at attention waiting to turn words into black-and-white certainties. The world is very simple and quite trustworthy when you take it one letter at a time. Just don't look around.

Mr Lynch comes out of the inner office and waves a pile of papers at her.

– Good morning how are you this morning, he says.

Oh I died in the night thanks and you?

– These are very urgent I'd like you to get straight onto them if you don't mind.

She takes the papers and sits down and starts to type as fast as she can. Her mind empties and she follows only the tap tap tap comma space tap tap tap. She works so fast that by lunchtime all the letters are lined up in their uniform shrouds and the IN tray is empty. Every pencil is in its jar and the stapler is lined up next to the liquid paper. An orgasm of elimination she thinks and has a sudden urge to speak to Martin. She calls his office. He went out an hour ago, the switchgirl drones. Didn't say where but he'll be out for the rest of the day can I tell him who called. She shakes her head although she knows the girl can't see her. Shakes her head and puts the receiver carefully back on its cradle.

Mr Lynch comes out in the nick of time with more letters

and she types them with great speed.

Deqr Mr Mortimer
Dear Mr Moetimer
Deat Mr Nortimer
Dear me mortimer

Come on you're going too fast just slow down and don't panic.

Dear Mr Mortimer

She feels relieved with every clickety clack space clickety clack carriage return but when she takes the letter out she sees she's put the carbon in the wrong way round and the back of the letter is a code of mirror writing. She stares around the office wondering what's going on. The Office Monotony Pad stares back at her and she has to look closely before it becomes again the Office Economy Pad. The directions for the telex machine appear to be Clown Copyright. I know that can't be right that just isn't right where has he gone?

She blinks hard to clear her vision and grips a pencil tightly and tells herself to breathe deeply it will all be perfectly simple in a minute. The pencil snaps and a piece lands at her feet. She stares at her foot next to the piece of pencil. It's just my foot. In its shoe. With a piece of this pencil I've just snapped. Nothing to worry about. And this, yes, this is my hand lying here on the desk, it's mine, I am all right and everything absolutely everything is 100 per cent okay.

She dials home and sits gripping the receiver hard, listening to the ringing tone and reading about all the emergencies there's a phone for. Police Fire Ambulance. What about the other kinds? She hangs up and dials again a few minutes later maybe I dialled the wrong number. It still rings emptily. She puts the receiver down slowly, listening to the ringing sound until it's cut off. She's run out of letters to type but in a frenzy of activity she rolls paper into the typewriter and starts pounding away like someone whistling in the dark. qwertyuiop the quick brown fox jumps over the lazy turd.

She stops, overwhelmed by this little machine that makes words sit up and beg one at a time. She looks at the plants yearning with their last feeble strength towards the light and at the terrible tidiness of her desk.

Dear My Lunch,
As I am not feeling very well I have gone home for the rest of the day

She looks at this and giggles until she runs out of air and breathes in, feeling her ribs jump and her stomach contract. She gets up clumsily and knocks over the jar of pencils but she doesn't look back she has to get out. The telex machine barks at her as she passes. She hits her hip against the door as she goes out and it tries to slam back and hit her. Pulling her coat on, she pushes past blindly but one sleeve has disappeared. Where is it where is it where is he?

The quiet streets spring at her. GROUP URGES PUBIC PROBE a headline sniggers. The Venereal Heating Centre tries to take her by surprise. A bus roars past advertising Hell Tours and a man with a limp goes into an On-The-Spot Hell Bar. The drinkers outside the Punch of Grapes stare at her as she passes Fiend's House. Then there's the Cobra Hotel where the desk clerk sits under a neon sign that says DECEPTION.

She breaks into a run but her coat wraps itself around her legs and flaps in front trying to stop her. An old man stands in the middle of the pavement in front of her with his arms wide apart as if turning back a cow. Easy easy he smiles as she pushes past. A bus grinds along close to her ear with an ugly roar like the world crushing itself to bits.

At the mouth of the Tube she hesitates and wonders if she should go back to work after all. She keeps her eyes on the ground as she goes through the tunnels and down the steps and waits on the platform. When the train pulls in she thinks of throwing herself underneath. Sweat breaks out on her palms as the moment passes.

Although it's an earlier train than the one she usually takes it's still crowded. She clenches her fists in her pockets and fights the urge to grab the grey suit next to her and shake the padded shoulder until something snaps. Inside she feels a great wail building up and thinks how easy it would be to open a hole in her face and let it out. Aaaaaaaaaaaaaaaah. She licks her lips and stares woodenly at nothing but after a few minutes finds she's been forgetting to breathe. She takes a deep breath that turns into a yawn, huge, uncontrollable, her mouth opening wider and wider and the breath jerking into her chest in gasps. The grey suit glances at her with panic in his eyes and she knows he thinks that she's going to cry. She covers the yawn with her hand and stares him down.

The park near home looks strange and she tells herself it's because she's never seen the garbage heap at this time of day before. It gleams triumphantly in the shafts of sun, a lavish harlequin lily among the demure trees and grass. A puny fence at one side has been flattened by its sprawling weight and the bus-shelter is engaged in intricate embrace with a tangle of wallpaper. The pile is already bigger than it was this morning, engorged with more furtive bags. Even as she watches a man comes over to it and shamelessly throws his garbage onto the heap. One bag bursts in the ecstasy of its flight and rubbish sprays out like confetti.

On the edges of the heap the vultures are already starting to scavenge, the parasites on this vast bloated whore lounging at ease in the park. People swarm all over it or stand chatting, holding picture frames and cracked plates. An old man picks out bottles and lays them together with palsied laborious care. Mrs Laundromat stands legs astride holding a stool by one leg like a doll. Funny what people throw out she agrees with the greengrocer who shows her his booty. You know how much these pliers cost in a shop? Good brand this.

She walks up the front steps reluctantly, but there seems nowhere else to go. Sitting curled up in the big armchair she watches the hands of the clock move around to 6 o'clock. She doesn't know what she's going to say and can't decide whether she'd rather be crazy or sane.

The clock strikes the hour and there's his key scratching at the lock. She hears him come in and stand inside the front door listening to the silent house. She holds her breath. He takes an uncertain step forward as if into darkness and stops again. The dense silence hums in her ears.

– Ah . . . Rosalie? You home?
– I'm here.
She hears him move towards the living room.

– It's OK I know all about Anna.

He stops and there's another long silence before he appears at the door and stares at her. Slowly, his eyes never leaving her face, he unwinds his scarf and sits opposite her, folding and refolding it. He waits. Oh my god oh my god so this is how it happens she thinks. There's no way out nothing to be done no escape too late now. She watches his hands smoothing the scarf on his knee as he waits for her to speak.

'Who Was That Masked Man?'

TONY MANIATY

I am in the city of Zorro, of the Castilian Queen, of the Princess of the Enchanted Night, of Zapata and the Hawaiian Beauty, of the Anonymous Cosmonaut, of Chaplin, of the Red and White Mushroom Ladies and the Bandaged Man. I have arrived in the old man's country, a kind of ancestral home. It's late on a February evening and there's a lively parade in the distance. . .

Lying on a lumpy mattress, Harry observed the lone mosquito. It was already flying away. He tossed and couldn't sleep properly. The flowers of spring and the first bugs had arrived too soon, and Easter was coming on. He sat up, annoyed. The hard pillow was turning into a rock, or more than one – shifting every minute under his aching head. He was unable to catch up, to catch Athens. When he managed to sleep the City awoke and whenever he came to life the City was closing its metal shutters and turning off those bare electric lights. Back in his father's city. Another mosquito bounced off his flaying hand. 'Get lost,' he shouted in a whisper. It was as though he'd entered not the bustling Greek capital but a ghost town; or was hanging on as a foreign ghost among the living dead. He lay awake, and listened. Odd sounds came off the plumbing, the heating pipes against the wall belched with the uneasiness of worn intestines; of a stomach full of airline food, he remembered. And then from the street came the comforting smell of yeast, of fresh loaves building up and slowly

161

assaulting his nostrils. From all over Athens it entered his room. And wide awake now, Harry the Australian son imagined a city full of expanding ghosts in dusted white aprons who worked throughout the night and slept all day. He pounded the pillow hard, in despair.

On his first afternoon, Harry Tekaros could hear people eating behind those faded blue and red shutters; and then sleeping or probably making love in some Greek way or other. He surveyed the empty backstreets on foot, disturbing the mandatory silence with more silence. Every now and then he stopped to read a taverna menu. It was odd, not easy reading *moussaka* in English and *icecream* in Greek. At one point, a dozen stray cats rushed out to meet him. Harry went in. He ate little and eventually drank too much wine; and found himself in earshot of two sniping English tourists.

'Look, they're speaking French,' the woman exclaimed. 'I'd forgotten about the French. They don't look French. They're very dark.'

'Oh, the girl does,' replied Jack knowingly. 'She's got a sour look.'

'I thought the French had more of a whitish look. . .'

'They come from Marseilles, they're dark around there.' Jack stalled, and got up. 'I must have a pee, otherwise there'll be a nasty scene.'

'Oh, ok.'

Further away, a large Australian girl with dark glasses was laying into her Greek escort. He was clearly baffled.

'I came alive,' proclaimed Glenda. 'I just came alive. I mean, bloody hell. . . The first year I worked my arse off, right?'

And so Harry stumbled onwards. Clouds were forming around the Acropolis in the early night, and coloured balloons were sweeping in all directions. He slowed down. Had he really been away from the hotel for three hours? Or even longer, surely not. Again he moved on, up the hill. But no sooner had this mild confusion passed, than a new one took its place. Harry steadied himself, incredulous at the unfolding scenes around him and below. In the Plaka where he was standing – at its crumbling, ancient fringes – the inhabitants were belting each other with clubs, of soft plastic. Orange and green, and bright Aegean blue. At the corners, out of sidestreets the local Greeks were streaming; dressed in the hideous costumes of madmen and heros, and even saints. What the hell was going on? A ragged procession of cowboys, old movie stars among them, hack politicians, ageing European queens and zombies – all flaying each other and out to baffle the sleepless Harrys of the world. But then confusing themselves too, he noticed. The gay panic subsided; the beltings, the screams and shouts fell to whispers. They cleared a path for a nun, a young and very sensuous girl in habit. Nobody could tell if she was real or not; and she – coy, but smiling – wasn't about to confess. For this was Carnival time, with its mad costumes and masquerades.

Harry pressed into the self-heartening crowd, being assailed with pink and turquoise clubs – his inner spirits inflated at one corner, and crushed at the next. Athens was coming alive, the night full of pre-Easter celebrations. Its horny Devils were not only wide awake but attacking any obvious lack of enthusiasm, while pillow-pregnant Damsels cheered them on. Bang, slug-thump, bash! All around the Greeks were having it out. They were also belting Harry senseless, urging him to join in or give up. 'Ella, ella,' they called and laughed. I shouldn't have left the plane, he thought. Or even boarded it. . .

A boy dressed as the Lone Ranger was tugging at his sleeve. He was offering – what? – something like a black garter. Harry held it up and smiled clumsily. He stuffed the flimsy contraption into his pocket, but the boy insisted. Harry took it out again, and held it to the neon lights. And seeing its purpose, he pulled the spare black mask over his head and bleary eyes. At once he became a typical Athenian reveller and a total stranger too. But it offered him no rest. He was still being pushed along by people who had no intention of sleeping, or making sense; or showing any reason on this planet, he realised. Just a Carnival madness, to which he could offer nothing more – tonight, at least – than a cowboy mask and the mild belligerence of the outsider. And the traveller's crumpled brain. Oh god, he remembered the pillow back at the hotel; the sheer density of it. And he downed a few drinks more, if only to carry on.

His dreams were lost almost as quickly as they began. But in one Harry Tekaros was floating into a tidal jungle: the waves were constantly shifting and he bumped into trees with trunks the size of elephants. He was the Phantom in another, only to be woken by a barking dog; or as it turned out, by waves of delinquent strangers running and barking into the void. There would be no more dreams in the city of Make-believe, of course; in the Land of Immeasurable Darkness and the Dry Throat. And just as he'd desperately wanted sleep, and failed; now Harry wanted nothing more than the morning proper – for the first light to carry him out of the dreadful abyss and into a new day. He was even prepared to face the worst; for beneath the eternal jet lag there was a mighty hangover in the making, full of corrosion and not so simple.

He got off the bed slowly and opened the faded curtains, and worn shutters. It wasn't night, but already day. A flood of business and traffic noise came up to his ears and daylight poured into the room. Harry stepped out, at once amazed and dulled by it. He bent over the railing. The people in the street were dressed not as Sea Monsters or Nocturnal Idiots but in sober winter suits and coats, rugged up to the final button and scurrying to work. And not a streamer or balloon in sight. Under cloudy skies the people of Athens were going about their lives with purpose, efficiency and gusto.

Harry pulled back quickly, trying to conceal his stained blue shirt and yesterday's jeans. Like a layabout in his father's land. He retreated to the mirror – and there he was, still in the crazy black mask of the Lone Ranger. For a second too long he waited, filling his empty mind with the night's long journey. The stranger's face before him was utterly sleepless, and his eyes refused to part correctly. He could use only one at a time, or two halves; and in that second he wondered if being a real alcoholic was like this too. He decided not and slowly peeled off the mask, along with the rest of his clothes. In the shower he began to sing. 'I am in the City of Bad Dreams,' he shouted to no particular tune, 'of Cruel Demands, of the Fifteen Rounds with Sonny Liston, of Factor X – and of the Never-ending Curse.' He turned off the taps, and dried and dressed as though surfacing from a deep well. And in the Carnival city which had so far refused to accommodate him, in which Harry Tekaros could find no reference to normal time, and where he was lost the minute he left this room – in Athens of all places, he resolved to go out and buy a decent pillow.

Standing outside the hotel, he expected to wake even now from a dream. On the footpath directly opposite was a pillow shop. It had been there not only since his arrival – one, two days ago – but for a good century, judging by the signs. How could he have missed it? A couple of naked lights hung from the ceiling, radiating off the gold and crimson satin of a hundred cushions; and behind these sat the ordered piles of white and floral pillows. And as Harry took his chances with the noisy Athenian day, a man as round and padded as the goods he sold appeared at the doorway. In quite deliberate English, he said: 'You want to buy a pillow?'

There was no time to waste. He struggled past the hotel owner with a smile and up to his room, laying down the parcel of his dreams. To start again. He unknotted the yellow twine, tore off the brown paper and the plastic dust cover; and buried his face in that sea of printed flowers. Only then did it occur to him – that the happy proprietor of the Providence Hotel was probably the brother of the pillow-shop man. All this could have happened before, to others. He pressed his cheeks into the lightest foam and smiled. For three dollars of pure bliss, did it matter? To catch up at last, to sleep through the afternoon siesta while the Greeks – his fellow Athenians, he meant – ate and slept too; and to rise at sunset for a lively night of Carnival fun. Above all, to get ahead and whisper 'Sleep. . .' before the shutters came rolling down and the City closed for lunch.

Harry fell back, and waited. There were no mosquitos now, the weather was getting cold again. He waited for the sleep of a lifetime. Beyond the windows and walls – still – he could hear people arguing and laughing loudly in the street. He could smell the yeast of a newly-baked pillow, and last night's indulgence began to hammer in his head. And then his eyes didn't shut but began to flicker. They were opening, wider, and wider. They were taking in every detail of that ceiling, that convoluted ceiling. Every nuance of Greek light. Slowly he took up his mental pen and began to write.

I am in the city of Zorro. . .

The Waters of Vanuatu

CARMEL KELLY

And the waters drift so gently in the tide, carrying their load of seaweed, coral and exquisitely coloured fish. The hotel has set out a real feast tonight for the tourists. Tables groan under the burden of tropical fish and vegetables baked in fires and wrapped in coconut leaves. The tables are lit with coloured lights and the guests choose the fish they'll eat. We are warned not to eat the iridescent blue and vermilion fish which can give you a strange stomach virus. Tables of various national dishes call their wares, Japanese, Indonesian, Melanesian as the guests line up to taste and savour. There is something slightly obscene about this over-abundance.

We had chosen a hotel near the lagoon made from woven pandanus palms, where the staff came and went slowly, serving fruits. The women wore long green flowered frocks. They talked and laughed in various tongues. You could sit all morning on the breakfast terrace, alone, overlooking the lagoon and no one would come to serve. You had to go searching for a face hidden behind the doors and say, 'Look, I'm hungry. I need breakfast. Feed me.' And then they would think about it. A huge plate of fresh paw paw and melon would be brought to you. Maybe an omelette made with many eggs and a choice of different teas. And the people talked behind the woven pandanus serving bars, oblivious in some ways of the tourists who after all were just visiting. The mornings were

167

slow – lethargic. And there was no urgency. I was prepared to sit waiting forever for my plate of fresh fruit. Later, I would walk back to my hotel room, through the lemon and yellow hibiscus.

See that cat? See that black cat? She has kittens hidden in the roof. One by one she will bring them down and the staff will try to kill them if she does not hide them fast. This hotel breeds cats and they are as thin as skeletons. I feed the mother secretly at night. She calls to me from the woven pandanus roof of the hotel. I feed her with fish in tins from the French delicatessen in Port Vila.

We had come to the island in order to recover from the death of someone who had been close to us. Can you forget such nightmares stalking the stage by going to a place of incredible beauty? Or does it simply remind you even more? Humans must have hope in order to live, and I am one to exaggerate the exigencies of life. But many times, my own exaggerations have been put to shame by the outright horror I've been confronted with.

To talk about the ones you deeply love who have died is impossible and sacred. You cannot use print for it. You cannot use it to make a story. Some peoples will not speak of their dead. The grief and pain are too great. But nonetheless I'm telling you.

The beauty of our surroundings was like a promise, an excess of beauty we witnessed all around us. We were on the run didn't you know? Would we erase the brutality of what we had seen? Our powerlessness to control events? Could we find a mirror within the touch and taste of our own bodies, minds, the communication humans use to express love? A mystery. Something beyond our own experience would have to happen. The environment itself created this expectancy.

Every morning the foyer to our hotel was freshly decorated with tropical flowers. Every new guest experienced the same delight in coming to a hotel designed with such taste. A Japanese consortium now owned the hotel. The architect had designed it to resemble a Melanesian longhouse. Big wooden beams in the dining room. All the intricate palm weaving along the walls and ceiling had been done in New Guinea. And the furniture was cane – large generous chairs and lounges, overlooking the lagoon.

The golf course near our hotel – so quietly manicured. Every morning the fine spray of the sprinklers sent rainbows into the air near the pandanus palms. And the man who mowed the lawns putted quietly across the green. There was never anyone using the golf links. Perhaps they were for decoration.

We took food back to our hotel and kept it in the small refrigerator for those moments when hunger struck. We started to visit a new eating place each night where we could try out the French food. And in this silence which belongs to a couple, we lived like two strangers on a new planet, observing, watching the exotic life around us, trying to plumb what was largely unknown. As I walked down the street, men smiled at me unselfconsciously. It was a joy not to feel like a sex object, a sensation of freedom.

The French restaurants did good trade with the tourists. They had merged their cuisine with the coconuts, coconut crabs, and local fruits. The cheeses and soft French breads – tempting. Everywhere you heard the radios broadcasting in pidgin, French, English and various native dialects.

Many nations had stopped in this seaport, sailors from all over the world. The native women wore the ghastly Mother Hubbard dresses dictated by missionary influence, the frock that belongs to a child. It has a yoke, puffed sleeves, but the people had changed and modified the modesty garment. They sewed pieces of bright lame to the sleeves, blue and red and gold. They decorated the yokes with lace, they made the smock into a celebration. But no one could alter the childlike image of the dress.

We decided to go out deep sea diving. My lover was quite fearless, but I was content to float near the boat with goggles and flippers savouring the beauty of the world beneath me. Sometimes when I surfaced to breathe, my eyes would search along the long slow cusp of beach fringed with palms. I wondered at the absence of people. Just a few children could be seen, black dots on the beach, running along the sand, but mainly silence, emptiness. It was an extraordinary perspective. First, the coral beneath us in the palest of blue melting forms, quiet and creamy at the edges, blue and pink, soft but hard. A forest of fish that came and went in shoals. Parrot fish in blues and greens and reds, a bank of peacock blue fish turning and jiving against the current, shifting direction, colour as they moved. A tropical forest, underwater. Then, intervening, the surface of the sea, the dimension of blue space that existed there. The beach in the distance, the electric green of plants with their intricacy of leaf and shape, and finally above, the sky – a blue bulb hanging overhead. Swimming on the surface was like looking into a hologram. Each moment created a new depth, colour and scenery. Altogether it made for the perfect universe. But an indefinable sadness ran through all this.

Our drive around the island of Efate had been disappointing. People sought their privacy in the depths of the vegetation. There was a ghostly feeling. The small bays were deserted. Why weren't there people in the water, on the sand? I heard voices behind the sandhills, near the jungle, faintly murmuring. I saw a family group bathing in the sea, their black bodies in the green water, splashing, swimming, talking to themselves. Where were the people? Were they all on the other sixty islands of the New Hebrides? Tanna, Pentecost? I saw one longhouse through the trees, near the side of the road and that was all. We didn't see other villages and it took us a whole day to drive around the island.

I sensed some tragedy of a frightening nature but I had not connected the parts. Some people travel with a lot of information in their heads before they arrive in a new environment. I prefer to savour first impressions, take them where they will lead me, pursue the meanings that I crave. I did not like the feeling on the island of Efate. I did not like the stillness overall, the emptiness at the centre of the island. I did not like the huge coconut plantations where native villages should have been.

I began to read the books I had bought about the history of the New Hebrides and a picture came clear to me.

Natives of the various islands had been used as slave labour on the French coconut plantations. White diseases had decimated them as they had the Australian Aborigines. Australian blackbirders had been ruthless in deceiving natives into coming aboard their boats. Whole villages had broken down under the impact of kidnapping, forced labour and disease. I read the story of a native who had returned to his village after a period of indentured labour and hung himself because he could not find any traces of his family. His village was a wasteland. From the time the sandalwood trade first started, over one hundred years ago, there had been a decline of over one million in population.

And so, the empty beaches, the foliage which hid no people, the echoes of voices in the long grass, the sense of a great beauty having been betrayed. The French colons. The new government building was housed in the old French embassy. The British Governor's house was on an island off shore. The joint management of this condominium had ended only the year before when the New Hebrides became independent Vanuatu.

I heard that a church service was to be held on the island, the first to be held since a cyclone had caused damage some years previously. The people had moved their village back to the mainland. I woke early and took the boat alone over to the island.

The barge drifted slowly across the lake. The water drifted thick as spun glass beneath me. The Efate man steered the barge. The fish, the coral, the cold blue wash beneath me. I drifted to the quiet purr of the engine. I was drifting between two worlds – mainland and island.

The humidity was already in the air. Several tourists had gathered for the service which was held outdoors. The minister was a young islander, wearing a delicately woven palm bag from Pentecost over his shoulder. I thought of the tourist shop in the hotel crammed with the artefacts of the Pacific islands and these small tightly woven bags which had been the rarest of all to buy. He read the service in pidgin and then in English. The old men and women from the village were present. They seemed extremely shy and self-conscious at the presence of the tourists but nevertheless determined. When they began to sing, a feeling of pleasure went through me. They sang in harmony in several parts, the high clear voices of the women rising above the men. They sang exquisitely. The minister spoke of the need for harmony in the village and the need for the older people in the community to respect the young. When the service ended, the villagers lined up to shake hands with the guests. As I filed past the children, the older women, I felt the tears welling. The old woman who shook my hand must have known relatives who had disappeared within her own lifetime. Many kanakas who had been repatriated had been dumped on hostile islands along the way, never to see their fellow villagers again. I looked into the eyes of the old woman, her lined face. It was like my own mother's, so warm and kind and loving. The tears streamed down my face into the blue sea, the blue wash. It seemed as if, for some mysterious reason, these people had abandoned hatred. The other side of terror could not be this acceptance.

If we live with any hope at all, it is that the obscenities of the past have been left behind us. But it is not so. The human race is dreaming up new horrors for itself. At least, to be more accurate, some sections of the human race who do not deserve the consciousness they were born with and who have betrayed us all with their inability to worship.

My lover and I clung together. Through the glass the lagoon glittered like mica. We held each other tight in warmth and tenderness. We were fleeting, we knew that, cast up like flotsam against the tide, brief in our moment upon this earth, in a country also shipwrecked, loving each other amidst this dislocation of human beings, suffering, cruelty and misadventure. The red hibiscus, that bright vermilion in the hair of the people. Like blood. Life is hard enough, I say, without wars. Just surviving from day to day is hard enough. There are enough battlegrounds and tragedies without war, pillage and barbaric cruelties.

My beloved. I took you to a place I barely knew the history of, that in its outward form represented a kind of paradise. Peel away the surface and once again we are sent reeling back. The Japanese have cultivated an aesthetic of pleasure from very beautiful things. How do they deal with pain? Do they have some art, some skills that we can learn? Is it just as hard to reconcile suffering and beauty?

Our love is still there, in the memory of that island. The damage that had been done would never be repaired by that journey. It was to be our last moment of happiness. Our last retreat. Unfortunately into other people's pain. But how were we to know that? We took what pleasure we could find.

And the waters of Vanuatu run quiet out there, in the dark, black as ink. The barge still goes out to the island, carrying visitors back from the restaurant. We can hear the purr of the engine, the plop of fish. And the rivers of Vanuatu run warm, they say, in this season.

Eighteen
Hours in Frankfurt

MICHAEL HAIG

Hugh had learnt German at school and was determined to speak it.

'*Hier ist mein Pass,*' he said boldly to the customs official at Frankfurt airport.

The official turned the untainted pages of Hugh's passport. '*Du hast Deutsch in der Schule gut gelernt,*' he smiled.

'*Danke,*' said Hugh dubiously. With a shrinking feeling he wondered what the official was smiling at: his accent? his grammar? his clothes? He looked down at his white paper jacket, his jeans, his blue vinyl moonboots. This outfit was his parents' idea: 'Oh no, son, don't wear sandshoes, you'll get cold. They all wear ski-gear over there, you know. We hear it's the fashion.' As if you'd know, thought Hugh, disgruntled.

In the back of his mind was the expectation of some distinctly German culture: Gothic buildings, beer halls – maybe even a few buxom wenches. He bought a postcard depicting the weathered facade of a Gothic building veiled in an elegant mist. 'Dear Mum and Dad, Paper jackets and moonboots are not in fashion this year,' he wrote on the back.

He was due to catch a train at 5.30 p.m. – eight hours away. A railway line ran straight from the airport to the centre of the city. He struggled with his suitcase down onto the platform.

Shortly a Negro with hair as fine and short as sprinkled pepper approached him. Is this where you catch the train to town? he wanted to know.

'I think so,' said Hugh.

The Negro put his bag down next to Hugh's. 'Where yuh goin?' he asked.

Hugh guessed at the level of the question: 'I'm on my way to London.'

The Negro nodded.

Hugh had a sudden thought: 'How did you know I spoke English?'

The Negro shrugged: 'Ah guess yuh jest look un-German.'

'I'm Australian, actually,' said Hugh.

The train glided up to the platform, snug in its tunnel.

Hugh clambered aboard and sat down opposite a burly, pink-faced American in a lumber-jacket. The Negro sat down next to Hugh.

'This a smokin cabin?' the American asked the Negro abruptly.

'It don say,' said the Negro.

'But sure as hell you light up somebody'll come runnin in here and tell you . . .'

Hugh cut this spiel short by drawing the American's attention to a non-smoking sign above his head.

'Where're you from?' the American asked the Negro, ignoring Hugh and, with his mouth, dragging a cigarette out of a packet.

'Long Ahland, Nu York.'

'Scranton, Pennsylvania,' the American replied. The Negro nodded.

'D' you know any Australians over there?' said Hugh, poking around for something to say.

'Nope, not dat ah know ov,' said the Negro.

'Can't say I know of any neither,' the American chipped in.

'Ah'd hafta say,' the Negro continued, 'yore de first ah ebber met . . . in fact, ah always thought dey were black and wore dem – wadaya call 'em?' He framed his loins with his fingers – 'loincloths, dat's it . . .' He peered at Hugh, 'Yuh got 'lectricity?'

'Course they got e-lec-tricity!' snapped the American. 'Can't you see he's civ'lised?'

In the *Stadtmitte,* the centre of the city, Hugh walked at

random through the streets: he found sex shops which displayed their wares in the window and peep shows open to the street; a steady stream of bright red facades flowed amongst the other dress shops, electrical shops, jewellers and restaurants. '*Komm rein! Komm rein!*' the doormen urged him, smearing their greasy fingers on his paper jacket. From the footpath he could see the queues of customers and the rows of inscrutable doors. He looked up and down the street, wondering which direction to take: the city seemed to lead him nowhere at all, no sight lead onto another as he'd imagined they would; the city possessed no apparent logic.

He wandered aimlessly back to the central station where he ran into Ricky – the Negro with sprinkled pepper hair – who was drinking coffee at one of the outside cafes. He made room for Hugh at his bench: 'What chu doin?'

'Just looking around.' Hugh looked at his watch.

'Train's not due till 5.30.' It was 12.

'Ah'm goin' out,' said Ricky, 'to de 'merican barracks at Giessen.' He had once worked there as a soldier. 'Why don' yuh come 'long fer de rahde?' he asked Hugh.

'Ah . . . all right,' said Hugh, shocked into agreement by the unexpectedness of the question.

The barracks were familiar to Hugh; on TV he had already seen the jeeps and official cars drive up through the sludgy snow, the cases of ammunition unloaded, a freckled private wearing a baseball cap loudly rebuked by a hamfisted sergeant. Only the stink of petrol, tyres, khaki, lent the place a slightly frightening reality.

Ricky was spotted by a couple of old friends. 'Hey Ricky, where yuh bin?' they exclaimed.

'Back home tah see mah folks.'

These soldiers, obviously suffering from homesickness, plied Ricky for news of the States: 'Whatzhappnin back there, man?'

'It's snowin lahk crazy – asshole deep in places.'

'Shee-it!' they shouted. 'Shee-it!'

Hugh tried to talk about the hot summer of Australia, Christmas days on the beach; but for them he simply had no existence. He looked across the road at an old-style *Konditorei,* dwarfed beside the high wire fences of the barracks. A woman, hair tied up in a scarf, ambled past holding a washing basket.

Ricky was voluble about himself after this encounter with old buddies. 'Dere's a heap o' prej'dice in de States, man, 'specially fer de brownies . . .'

'Brownies – ?' Hugh wondered.

'Yeah . . . what ah am. Half-black, half-wahte . . . D'yuh think ah wuz a nigger or somethin?'

'Well . . . yes,' said Hugh cautiously.

'Shit, man, dis skin ain't black.' Ricky was taken aback. 'Needer de wahte nor de black lahk mah kahnd. So 'times ah git into fahts, if some guy smartass me roun'. Ah know how t' handle mahsel, and dat's de truth. Any guy gimme shit 'n ah'll whop 'im. But de fact is, ah don' go out in de streets much – less . . .' Ricky leant forward and grabbed Hugh by the jacket – 'less ah'm lookin fer some pussy.'

As the train pulled back into the central station, Hugh suddenly remembered. Ricky woke from his reverie: 'What's de madder wid chu?'

'My train!' Hugh glanced at his watch: 5.25 – it was due in five minutes. Oh God, oh God . . . probably time . . . trains are always late, anyway, he thought vaguely.

'Well, go on, slackass!' Ricky prodded him.

'OK, OK, . . .' Hugh grabbed his bag and leapt from the train.

At 5.28 he pulled his suitcase from the lockers. By 5.30 he was approaching the platform and could see the train waiting. Everything was working like clockwork. They can see me now, he thought. I'll take it a bit easier. He slowed from a crouching run into a sort of lopsided tortoise step, shifting the case forward with a stiff right leg.

He was less than five feet away from the first carriage: the train started pulling out – without blowing its whistle, without guards checking the platform; slowly but surely the steps were moving off. In desperation Hugh attempted to hurl the suitcase and himself onto the receding steps, but the effort merely wrenched his shoulder and rushed stars into his head. 'I have to meet someone in London,' he yelled. Passengers' faces, some curious, most indifferent, flashed at him as the train accelerated. 'You bastards!' he burst out.

The next train was due at 5.30 the next morning – sharp! Hugh quipped to himself, turning away from the timetable in disgust. What kind of fucking country has trains that leave on time? What do they expect me to do for the next twelve hours?

At midnight Hugh was in the toilets at the central station. He'd filled in time reading newspapers, walking in and out of shops, eating, drinking coffee. His hair was streaked with grease, his fingernails lined with grime, his hands sticky – no soap and water! He found a vending machine of moist towelettes on the wall. He pushed a coin in the slot. No result. Shit! He bashed on the machine. He turned round to a man standing behind him '*Es klappt nicht!*' he blurted out – just a bit cheered up for knowing how to say it in German.

The man, well-groomed in a beige overcoat, replied with some light remark. It's all right, my friend, he said, these machines often do not work. In a French-sounding voice the man fired off a reel of questions at Hugh: What are you doing here in the middle of the night? What are you waiting for? He discovered that Hugh's train wasn't due for another five hours. Would you like to spend the time at my flat? He continued. It's just close by . . . no, never mind, I will drive you back for your train later . . . yes, no problem . . . you can come, yes? . . . OK, come on then. He bustled Hugh off by the arm and into his Mercedes parked nearby.

'*Wie heisst du?*' the man wanted to know as he started the car.

'*Bruce,*' said Hugh, thinking of the first assumed name.

'*Broose –* ?'

'*Ja.*'

The man pulled out onto the road. 'Manfried,' he said patting himself on the chest.

Hugh peered at Manfried: he looked close on forty – almost old enough to be his father. He acutely felt Manfried's foreignness: the stroking of his moustache, the courteous bow of his head dipping into unknown space. He felt uncomfortable: his parents had told him to avoid loitering strangers.

In the corner of Manfried's flat stood two life-sized porcelain greyhounds, pompoms slung about their necks. A black-faced Buddha squinted over the opened pages of an ornately bound book. A wooden table sprouted the carved legs of a lion. On the walls were photographs – poster-sized – of Manfried in black leather holding a coiled whip.

Take a seat, said Manfried hospitably. One moment while I dress for bed. He disappeared into the bathroom.

Hugh nodded, shocked; he had heard of young foreigners dumped in the snow, raped and murdered. He scanned the table before him. His eye caught the address on an opened letter: *M. Robert Dubois.*

At that moment Manfried/Robert emerged from the bathroom, his hairy legs showing beneath his bathrobe. *'Kaffee?'* he inquired.

Hugh nodded.

Manfried/Robert disappeared into the kitchen.

God, what am I going to do? Hugh panicked. He could hear a clattering noise coming from the kitchen. His heart thumping, he rose from his seat, slunk across the room and secured his bag. He crept towards the door, cringing: his paper jacket was crumpling loudly at every step. He put his hand on the doorknob. Manfried/Robert, holding coffee cups, emerged from the kitchen.

'Gehst du irgendwohin?' Manfried/Robert looked at Hugh's hand which was still on the knob.

'Nein, nein . . .' Hugh hastily let it go.

'Schoen,' said Manfried/Robert cautiously.

Hugh sat back down in the fortress-like security of an armchair, too faint-hearted now to attempt a second, more obvious escape.

'Mein Gott, bin ich aber muede,' yawned Manfried/Robert after a pause.

Muede, muede . . . Hugh repeated to himself, trying to jog the word's English equivalent from his memory. Happy? ready? willing? able? tired? – yes, that's it. He sat rooted to the chair.

'Bist du nicht muede?' Manfried/Robert was wondering as he smoothed his moustache.

'Nein.'

'Aber Broose, du musst schlafen.'

'Warum?' Hugh recalled *du*'s connotations of intimacy.

'*Morgen muss ich frueh aufwachen.*'

Hugh eventually established that he wasn't going to budge an inch from the armchair until 5 a.m. when he, Manfried, would drive him, Bruce, back to the station.

Manfried/Robert took the soothing approach; Come on, Broose, don't be frightened, I won't hurt you. Sleep now, you will feel better in the morning. He put his hand on Hugh's shoulder: it was slapped away. He became angry: Do you think I am a robber, that I will steal from you? . . . You think then that I am a pervert, that I will screw you? He let out a wheezing laugh which froze Hugh's blood. In panic Hugh broke into English. He stopped laughing: No, you speak German as you did before . . . What's that you say? . . . You cannot trust me because you are foreign and cannot speak so good. He turned and walked over to the front door: So you don't want my hospitality, you bastard. Well, get fucked then . . . Here, this is the door. He grabbed Hugh by the arm and shoved him down the stairs.

By 4.30 Hugh was back at the central station sipping coffee in an all-night bar. He had walked most of the way from Manfried/Robert's and then hailed a cruising taxi. He'd drunk too many coffees and his tongue felt like leather.

Sensing Hugh's foreignness the bar's drunken clientele stared at him — his sun-tanned face, his white paper jacket, the square cut of his jaw. A drunkard at his elbow brought his face close. '*Schade, Schade, Schade,*' he rasped, pouring a heat-wave of alcohol over Hugh through a jumble of yellow teeth.

'Bugger off,' Hugh moaned.

'*Schade, Schade, Schade,*' the drunk wagged his head. '*Schade, Schade, Schade.*'

'*Was wuenschen Sie?*' asked Hugh weakly. He could see people around the bar watching the drunk with amused, brotherly interest. He attempted in vain to catch the connotations of what the drunk was saying. He had an urge to smash the drunk in the face, to stop the glazed quivering of his eyes, the lips forming the noise. Shithead! Hugh strode from the bar.

At 5 he was on the platform in the aching cold.

At 5.30 the train pulled in. Hugh clambered aboard and

found a vacant seat in a smoking cabin among four other passengers. In the two window seats sat a middle-aged husband and wife; they wore a vague air of gentility, an abdicated gentility; her mauve outfit frayed about the sleeves; he sagging in his tweed coat. Beside Hugh was a bald-headed man who compensated for the dearth on his head with a pendulous beard. Near the door sat a pale, diffident youth slumped in a bikie jacket. They're all a bunch of phoneys, thought Hugh, catching the would-be bikie's eye. Gloomily he recalled the people he had met since arriving in Frankfurt: half a Negro, a French Manfried, a drunk . . . when would he meet *ein echter Deutsche?* . . . maybe this is how Hitler felt: the race must be purged of alloys.

The smoke in the cabin was thick and hot; a wave of nausea rushed to Hugh's forehead.

Night was nearly at an end. Hugh's companions were falling asleep. The husband and wife slumped forward, their mouths open.

Exhausted but unable to sleep, Hugh felt the train rushing along on its iron seam, turning blindly, irresistibly around the hard curves. The drifting smoke clung to the air. The faint beams of morning crumbled through the window and into the layers of smoke. Hugh felt strangely blank, a blackboard rubbed clean. The trees flicked past outside like strands of hair through a comb. The train's iron wheels clattered hypnotically. He looked out at the snow-covered landscape: the concentrating light caught the whiteness of the snow. He looked back at the motionless, intentionless faces. He felt he could have been anywhere, at any time; nothing different, not a face altered.

The Beautiful Journey

PAULINE MARRINGTON

'Ithaca has not deceived you. . .
She gave you the beautiful journey. . .'
Cavafy

By the time she reached the dining room the cruise passengers had already formed into groups at the tables. As Thelma followed the steward across the room she was conscious of moving inelegantly, despite her Spanish shawl.

The five people at the table looked faintly hostile, as people do when interrupted in mid-topic. They acknowledged her to the point of making introductions and kept the conversation to themselves, tossing the words about as though they were ping-pong balls. Thelma longed to join in; she kept silent, having been taught that she had nothing to contribute.

Her mother had said most things for her, even when someone asked Thelma a question, and her recent death had left a silence that hung, miasmic, over the carved mahogany furniture. The family solicitor, a kindly man, had urged Thelma to travel, hoping that it was not too late, while admitting that forty-three years is a long atrophy.

'Is this your first visit to the Greek Islands, Miss Prentice?' Mrs Rogers, who had lost the thread of the conversation, thought it was time to 'place' the newcomer.

Thelma nodded. She hated these 'Have you been to. . .?' questions.

'We,' Mrs Rogers' ring-bound fingers associated themselves

with her husband's sleeve, 'have been just about everywhere, haven't we, Daddy?'

'Daddy' nodded, lost in the introspection of his own flesh and profitable business deals.

'It would take a lifetime to do justice to the Aegean Islands – let alone the mainland.' Miss Oldershaw could have been addressing her sixth form.

'So, what has brought you to Greece, Miss Prentice?' Professor Heinrich was fond of asking this sort of question. He smiled at Thelma, the upward pressure of flesh increasing the moisture in his eyes. They were large and brown and could, at any moment, break the bounds of their iris.

'I had no particular reason,' Thelma was forced to admit.

'All that history, I suppose,' Mrs Rogers said vaguely and looked at the ex-headmistress for confirmation. The company was dull, Douglas would have to tell the steward to change their seating. She looked around to see what the room had to offer.

'Miss Prentice comes, like Byron, to see where Sappho burned.' Bernard Lynch was a poet and could be expected to be fanciful.

Miss Oldershaw had read some of the young man's work and had not been impressed. She disliked the abstraction of most modern poetry, condemning it on the grounds that it offered more shadow than substance.

After dinner they regrouped for coffee in the vinyl stonehenge of the 'Dolphin' room. Ten days' cohabitation stretched like grey elastic. Thelma pretended she did not play bridge and went on deck.

The night air was soft – she felt its cashmere touch – and silent except for the thrust of the propellers. Why had she come to Greece? She had not needed a reason until Professor Heinrich raised the question. Nor did she now but was, by nature, truthful.

Perhaps she had come to spite her mother. 'Greece is out of the question, Thelma.' Mrs Prentice's voice had left no room for argument. They had gone instead to the safer regions of the Lake District.

Thelma was not prepared to define just what it was she expected to find. She thought of Bernard Lynch's words (he had introduced himself less formally than the others although no one had, as yet, addressed him by his Christian name) and she was curious as to their meaning.

Her father had had his private moments of poetry. Thelma had found an exercise book – tossed out when her mother went through his papers. 'How lonely the heart when the only hands that touch you are your own.' The lines were as sensitive as sea anemone, Thelma was glad he had not exposed them to the strong light of criticism. She wondered what sort of poetry Bernard Lynch wrote and thought it might not be unlike her father's.

'You were wise,' Bernard Lynch materialised beside her, 'Mr Rogers plays post-mortem bridge.'

Thelma laughed without meaning to be unkind.

'Cards are for another time and place.' He indicated the alternative of sea and sky.

Thelma responded to his mood but did not reply. Not quite at ease. Here, alone, at the ship's rail.

'Why is it all so predictable?' he gestured. 'Cards in the "Dolphin" room, an indifferent movie in the main lounge, and music' – a band could now be heard under the awning of the lower deck – 'in case silence is mistaken for boredom.'

'People expect it.' Thelma was diffident although he was younger than she.

'I had hoped for Orpheus's lute and gymnopaedia.' He shrugged at over-optimism.

'Ah, there you are!' Miss Oldershaw sounded pleased to have found them. Perhaps she too was dissatisfied with routine amusements. 'We are due to dock at 6 a.m. I am half-inclined to make myself comfortable on a deck chair so that I may have the pleasure of seeing Crete come up out of the dawn. Would you care to join me?'

Greeting the dawn barefooted, to the music of lutes. Thelma excused herself and went to her cabin.

The steward had turned down the bed. Her nightgown, which she had put under the pillow, lay on top. Spread out, the waist pinched in. There was a suggestion of intimacy as though the man knew how she would look in bed. Thelma snatched up the garment. She would leave it in her suitcase in future.

The buses waited at the quay. The drivers lounged under the shadow of the stone walls, fingering their worry-beads with pocketed hands.

The passengers tested the gangway. Some paused, looking anxiously towards the coaches, as though they feared they would not reach them in time. Or find themselves without a seat. And when they found one, sat peering out of the windows, wondering if the air-conditioner would function. They would not have come to Greece if they had known about the heat.

Thelma pushed her way back up the gangway, for forgotten sunglasses, and was the last to cross the quay. The cavalcade of coaches was already setting off and the driver of the one that remained was revving up the engine. Thelma ran feeling red and unsightly and the focus of impatient eyes.

She had no choice of seat. The only vacant place was beside Bernard Lynch. The lurching bus jostled their thighs together. Should she apologise or pretend she had not noticed?

The poet looked heavy-eyed and had not come to breakfast. Thelma hesitated to ask if he had kept Miss Oldershaw company on deck.

'We would not have let the driver go without you.' Mrs Rogers rose and leaned forward from the seat behind. Her head hung above them like John the Baptist's.

Thelma thanked her and was grateful when the face withdrew.

'Miss Oldershaw had the right idea,' Bernard Lynch made the effort of conversation, 'the sunrise must have been spectacular.'

'It was. I watched it from my porthole,' Thelma did not add that she had been obliged to close her eyes: one could have drowned in so much liquid gold.

'It is not something to be watched through glass,' he made it sound like a reprimand. 'One should be out of doors to greet the dawn.'

Thelma felt that she had said something foolish. Embarrassed, she turned her head away and looked out of the opposite window.

The tour buses had left the narrow, bazaar-like streets of the town and had begun to climb until at last the recurring glimpses of sea and sky fused into dazzling unity. The coaches drew off the road so that those who wished could stretch their legs.

Mr Rogers's 'Leica' caught the group at the cliff edge. Long after they had forgotten each other's names the photograph would recall Miss Oldershaw's sensible walking shoes, Professor Heinrich's round, amiable face and the pennant of Mrs Rogers's silk scarf, Bernard Lynch – looking not unlike a poet – with wind-blown hair and ballooning corduroys, and Miss Prentice, who could have been attractive if she had allowed some of herself to escape.

'Will you write about all this when you return to London?' Thelma had ventured a question when they were back in the coach.

'Not immediately.' He made an indecisive motion with his hands. 'The true impressions are those recalled months, even years, later.'

'That can apply to people.' Thelma was thinking of her mother. Time was giving her image the sharpness of broken glass.

'Yes, of course.' He looked at her, surprised at her perception.

His eyes, seen at close quarters, were disconcerting. The guide's voice saved Thelma from having to elaborate on her remark.

'Crete is the legendary birthplace of Zeus,' the woman said. She was small and passionately Greek and repetition had not staled her enthusiasm for what she saw around her.

Thelma would have preferred to make her own assessment of the cypress and olive trees, the limestone hills, the dusty villages enlivened with bougainvillea. Her father had taken a scholar's interest in Greek mythology. Thelma wondered if he had found his wife's rejection of it disappointing. She thought of his gentle, withdrawn face. What other disappointments had there been?

The guide had passed on to the legend of the Minotaur – the monstrous progeny of Pasiphaë and a bull. No labyrinth, the woman was saying, had been found. The maze of passages beneath the palace had been identified as drains.

The coaches, smelling of leather and the press of bodies,

returned to the quay. There was time for a shower before dinner.

Thelma lay on her bed in her dressing gown sorting out the day's impressions.

The knock was unexpected.

'Yes? Who is it?' She was not yet ready to open the door.

'Mikos. The steward.'

He looked very clean. As if he, too, had recently showered.

'You have good day?'

'Yes. Very nice, thank you.'

'You like Greece?' He smiled, showing good teeth.

'Yes. I do.' Thelma wondered at his interest.

'You want love in Greece?'

'I beg your pardon?'

His smile broadened. His glance assessed what the dressing gown hid.

'Ladies travel alone all times want love.'

'How dare you!' Thelma shut and locked the door.

He knocked once more but without urgency.

'Go away! Away, do you hear? If you bother me again I shall report you to the captain.'

After that there was silence.

Thelma sat on the edge of the bed. The impudence! Surely she had not given him grounds to suppose...'

She got up and washed her face with cold water. She looked at her reflection in the mirror above the wash basin.

Did she want love in Greece? Was that what she had come for?

The ship skimmed across the Aegean like a giant beetle bearing the curious to Mykonos, Patmos, Delos. The groups in the dining room reflected the stimulus of discovery.

'Such heavenly jewellery. And so cheap.'. Mrs Rogers was weighed down like a Mycenaean princess. They had not changed their table; Douglas had not thought it worth the additional tip for so short a voyage.

'They did not allow us enough time to do justice to Ephesus.' It was Miss Oldershaw's standard complaint.

Thelma thought of the poppies springing up between the stones '. . . as where some buried Caesar bled . . .' and the timeless message of the graceful, female footprint pointing the way to the brothel. Only the men of the party had been allowed inside – and had come out laughing.

'I discovered a pride of stone lions hiding in the tall, bleached grass.' Bernard Lynch hoped the impression would translate well into iambic metre.

'Did you hear that, Daddy? You missed the lions while you were looking at that pri . . . priapic – whatever it was.' Mrs Rogers wished Douglas would not try to confuse her with technical words. She wondered why Professor Heinrich found her remark amusing.

Miss Oldershaw also understood the reference and diverted the conversation. 'Rhodes will be the most interesting island of all, in many respects,' – she could not resist a platform – 'the city itself is a survival from the Middle Ages, when Greece was dominated by Turkish rule, while at the other end of the scale you have the classical gem of Lindos which is considered to be one of the most beautiful and best preserved Acropoleis. I hope you will make the most of the overnight stay.'

The coaches, genetically linked from island to island, transported the adventurous to Lindos.

The hotel faced the beach. Thelma opened the shutters of her room and let in the hot, clear afternoon light. It made her feel – if one could use the word – scarified. And liberated. She was not prepared to follow that train of thought, she changed her clothes and went outside.

A team of donkeys had replaced the coaches. For a few drachmá one could ride to the summit.

The camera lens reflected Miss Oldershaw astride her stoic mount, showing more knee than she normally cared to expose. Presently – although she was out of sight – her assembly-hall voice could be heard rebuking the guide for goading his beast with a battery-stick.

The beauty of the temple compensated for the indignity of the ascent. It perched on the edge of the cliff, its chalk-stick columns sharp against the sky. From the cella one looked down into the peacock waters of the bay where the secrets of the sea-bed were exposed as though through plate glass. Fishing boats, moored to the jetty, duplicated themselves in perfect detail.

Thelma felt an overwhelming need to share the moment. She looked for the poet but could not see him.

'I'm sure I can see bones down there.' Mrs Rogers shuddered. 'Just think of all those poor girls being thrown to the gods.'

'That was at Chichén-Itzá,' her husband corrected her.

'Well, wherever it was, I can't help feeling sorry for them.'

Professor Heinrich returned to the topic as they sat outside the hotel after dinner. 'The Rhodians made an annual sacrifice to Helius, to whom this island belonged, of a chariot and four horses which were flung into the sea.'

'I can almost see it,' Bernard Lynch indicated the cliffs. 'The red, fear-stretched nostrils, fringed tails, forelegs extended to take the impact of the sea.'

'How cruel,' said Thelma, feeling the terror of their descent.

'They don't exploit these places properly. Think what a tourist attraction it would be if they revived the custom.' Mr Rogers's cigar exuded economic possibilities.

'Horses are not as bad as humans.' Sitting safely on the hotel terrace Mrs Rogers could afford to pleat her predominantly orange chiffon skirt.

'The Greeks, of course, were no strangers to human sacrifice.' Miss Oldershaw rearranged her posture in readiness for discourse and found that she had lost her audience.

Someone was playing a bouzouki. Its haunting, compelling sound enticed the hands and feet and a group of men from the village began to dance. Graceful, rhythmic, united by arms and shoulders, yet self-absorbed; each might have been dancing alone.

The onlookers caught the contagion and began to clap in unison. Bernard Lynch was on his feet accompanying himself with clicking fingers. Thelma felt embarrassed for him.

'Let's show them what we can do, Daddy,' Mrs Rogers coaxed.

'Only the men dance in Greece,' Miss Oldershaw reproved her.

But had not allowed for the magic of the music. People were standing up. Reaching for hands. Pairs became fives, eights, joining and spreading like beads of mercury.

'When in Rome', said Miss Oldershaw, securing Bernard Lynch's hand, and signalling to Thelma. 'Come along, Miss Prentice.'

With a sense of desperation Thelma reached for the poet's other hand. It was warm, and softer than she had expected – she could have mistaken it for Mrs Rogers's who was on her other side.

The human chain took on a life of its own. An animated frieze that wove between the tables and stretched out along the sea wall.

She was dancing like a bacchante. Thelma suspended belief. She no longer avoided the concept of liberation. She wanted to lose her shoes, her clothes. She ventured to look at her companion – did he have similar thoughts? But his eyes were closed, intent upon some inner vision of his own.

Had Thelma been less engrossed she might have sensed the watching eyes beyond the circle of light. The ancient, tired eyes of Greece, long-wearied by recurrent themes.

'Oh, my goodness,' Mrs Rogers found the incantation for normalcy. 'I must sit down.'

Thelma was too affected by the evening to sleep well. Now wide awake, she recalled how they had sat talking and sipping the libations of ouzo Bernard Lynch had continued to order until the terrace was almost deserted. Thelma admitted to herself a feeling of affinity with another person such as she had never known; neither at school nor in the half-hearted friendships of her later years.

'You were born to be single, Thelma. Some women are.'

Thelma sat up in bed angered by the intrusion. There was a suggestion of light above the sky, she got up and went to the window.

The terrace was empty, the beach deserted, the sea's rhythmic assaults upon the shore recalled the movements of the dancers.

The sea front was not deserted, Thelma saw that she had been mistaken. There was enough light to recognise Bernard Lynch. He was walking purposefully in the direction of the road that led from the village to the cliff top. To watch the sunrise? She now understood what he had meant.

Thelma began to dress, not allowing herself time for doubts

or hesitation. He would be surprised – but not offended – to see her.

The white-washed houses were still shuttered. The bright-eyed geraniums kept watch.

The ascent had not seemed so steep by donkey. Thelma paused for a moment before the final effort of the temple steps.

The sky was flushed, small clouds clung to its fragility like gorged, pink leeches.

Thelma thought she heard voices and could have wept with disappointment. Surely Miss Oldershaw had not attempted the climb?

A few more steps gave her a clear view. Bernard Lynch stood facing the sea, his arm around the shoulder of his companion.

The sun had risen and was red-pencilling the purity of stone. It shone on flesh that was already golden. The poet's hand traced the anatomy of the youth's back.

It took the watching woman a moment to grasp the implication. Then, suffocating with grief and embarrassment, she stumbled across the fallen masonry, scattering the dust and stones of the road with the urgency of her flight.

'Well, Thelma, I hope that answers your question.'

'I don't care,' she shouted at her tormenter. 'I don't. I don't.'

She withdrew into her skin and wished there was a safer place to hide.

Snap

ALLAN BAILLIE

The camp was a great brown stain in the forest, with a few splashes of bright blue. Low thatch huts jostling for room, leaning on scarred and stunted trees. Sometimes with a patch of plastic sheeting to make the roof work. Tired, bored groups settling around a thousand pots of simmering rice in the light haze of the low fires. In the centre of the camp, a man was prancing like a monkey with his cameras.

A one-legged man leant on his crutch and watched him curiously. He was standing before a large thatched hut with a group of veterans and a gold-toothed woman, but he was apart from the others. He shook his head very slowly as the man with the cameras dropped to his knees before a girl carrying sticks and ran to get in front of a bullock cart and its arrogant owner. Finally the one-legged man called to him.

'Oy!'

Brien glanced across at the large hut and saw a man waving a long stick at him. He ignored him while he shot a woman holding out a blackened melon in a sparse market, but he called again. Brien measured the sinking sun and clicked his tongue in anger, but he walked towards the man and his hut.

The hut was probably the biggest building in the camp beside the blue plastic circus tent they used for a hospital. It had been built carefully of stripped saplings, straight twigs and the essential grass thatch. It even had a painted sign on one of the front poles. Cafe de La Bohème.

'Francais?' The man had been waving an aluminium crutch,

and he had folded his arms over it. He had no right leg.

Brien dropped into a clumsy squat and took the man and the sign together. Nice shot. 'Un peu.' He shrugged.

'Never worry,' the man said. 'I am very fortunate with the English.' Deep brown eyes with an astonishing streak of grey in the right pupil. Somewhere between twenty-five and fifty years old.

'Come and have tea with us,' said the man, indicating the other men and the gold-toothed woman.

Soft focus for the woman? 'Well . . . I've only got a moment . . .' Brien stalked the woman and she looked a little frightened. Ideal.

'She is La Bohème.' the man said, and laughed.

'Pleased to meet you.' Brien nodded at the woman and stepped into the cafe.

No windows, just open walls and the shadow given by the large roof. No floor, just beaten and immaculately-swept earth floor. The cafe's seats were untreated benches anchored in the earth, the tables were picnic tables, but covered in blue plastic pulled taut to eliminate wrinkles and pinned at the edges with old drawing pins. A painting of someone's dim memory of Angkor Wat faced the tables, a crude altar piece.

'You know that?' The man was at his shoulder. His breath was heavy with garlic.

'In Kampuchea.' Brien was reaching for his flash.

'No.' The man shook his head, almost violently. 'No, it is Cambodia. Cambodia before . . . everything.' The man shrugged. 'I am sorry. I am not polite. I am Phan Mang. You are a newspaper. Yes?'

'Yes.' Keep it simple. They understand a newspaper, maybe even a magazine. But they are not going to understand a freelance are they? Get the low sun on their faces.

'You are late,' Phan said, accepting a chipped Chinese teapot and two small glasses from La Bohème. 'We thought newspapers had finished with us. Long ago you forget about us.'

'Oh, no, I never forget.'

Phan rolled his glass in his fingers. 'You come here before?'

Brien fumbled awkwardly with his camera. 'Ah, no. But I know about you –'

'There is not much thrills here any more. No hungry babies now, no fights over rice, no more Thai black markets, we have no gold left for them. No Viet shells, they fight the bloody Khmer Rouge in the hills there, not here. There is nothing for you now.'

'There is always something.' Brien could still remember his bushfire scoop. He had been too late then, the fire had roared past a town and had begun to die in a black forest, and the journalists and the firefighters had left for their phones, their homes and their pubs. Except five firefighters had saved a house and were too tired to leave and he had got them. It's never too late. Brien panned the camera around the faces.

'What newspaper?'

Brien looked up from the camera. 'What?'

Phan flapped the air with his fingers. 'I know *Newsweek, Chicago Tribune, New York Post,* the *Guardian.* What are you?'

Brien placed his camera on the table before him and studied Phan's face. He somehow felt at bay. Which was ridiculous. 'Ah, all of them, and none of them. Whichever pays the best.'

Phan grinned. 'Ah, yes, I know this. Many bosses, but little money. Which boss wants Nong Samet even now?'

This had gone far enough. 'Look, I'm not worried about that now. We'll see what I get first. I've got to see the camp before the light fades.' Brien moved to the edge of the seat.

Phan rammed his crutch into the earth and swung clear of the table. 'I will show you.'

Brien half-stood and stopped. He didn't want this smart little man around any more. 'I don't want to tire you . . .'

Phan laughed and reached the door in a long single hop.

'Come. You don't worry about me. Nobody worries about Phan.'

Brien reluctantly nodded his farewell to the cafe and followed Phan across the camp, passing a group of men repairing bicycles under a tree with less than a handful of tools and some shouting men throwing themselves at a volleyball. Men, rarely ever a youth. He clicked his cameras and caught Phan looping through the trees, an old hawk flying – just – on one wing.

'Wouldn't it be better with two crutches?' Brien said.

Phan waved his free hand. 'Then I lose this. I cannot carry things. But with two I make a lot of baht.'

They passed a girl of about seven, staggering along the path under a yoke of kerosene tins filled with water. Brien turned and squatted. 'How?'

'Sometimes it is from the doctors – you are very late here, now, the doctors have gone from here. They leave before you come. Maybe you better come tomorrow.'

'The sun is still up. How do you make money from the doctors?'

'Ah, most it is from the newspapers at Khao I Dang. The doctors, they get to know me and they say, "Aihah, it is Phao Mang again, we must sit on our purse." But the newspapers, they are new, they fall into my trap.'

Brien snapped the girl brushing her hair back from her face as she walked into the camera. 'Yes?'

'Ah, when we see the newspapers we have races outside the hospitals, the crutches and the chairs. Slow races, you understand? And they take pictures and then we make bets that I can race a newspaper. The newspaper thinks it is a big joke so he begins to run soso and then it is too late to catch me.'

'It would make a good pic,' Brien said warily.

'I don't do it now. It is not dignity.' He tripped a running boy with the crutch and grinned.

'Why aren't you still at Khao I Dang?'

'What do I want with Khao I Dang?'

'You wanted to come here? Really?'

'You also wanted to come here.'

Brien stopped for a moment, surprised and a little off-balance. 'That's different. I've got a job to do.'

'I've got a job to do, here.'

'Khao I Dang is ten times better than this place. It's almost a town. You can live comfortably there, in houses instead of huts, eat good food and they'd get you a new leg.'

'Khao I Dang is a prison. Full of Cambodians who want to go to America, France, even Australia, anywhere but back to Cambodia. They can't do anything there but build bamboo huts and wait. They don't need me there, they need me here.'

Brien slowly lowered his camera.

'In Khao I Dang I am just one of the beggars waiting for a bag of rice and a tin leg. Here I am a soldier, a king.'

Huts chest-high and nuzzling each other. A long way from the hospital now, but some still with a piece of blue plastic, a bit of rice matting to sleep on, a little pot of rice, a pile of sticks, a tin of water. A string running from the hut to a tree or to another hut, carrying tired clothes out to dry. Women laughing and holding up babies for the camera.

Phan saluted an old man limping towards him with a load of sticks on his back, and the old man whooped with laughter.

Brien frowned. 'You were a soldier before . . .?'

'Before?' Phan laughed suddenly. 'I was not even army cook.' He stopped by a low hut containing two young boys and a quiet woman. 'This is my family now. Saro. Khim. Moung.'

Saro bowed her head and allowed her hand to be taken with a smile, while the two boys stared at Brien and giggled.

'May I take a shot of your family.' It was the first time he'd asked.

'Oh, yes.' Phan lowered himself on his crutch and swept his family about him. 'But, not my family. Saro is a widow, I am a widow, it is a camp of widows. You have a wife?'

Brien rewound the film. 'I had.' See, it doesn't hurt any more. Much.

'Ah. How did she die?'

Always the questions. 'We were divorced.'

'Ah yes. I know.' Phan watched Saro argue softly with Moung. 'You have children?'

'No.' And that is just about enough.

'They are trouble . . .' Phan scratched in the ground with a stick. 'It is a funny thing, this wars, you know that?'

'Screaming.' And you've got to move.

'Before, Saro does not know me, never speak to me, you understand? She is Royal Classic Dancer, I am itchy bug cyclo rider. I learn a little English when I take newspaper from Royale Hotel to the bars, to the war, where they want to go. Then I am nothing, maybe I will be nothing again if we ever go back. But now Saro has my baby. See? It is very funny.'

Brien nodded and hoisted the camera bag on his shoulder and started to leave. 'I want a few quick shots as the sun sets . . .'

'But maybe if I go back I can drive a bus. Eh, you got a pretty good job. You get all over the world.'

'Ah, you get around . . .'

'Seeing presidents and movie stars, eh?'

'Everyone. Taking photos of men on the way to the moon, admirals . . .' And Brien petered out. For a moment he just stood there in silence and stared at Phan.

Jesus, what are you trying to do, start a fan club? Why don't you start again and tell him what a marvellous wedding photo man you've become?

Brien jerked his eyes from Phan to Saro, and to the gentle swelling of her stomach. 'The doctors? You said they have left?'

'Until tomorrow. You should leave also.'

'What happens if there is someone – sick – tonight?'

'We have some Cambodian nurses in the hospital.'

'Why have the doctors left?'

'They have been ordered to leave the border at 4 o'clock all the time. We have a little trouble.'

Brien lifted his head. 'What sort of trouble?'

'Khmer Rouge.'

And Brien was not as hot and tired as he had thought he was. 'Here?'

'For a long time. The army lets them stay and they stay to steal our food. We watch them, but what can we do?'

'Where are they? I've got to see them.'

Phan pointed. 'Come back tomorrow. They are safe in the day but very dangerous at night. They want to control the camp.'

Brien felt something twitch along his spine. He wanted to go back to his car by the hospital and drive away, but this was what he came for. 'I'll only be seeing them for a few minutes.'

'I cannot come with you.'

'That's all right. Are they armed?'

'Yes.'

'Good.' Brien took a step away from the hut, then half-turned, remembering an old question he had forgotten. 'What happened to the leg?'

Phan shrugged. 'They use iron bars. Take care.'

Brien waved and walked quickly through the thinning camp. The shadows were now long ghosts among the trees. He had wasted too much time, but he could sense a photo story bare minutes away. He hadn't felt that kind of excitement since the bushfire.

He had to remember that. The one time he had been on top of the world. When a bright kid with an ancient Pentax had staggered from the smouldering black scrub, shirt ripped open, burns throbbing where the falling branch hit, sweat dripping into the eyes . . . But five exhausted, streaked black men were leaning against a scorched little weatherboard house with smoking stubble all around them, and they were sharing a water-bottle and one had his thumb in the air because they had whipped the fire.

Brien strode toward the edge of the camp, and Cambodia and the killers. He felt the old adrenalin pumping for the first time in a long, long time.

Then, he'd dropped to his knees and with shaking hands framed the house, the stubble, the men, and he'd known that it was a beauty, a classic, and it was his. There was nothing like it. Front page, huge byline, nationwide spread, even a showing in Fleet Street. Then money, marriage, models, clicking away for Myers and the Trak brigade. Until you forget why you picked up a camera in the first place.

A single report. Like a bursting paper bag.

Brien stopped in the path.

A shot? Don't be silly. But that's what you came for. Something like that. You did it before, you can do it again.

Another report. Louder, to the right.

You did it before. You can do it again. Brien looked down at the Nikon quivering in his hands and forced himself to move toward the reports.

Suddenly a woman dragging a panting little girl brushed past him at a run. She was watched in silence by the families sitting outside their huts, then one family got up and followed her.

Brien began to pass empty huts, the fires still burning, the pots still bubbling on them.

This is getting very stupid.

A short string of heavy impacts. An automatic rifle?

Perhaps you should warn Phan. He can't run.

A man rushed at him, his mouth wide open and gasping. He

could smell the sweat as the man bolted round him and away.

He looked down at the camera and realised, dully, that he should have whipped it up to his face the moment the man had appeared. This was it, all that he could ever have hoped for, Brien's private little war. All he had to do was just stay here and fill the films. Easy. Isn't it?

A handful of children, a screaming woman, a bunch of men running low and fast, more children, more women and they were all jostling him, pushing him aside, running over him as if they could not see him. A quick hop and a stride and someone was shooting towards him and he was only a part of the seething torrent of isolated people.

He felt his camera bag pounding hard against his leg, thought for an instant of throwing it away, then he heard a shuddering string of explosions and a man shouting once in anger and pain almost beside him, and he forgot the bag. But he wasn't in a panic. He would just run out of the rush so he could see what was going on. He just wanted a few moments . . .

The rush suddenly reached the Cafe de La Bohème and the hospital and his car and began pouring into the huge trench the Thai army had dug to cut the refugees from Thailand. Brien swam against the flood for long enough to reach the front seat of the car. He threw his camera bag from his shoulder and fumbled his dripping fingers after the keys without thinking.

A woman shrieked through the trees, more rapid shooting and an explosion. Getting closer.

Tried one key, trying another, but can't find the hole.

A black wave of men flowed from the forest, eddied round the car and thrashed through the grass.

The key sinking in, turning, the starting motor rocking the car, pumping the accelerator.

Woman sprawled across the bonnet, staring with empty eyes.

It won't fire. Brien pulled his hands from the key and wiped it on his shirt.

Rattle of gunfire through the trees, close enough to see.

Jesus, Jesus. The engine turning, turning and beginning to flatten and wheeze. Brien kicked at the car.

A burst of fire from ten metres.

Brien threw himself across the seat. Someone panting up to the car. Jesus.

'Allo.' Phan, face gleaming with sweat and eyes alight. Leaning against the car with an automatic rifle in his free arm.

Brien pushed himself upright.

'It will not go?'

Brien tried to say something, but his throat was locked.

'They want to fight. Good. You want to go? It is better. Huah!' Phan shouted at the trench. Shouted again, in anger.

Slowly a man crept from the trench, followed by three others. They got behind the car and pushed.

'No light, OK?' Phan stepped from the window.

Brien released the brake and more men and women ran to get a handhold on the car. Brien turned and straightened, dropped the gear into second slowly raised the clutch and heard the engine cough into life. For a few seconds the engine was drowned in shouts and whistles as the car moved away.

Brien looked into the mirror and saw the crowd evaporate, leaving a one-legged man standing alone on the track, leaning on a single crutch with a rifle in his hand.

He thought, You did it before, you can do it again.

And accelerated for home.

The Fellow Passenger

ELIZABETH JOLLEY

Dr Abrahams stood watching, for his health, the flying fish. They flew in great numbers like little silver darts, leaping together in curves, away from the ship, as though disturbed by her movement through their mysterious world. Nearby sat his wife with her new friend, a rich widow returning to her rice farms in New South Wales. The two women in comfortable chairs, adjoining, spoke each other softly and confidingly, helping each other with the burden of family life and the boredom of the voyage.

'Who is that person your daughter is talking to?' said the widow, momentarily looking up from her needlework.

'Oh I've no idea,' Mrs Abrahams said comfortably. And then, a little less comfortably, she said, 'Oh I see what you mean. There are some odd people on board.' She raised herself slightly and, raising her voice, called, 'Rachel! Rachel dear . . . mother's over here, we're sitting over here.'

As the girl reluctantly came towards them, Mrs Abrahams said in a low voice to her new friend, 'I'm so glad you noticed. He does seem to be an unsuitable type, perhaps he's a foreigner of some sort.' She lowered her voice even more, 'And they do have such ugly heads you know.'

Their voices were swallowed up in the wind, which was racing, whipping the spray and pitting the waves as they curled back from the sides of the ship.

Dr Abrahams walked by himself all over the ship. The sharp fragrance from the barber's shop excited him, and he rested gratefully by the notice boards where there was a smell of boiled potatoes. The repeated Dettol scrubbing of the stairs reminded him of post-natal douchings and the clean enamel bowls in his operating theatre.

Whenever he stood looking at the front of the ship, or at the back, he admired the strength of the structure, the massive construction and the complication of ropes and pulleys being transported, and in themselves necessary for the transporting of the ship across these oceans. It seemed always that the ship was steady in the great ring of blue water and did not rise to answer the sea, and the monsoon had not broken the barrenness. Most of the passengers were huddled out of the wind.

When he returned to his wife he saw the man approaching. For a time he had managed to forget about him and now here he was again, coming round the end of the deck, limping towards them in that remarkably calm manner which Abrahams knew only too well was hiding a desperate persistence.

Knowing the peace of contemplation was about to be broken, Abrahams turned abruptly and tried to leave the deck quickly through the heavy swing doors before the man, with his distasteful and sinister errand, could reach him. There was this dreadful element of surprise and of obligation too. For apart from anything else, the man had an injury with a wound which, having been neglected, must have been appallingly painful. It was something that, if seen by a doctor, could not afterwards be ignored.

'All you have to do is to treat me like a fellow passenger,' the man had said the first night on board. He entreated rather, with some other quality in his voice and in his bearing which had caused Abrahams to buy him a drink straight away. Perhaps some of the disturbance had come from the unexpected shapeliness of the man's hands.

The Bay of Biscay, unusually calm, had not offered the usual reasons for a day of retreat in the cabin. Abrahams, excusing himself from the company of his wife and daughter, had again invited the man for a drink.

'What about a coupla sangwidges,' the fellow said, and he had gobbled rather than eaten them. A little plate of nuts and olives disappeared in the same way.

The two stupid old ladies, they were called Ethel and Ivy

and they shared the Abrahams' table, were there in the Tavern Bar. They nodded and smiled and they rustled when they moved, for both were sewn up in brown paper under their clothes.

'To prevent sea sickness,' Ethel explained to people whenever she had the chance.

A second little plate of nuts and olives disappeared.

'That'll be good for a growing boy!' Ethel called out. Like Ivy, she was having tomato juice with Worcester sauce. Already they had been nicknamed 'The Worcester Sauce Queens' by the Abrahams family.

Abrahams, with the courtesy of long habit, for among his patients were many such elderly ladies, smiled at her. His smile was handsome and kind. The very quality of kindness it contained caused both men and women to confide. It was the nature of this smile, and the years of patient, hard work it had brought upon him, that had necessitated a remedial voyage. For Abrahams was a sick man and was keeping the sickness in his own hands, prescribing for himself at last a long rest. He had been looking forward to the period of suspended peace, which has such tremendous healing power and is the delight of a sea voyage.

At the very beginning the peace was interrupted before it was begun, and Abrahams regretted bitterly the sensitive sympathy his personality seemed to give out. It was all part of his illness. It was as if he were ill because of his sympathetic nature. The burdens he carried sprang from it. That was what he allowed himself to believe but it was not all quite so simple. There were conflicting reasons and feelings which were all perhaps a part of being unwell, perhaps even a part of the cause. He tried to make some sort of acknowledgement, to reach some sort of inner conclusion in the all too infrequent solitary moments.

At the first meeting, Abrahams' feeling was, apart from a sense of obligation or the good manners of not liking to refuse to buy a drink for the stranger, a feeling of gladness, almost happiness, perhaps even a tiny heart-bursting gladness which could have made him want to sing. He did not sing, he was not that kind of man. His work did not include singing of any kind. There was not much talking. Mostly he listened. His work kept him quiet and thoughtful. He often bent forward to listen and to examine and to operate. He had good hands. His fingers, accustomed to probing and rearranging, to extracting and replacing, were sensitive and capable. If he frowned it was the frown of attention and concentration. It was his look of kindness and the way in which he approached an examination, almost as if it was some kind of caress, which made his patients like him.

In the bar that first night, he reflected, he had come near singing. A songless song of course because men like Abrahams simply would never burst into song.

Once he did sing and the memory of it had suddenly come back to him clearly even though it had been many years ago. Once his voice, surprisingly powerful, it could have been described as an untrained but ardent tenor, carried a song of love across and down a valley of motionless trees. Throughout his song the landscape had remained undisturbed. He had not realised how, in the stillness, a voice could carry.

'Heard yer singin' this half hour,' the woman had said, holding her side, her face old with pain.

'Oh? Was I singing?'

'Yerse, long before you crorsst the bridge, I heard yer comin' thanks to God I sez to meself the doctor's on his way, he's on his way.'

It was during a six months locum in a country town. That day he sang and whistled and sang careering on horseback to a patient in a lonely farm house. He remembered the undisturbed fields and meadows, serene that day because he went through them singing.

The stranger's voice in the bar, and his finely made hands taking the glass from Abrahams, brought back so suddenly the song in the shallow valley.

On the track that day he thought he'd lost his way and he was frightened of his surroundings. The landmarks he'd been told to watch for simply had not appeared. There was no house in sight and no barn and there were no people. He'd been travelling some time. Joyfully he approached some farm machinery but no one was beside it. He almost turned back but thought of his patient and the injection he could give her. In all directions the land sloped gently to the sky, the track seemed to be leading nowhere and he was the only person there.

He came upon the man quite suddenly. He was there as if for no reason except to direct Abrahams, though he had a cart and some tools, but Abrahams in his relief, did not really notice. The man's eyes shone as he patted the horse and Abrahams felt as if the intimate caress, because of the way the man looked, was meant for him. He continued his journey feeling this tiny heart-bursting change into gladness, which is really all the greatest change there is, and so he sang.

As he walked or stood on the deck he thought about loneliness. The crowded confined life of the ship was lonely too.

'Give me some money,' the man said 'It'll look better if I shout you.' So in the temporary duskiness between the double swing doors Abrahams gave him some notes and small change and followed him as he limped into the bar.

'What'll you have?' the man asked the old ladies. They were there as usual, before lunch, their large straw hats were bandaged on with violently coloured scarves. They sat nodding those crazy head-pieces, talking to anyone who would listen to them.

They were pleased to be offered drinks. Abrahams had a drink too, but it was accompanied by disturbing feelings. The thought of his illness crossed his mind. The man's hands had an extraordinary youthful beauty about them, out of keeping with his general appearance. As on the other occasions when glasses had passed between them, their fingers brushed lightly, but it was not so much the caress of fingers as of a suggestion of caress in the man's eyes.

Abrahams, with a second drink, found himself wondering had he been on horseback that time in the country or in a car. Had that other man touched the horse or merely put a friendly hand on the door of the car? With his hand he had not touched, only the expression was there in his eyes. This time, all these years later, it was a touching of exceptional hands together with an expression in the eyes.

In the afternoon there was a fancy dress party for the children. Mrs Abrahams had been making something elaborate with crepe paper. Already the cabin blossomed with paper flowers. Abrahams discovered his daughter sulking.

'Look Rachel darling,' Mrs Abrahams persuaded. 'You will be a bouquet, we shall call you "the language of flowers",' she said holding up her work. 'White roses – they mean "I cannot", and this lovely little white and green flower is lily of the valley, it says, "already I have loved you so long" and here's a little bunch of violets for your hair, Rachel, the violets say "why so downhearted? Take courage!" and these pretty daises say . . .'

'Oh, no, no!' Rachel interrupted. 'I don't want to be flowers, I want to go as a stowaway,' and she limped round and round the cabin. 'Daddy! Daddy!' she cried with sudden inspiration. 'Can I borrow one of your coloured shirts, please. Oh do say I can. Do let me be a stowaway, please!'

Abrahams took refuge among the mothers and photographers at the party. He joined in the clapping for the prize winners, 'Little Miss Muffet' and 'Alice in Wonderland'. 'All so prettily dressed!' Mrs Abrahams whispered sadly. A girl covered in green balloons calling herself 'A Bunch of Grapes' won a special prize. The applause was tremendous.

'They must have made a fortune in green umbrellas,' the rice farm friend said with delight.

'Spent a fortune on green balloons,' Abrahams muttered to himself, almost correcting her aloud. He was unable to forget, for the time being, his sinister companion who was somewhere on the decks waiting with some further demand. Silently he watched his little daughter's mounting disappointment as she limped round unnoticed in one of his shirts, left unbuttoned to look ragged.

He thought he would like to buy her a grown-up looking drink before dinner, something sparkling with a piece of lemon and a cherry on it, to please her, to comfort her, really. If only she could know how much he cherished her. He longed to be free to play with her, she was old enough, he thought, to learn to play chess. But there was the fear that he would be interrupted, and she was old enough too to be indignant and to inquire.

'I am not quite well,' he explained to his wife after the first encounter with the man. 'It is nothing serious but I am not sleeping well.' He did not want her disturbed by something mysterious which he was unable to explain. So he had a cabin to himself and arranged for his wife and daughter to be together. Their new cabin had a window with muslin curtains and a writing table. Mrs Abrahams took pleasure in comparing it with the cabins of other ladies on board. Dr Abrahams called for her and Rachel every morning on the way to breakfast.

The children's fancy dress party was depressing. The atmosphere of suburban wealth and competition seemed shallow and useless. The smell of hot children and perfume nauseated him. But it was safer to stay there.

The ship remained steady on her course and the rail of the ship moved slowly above the horizon and slowly below the horizon. There were times when Abrahams felt he was being watched by the stewards and the officers, and even the deck hands seemed to give each other knowing looks. These feelings, he knew, were merely symptoms of his illness which was, after all, nothing serious, only a question of being over tired. All the same, he was worn out with this feeling of being watched. He avoided the sun deck for it was clear from the man's new sunburn that he lay up there, anonymous on a towel, for part of each day.

'You'd better let me have a shirt,' the man said. 'I'll be noticed by my dirt,' he said. He took a set of three, their patterns being too similar for Abrahams to appear in any one of them. He needed socks and underpants and a bag to keep them in. The nondescript one Abrahams had would do very well. It was all settled one evening in the cabin which Abrahams had said he must have to himself. The fellow passenger slept there, coming in late at night and leaving early in the morning. It was there in the cramped space Abrahams dressed the wound on the man's thigh with the limited medical supplies he had with him.

'Easy! Easy!' the fellow passenger said in a low voice.

'It's hot in here,' Abrahams complained. He disliked being clumsy. 'It's the awkwardness of not having somewhere to put my things.'

'It's all right,' the fellow passenger said. 'You're not really hurting me.' He seemed much younger undressed, his long naked body so delicately patched with white between the sunburn, angry only where the wound was, invited Abrahams.

'I'm not wounded all over,' he said and laughed, and Abrahams found himself laughing with him.

'Easy! Easy! don't rush!' The younger man said.

That laughter, the tiny heart burst of gladness was a fact, like the fact that the wound was only in one place. They could be careful. It was a question of being careful in every kind of way.

Abrahams knew his treatment to be unsatisfactory but there seemed nothing else to do in the extraordinary circumstances. If only he had not answered the smile in the man's eyes on that first evening; he should have turned away as other people do. Knowing the change and feeling the change, in whatever way it brought gladness, was the beginning and the continuation of more loneliness.

Incredibly the ship made progress, her rail moving gently up and persistently down.

Like many handsome clever men Dr Abrahams had married a stupid woman. She was quite good at housekeeping and she talked consolingly through kisses. Her body had always been clean and plump, and relaxed, and she was very quiet during those times of love-making, as though she felt that was how a lady, married to a doctor, should behave. Abrahams never sang with her as he sang in the cabin.

'Easy! Easy!' the fellow passenger said, he laughed and Abrahams put the pillow over his head.

'They'll hear you.' He buried his own face in the top of the pillow. He could not stop laughing either.

'And they'll hear you too!' Abrahams heard the words piercing through the smothered laughter.

Always unable to discuss things with his wife, Dr Abrahams did not want to frighten her now and spoil her holiday.

'Your husband is a very quiet man,' the rice farm widow said to Mrs Abrahams. 'Still waters run deep, so they say,' she said. That was very early in the voyage after a morning in Gibraltar, spent burrowing into little shops choosing antimacassars and table runners of cream-coloured lace.

'Did you go to see the apes?' Ethel inquired at lunch.

'Plenty of apes here,' Abrahams, burdened and elated by discovery and already bad tempered, would have replied, but instead, he smiled pleasantly and, with a little bow, regretted the family had not had time.

'You see Ethel and I have this plastic pizza,' Ivy was explaining to Mrs Abrahams and Rachel. 'At Christmas I wrap it up and go down to Ethel's flat, "Happy Christmas Ethel", I say, and she unwraps it and she says "Ooh Ivy you are a dear it's just what I wanted", and then next year she wraps it up and gives it to me, it saves all that trouble of buying presents nobody really wants. Thank you,' she said to the steward. 'I'll have the curried chicken.'

Rachel, accustomed to good meals, ordered a steak. Abrahams could not help reflecting that Ethel and Ivy had both the remedy and the method which simplified their existence. They appeared to be able to live so easily, without emergency, and without burdening other people with their needs. They could, of course, require surgery at any time, though he doubted that this ever occurred to either of them. Perhaps he too, outwardly, gave the same impression.

The fellow passenger's demand was both a pleading and a promise. At the beginning Abrahams had risen to the entreaty, but, as he understood all too quickly, his response was complicated by an unthought of need in himself. Walking alone on the ship he was afraid.

The begging for help had, from the first, been a command. Abrahams knew his fellow passenger to be both sinister and evil. In his own intelligent way he tried to reason with himself what, in fact, he was himself. At the start, but on different terms, it was a matching desperation of hunger and thirst and an exhaustion of wits. The fellow passenger had certain outward signs, for one thing, he had a ragged growth of beard which in itself was dangerously revealing. He was dirty too. He needed help, he told Abrahams, to hold out till the first servings of afternoon tea in the lounge, and until such time when the weather would improve and cold buffet lunches would be spread daily in the Tavern Bar and on little tables on the canopied deck by the swimming pool. To be in these delightful places, in order to fill his stomach, he needed to mingle in the company.

'It's dangerous,' he said. 'Being alone. Being on my own makes me conspicuous and that's what I don't want to be.' A companion who was both rich and distinguished was a necessity and it had not taken him long to find the kind of fellow passenger he needed.

'I better have a bit more cash,' he said to Abrahams. 'I'll shout you and them old Queens. They know a thing or two about life, those two. I'll take care of them.' His words sounded like a threat.

They had, without laughter, been sorting out what was to happen next. The cabin had never seemed quite so small, quite so awkward. He had plans to alter a passport, he knew exactly what had to be done, he needed a passport and it only needed the doctor to produce one.

Like many clever men Dr Abrahams was easily tired. He had come on the ship, as had the fellow passenger, exhausted, already an easy victim. Now, more tired than ever, he hated the man and saw him as someone entirely ruthless. It seemed impossible to consider what might have been the cause. It was clear that there would be no end to the requests. Abrahams realised that soon he would be unable to protect his family and quite unable to protect himself. The voyage no longer had any meaning for him. Together, the two of them went to the bar.

Ethel and Ivy were there as usual.

'It's on me today,' Ethel cried and made them sit down. 'You must try my tomato juice,' she cried. 'It's with a difference you know,' and she winked so saucily everyone in the bar laughed.

The fellow passenger drank quickly.

'Now it's my turn,' Ivy insisted. 'It's my turn to shout.' She watched with approval as the fellow passenger drank again.

'So good for a growing boy,' she declared and she ordered another round.

Dr Abrahams held his glass too tightly with nervous fingers. After the conversation about the passport he felt more helpless than ever. He could scarcely swallow. He should never have lost his way like this. Quickly he glanced at all the people laughing and talking together and he was frightened of them.

'More tomato juice for my young man,' Ethel shrieked. Her straw hat had come loose.

'Ethel dear, watch yourself!' Ivy shrilled. 'We're in very mixed company you know dear.' Their behaviour drew the attention of the other passengers.

'Steward! Steward!' Ethel called. 'Don't forget the-you-know-what-oops la Volga! Volga! It makes all the difference. There dear boy, let's toss this off.' She raised her fiery little glass to his, 'Oops a daisy!' Her hat fell over one eye.

While the fellow passenger drank, Ivy retied Ethel's scarf lovingly. She rocked gently to and fro.

'Yo ho heave ho! Volga-Volga,' she crooned. 'Volga Vodka,' she sang, and Ethel joined in.

'Yo ho heave ho! Volga-Worcester-saucy-vodka-tommy-ommy-artah – All together now – Yo ho heave ho-Volga-Vodka,' they sang together and some of the other passengers joined in. Above the noise of the singing and the laughing Abrahams heard a familiar voice, but it was much louder than usual.

'Go on dear boy! Go on! Go on! Don't stop now!' Ethel and Ivy cried together, their absurd hats bobbing. 'Tell us more,' they screamed.

It seemed to Abrahams that the fellow passenger was telling stories to Ethel and Ivy and to anyone else who cared to listen. Hearing the voice he thought how ugly it was. The ugliness filled him with an unbearable sadness.

'So you're wanted in five countries!' Ethel said. 'Why that's wonderful!' she encouraged. She bent forward to listen. Ivy examined the young man's shirt. She patted his shoulder.

'This is such good quality,' she breathed. 'Look at this lovely material Ethel dear.' But Ethel would not have the subject changed.

'Rape!' she shrieked with delight. 'And murder too, how splendid! What else dear boy. Being a thief is so exciting, do tell us about the watches and the jewels and the diamonds. You must be very clever. Ivy and I have never managed anything more expensive than a pizza and then it turned out to be quite uneatable.'

The fellow passenger did not join in the laughter. He began to despise his audience.

'Look at you!' he sneered. 'You two old bags and you lot – you've all paid through the nose to be on this ship. But not me, I'm getting across the world on my wits. That's how I do things. I've got brains up here,' he tapped his head with a surprisingly delicate finger. 'It isn't money as has got me here,' he said and he tapped his head again.

For the first time Abrahams noticed the ugliness of the head. He thought he ought to find the Purser and speak to him.

'It's all my fault about the head,' he would confide, and explain to the officer about the arching of soft white thighs and the exertion. 'It's like this,' he would say. 'When you see the baby's head appear on the perineum it's like a first glimpse of all the wonder and all the magic, a preview if you like to call it that, of all the possibilities.' The Purser would understand about the shy hope and the tenderness when it was explained to him. Abrahams thought the Purser might be in his cabin changing for lunch. He could find the cabin.

'What has happened?' he wanted to ask the Purser. 'What has happened?' he wanted to shout. 'What is it that happens to the tiny eager head to bring about this change from the original perfection?'

He walked unsteadily towards the open end of the bar. Really he should speak and protect his fellow passenger. He felt ashamed as well as afraid, knowing that he needed to protect himself. Of course he could not speak to anyone, his own reputation mattered too much.

He was appalled at the sound of the boasting voice and, at the same time, had a curious sense that he was being rescued. The fellow passenger was giving himself to these people.

Abrahams did not turn round to watch the man being led away by two stewards in dark uniforms.

'Mind my leg!' He heard the pathetic squeal as the three of them squeezed through a narrow door at the back of the bar. It was a relief that the wound, which he was convinced needed surgery, would receive proper attention straight away.

There were still a few minutes left before lunch. For the first time he went up on the sun deck. Far below, the sea, shining like metal, scarcely moving, invited him. For a moment he contemplated that peace.

'Yoo hoo Doctor! Wear my colours!' Ethel shrieked. Turning from the rail he saw the Worcester Sauce Queens playing a rather hurried game of deck tennis. Ethel unpinned a ragged cluster of paper violets from her scarf and flung them at his feet. Politely he bent forward to pick them up.

'You must watch Rachel beat us after lunch,' Ivy shrilled.

The pulse of the ship, like a soft drum throbbing, was more noticeable at the top of the ship. To Abrahams it was like an awakening not just in his body but in his whole being. He stood relaxed letting life return as he watched the grotesque game and, with some reservations belonging to his own experience, he found the sight of the Worcester Sauce Queens charming.

Acknowledgements

The following stories have been published previously in the sources mentioned:

'Blood and Wine', *Inprint*, Vol 4, 1980; 'The Voyage of Their Life', *Meanjin*, No 2, 1985 and *Triquarterly*, Winter 1985; 'Tourist', Marian Eldridge, *Kunapipi*, May 1986.

The editor and publishers would like to thank the publishers of the following stories for permission to include them in this collection: 'A Real Little Marriage-wrecker', from *Memories of the Assassination Attempt*, Gerard Windsor, Penguin Books, 1985; 'Through Road', from *Country Girl Again and Other Stories*, Jean Bedford, McPhee Gribble/Penguin Books, 1984; 'Islands', from *Vernacular Dreams*, Angelo Loukakis, University of Queensland Press, 1986; 'The Sun in Winter', from *Antipodes*, Chatto & Windus, 1985; 'A Thousand Miles from the Ocean', from *Postcards from Surfers,* Helen Garner, McPhee Gribble/Penguin Books 1985; 'Saint Kay's Day', from *Milk*, Beverley Farmer, McPhee Gribble/Penguin, 1984; 'The New York Bell Captain', from *Room Service*, Frank Moorhouse, Viking, 1985; 'Rosalie's Folly', from *Bearded Ladies*, Kate Grenville, University of Queensland Press, 1984; 'The Waters of Vanuatu', from *The Waters of Vanuatu*, Carmel Kelly, Sea Cruise Press, 1985; 'The Fellow Passenger', from *Stories*, Elizabeth Jolley, Fremantle Arts Centre Press, 1984.

THE STATE OF THE ART

Introduced and edited by Frank Moorhouse

A frenetic, talented guitarist, barely hanging on to a fragmented life; a canny Jewish uncle, frustrated without a family to organise; lovers seeking pleasure. Whatever the cost; an old woman, trundled from the home of one son to another, an intrusion, unloved . . .

These are among the characters, some innocent, some eccentric, some disillusioned, who are portrayed in this striking, innovative collection of short stories. Their diversity of style and content reflects the robust hedonism of contemporary Australian society.

TRANSGRESSIONS
Australian Writing Now

Edited by Don Anderson

Woman marries dog
Farnarkeling – state of play
Top odds at country race meeting
Conflict between black tribal law and white 'justice'

Not the news, but the newest and best in recent short prose – the state of Australian writing today by both established masters of the craft and newer writers.

Don Anderson has chosen work by authors like Carmel Bird, Barbara Brooks, Beverley Farmer, Helen Garner, Susan Hampton, Elizabeth Jolley, Richard Lunn, David Malouf and Frank Moorhouse for this excitingly various collection.

Here you will find the traditional at its most eminent and original, the leading edge at its most cutting and innovative.

HOT COPY
Reading and Writing Now

Don Anderson

Hot Copy is a wide-ranging collection of Don Anderson's book reviews and articles on literature from Australia, Europe and North and South America. Effortlessly combining literary scholarship and debate with the vigour of daily journalism, they show that a good review doesn't merely tell the story of the book – but is a piece of good writing in its own right which puts both book and author in context.

The authors covered include Helen Garner, Tim Winton, Kate Grenville, Italo Calvino, Edmund Wilson, Saul Bellow, Milan Kundera and Joan Didion. And along the way Don Anderson also deals with such varied subjects as our literary magazines, migrant writing, Australia's literary pensioners and the 1985 NSW Premier's Literary Awards. *Hot Copy* is truly a collection which will inform, entertain – and provoke argument.

'Don Anderson writes with flair; he is colourful, witty, stylistically agile, relevantly and accessibly erudite – and he is not afraid of plonking his sword in the scales with the decisive judgement, the wide-ranging judgement, the provocative judgement.'
Gerard Windsor

ROOMS OF THEIR OWN

Jennifer Ellison

Rooms of their Own is a collection of interviews with twelve authors of contemporary Australian fiction.

Jennifer Ellison's rapport with the writers and their writing has elicited surprisingly frank views on the relationship between authors and publishers; the place of writers in society; the role of gender in writing; and many other issues. Together, the interviews form a dynamic account of the creative, professional and personal motivations of some of Australia's most important living writers.

MEMORIES OF THE ASSASSINATION ATTEMPT
AND OTHER STORIES

Gerard Windsor

A man spars with his wife over his dead mother-in-law's unopened wedding presents; a deserted woman is visited by the father of her child; an old priest relives a tragedy in which his own youthful idealism was instrumental; an urbane gynaecologist discovers there are some parts of his women that retaliate . . .

The reach and range of Gerard Windsor's imagination has already been critically acclaimed: 'fabulist, moralist and humorist all at once'. His stories reflect experiences that span the sensual to the spiritual, the mundane to the macabre, yet beneath all their irony lurk subtle compassion and moral concern. This fine new collection can only assure his reputation as one of Australia's most deft and engaging fiction writers.

IKONS
A collection of stories

Even after thirty years, the Mavromatis family cannot understand their life in Australia. Until Peter Mavromatis's first exhibition as an 'ethnic' photographer clarifies everything.

In this collection of stories we follow the family fortunes. Old Yiayia has already lived her life in the old country. Christos and Eli wage a private war as confused as the motives which brought them from Cyprus. For Peter, their Australian-born son and proud hope for the future, life is a contest of shallow cultural identities and allegiances.

Ikons is a vivid and contentious protrayal of a family united only by society's view of them as outsiders.

NORTH WIND

John Morrison

Of the sixteen stories in this collection, 'North Wind' is the longest and most grimly compelling. It tells of a fierce clash of personalities, a conflict brought to its climax against the background of a raging bushfire.

Other stories are humorous, tender, philosophical – taking us through a wide range of human situations, from Melbourne suburbia and waterfront to up-country farms and sheep stations.

STORIES OF THE WATERFRONT

John Morrison

'John was born in England, but no native-born reflects the spirit of Australia more than he does. This country, of which he is so much a part, has absorbed and recreated him as one of its most significant voices.'

Alan Marshall

These imaginative and sensitive stories begin at a time when wharfies turned up at the docks to be picked like cattle, and often went home without work or pay. The events range from personal dilemmas like sharing lottery winnings to coping with pig-headed bosses and the tragedy of sudden death.

John Morrison worked for ten years on the Melbourne waterfront in the 1930s and '40s. His *Stories of the Waterfront*, collected here for the first time, give a realistic, yet unusually sympathetic account of the much-maligned wharfie.

JIMMY BROCKETT

Dal Stivens

Fiction – or fact? Jimmy Brockett is that archetypal character – charismatic, ruthless, playing for high stakes in politics, sport, business and the underworld. In the great tradition of Australian con men, he exploits the greed and weakness in others to build his own power.

He toughs his way from the Sydney slums to wealth, fame and influence. Brockett elevates the corruption and brutality in his personal and public life to a level which is bizarre but all too believable.

'. . . a work of importance, a thoroughly Australian work, written with an Australian idiom and tang . . .'

Jack Lindsay

A HORSE OF AIR

Dal Stivens

Harry Craddock – millionaire, ornithologist, idealist and buffoon – wrote this book, an intriguing account of his expedition to central Australia in search of the rare night parrot.

But all is not as it first appears. Craddock wrote his story while in a mental hospital, and the book also includes excerpts from his wife's diary, and comments from both his psychiatrist and editor. The result is an absorbing and multi-layered story, whose ultimate meaning or meanings must be decided by each reader.

'A brilliant novel, intensely moving, stimulating and puzzling . . .'
P. J. Rainey, *The Bush Telegraph*

'Stivens' master work . . . zestful, witty and intellectually first class . . . one of the few Australian novels in which artistic and intellectual triumph are one and the same thing . . .'

D. R. Burns, *Nation Review*

A BUNCH OF RATBAGS

William Dick

The bodgies and widgies of the 1950s were treated by the media at the time like monsters. William Dick's novel takes a close look at the human reality.

Born into the extreme poverty and harsh living condition of Melbourne's western suburbs, Terry Cooke grows through a tough childhood to the apparent glamour of the bodgie gangs.

Terry gradually begins to realize that there is more to life than the gang as the experience goes sour. The novel gives a vivid picture of the locale and fashions of the 50s, but the drama of teenage gang life remains relevant today.

KEEP MOVING

Frank Huelin

Keep Moving was the order given by police to the thousands of people like Frank Huelin, who roamed Australia during the 1930s appealing for work and handouts. Pushed from town to town, they jumped trains, slept under bridges or in shanties and, sometimes hilariously, made the best of very little.

The warm communal ethic which developed and the mateship of the road are balanced by the harsh facts of survival. The struggles for rights and dignity during the Great Depression are alarmingly relevant today with more people unemployed than ever before.

Alan Marshall says in his Foreword: 'This is history from one of the men who made it.'

'It works by understatement . . . a gutsy piece of work. I cannot remember a better one about the period.'

Melbourne *Age*

A WINDOW IN MRS X's PLACE
Selected Short Stories

Peter Cowan

Peter Cowan has been compared to writers as diverse as Hemingway and Lawson as he 'explores the responses of individuals to crises in love and work against a variety of Australian, especially Western Australian, land , sea and city scapes.'

This selection by Bruce Bennett allows his work to be 'experienced as a continuity, ranging from stories published in a variety of magazines and collections since the early 1940s. During that period, Cowan has established a well deserved reputation as master craftsman in one of the most difficult art forms.'

'One of the finest two or three short story writers now working in Australia.'

T. A. G. Hungerford,
Weekend News, 1965

MANNING CLARK
Collected Short Stories

Growing up at Phillip Island, solemn moments in church, memories of school, confrontations in academe, fishing with a son – this is the stuff of the short stories of the eminent historian Manning Clark.

This collection contains those stories originally published as *Disquiet and other stories* together with the later 'A Footnote to the Kokoda Story' and 'A Diet of Bananas and Nietzsche'.

"These are rare treasures from a writer of subtle eloquence – witty and compassionate observations on the human condition which give a lingering pleasure."

Mary Lord

Published by McPhee Gribble
Penguin

SCISSION

Tim Winton

SCISSION: 1. the action of cutting or dividing as with a sharp instrument, 2. division, separation, schism.

'Rosemary McCulloch is a model. She is the woman-model. She gives life to clothes, libido to car bonnets, meaning to vodka. She sets the pace for mothers and daughters who want to be like her.

Her husband is haunted by her reproductions, and her sons have learnt to hate her.'

Tim Winton writes of people struggling with change and disintegration, he writes of excruciating moments when love and loss are sharply focussed, and of a world that is somehow made more real for being slightly out of whack.

". . . bright, tough, physical stories, a stubborn celebration of the good in a frightening universe."

Helen Garner

LOVE CHILD

Jean Bedford

'My mother's name was Grace; she was graceful . . . I loved her, my vulgar, laughing mother.'

In blitz-torn London, Grace meets Bill, the older, sensitive Australian sailor. Their passion is swift and powerful and leads them to abandon their marriages and sail to Australia. There life sours as his solemnity overshadows her vivacity. Anne is the child of their days of passion – their love child.

Her parents' estrangement gradually casts Anne adrift as she moves from happy childhood into disturbed womanhood, unable to love her husband, her friends, her own child.